Letters To Bizzy

Letters To Bizzy

John M. Tabor

DREAMING BIG PUBLICATIONS

Letters to Bizzy
Copyright © 2019 by John M. Tabor

Content Editor: Emelyn G. Ehrlich
Copy Editor: Meagan Daquan
Editor-in-Chief: Kristi King-Morgan
Formatting: Kristi King-Morgan
Cover Artist: Kristi King-Morgan
Assistant Editor: Amanda Clarke

Printed in the United States of America

ISBN-978-0-578-56853-9

www.dreamingbigpublications.com

Table of Contents

Preface

Some of us will spend a life-time looking in our rearview mirrors trying to put a name and face to the hurts which haunt our psyche. And when I say some of us I mean most of us. These injuries aren't the accidental missteps that all are guilty of, but are in fact those caused by intentional insults; and, surprisingly many are subtle and difficult to discern. Those most problematic to describe in fact cause the greatest suffering. Would you be surprised if I told you we are most susceptible to the damage inflicted by loved-ones? Probably not, for by this time, in my short narrative, I have already awoken the little girl or boy in you crying to be heard, incensed by the lie that time heals all wounds. And it is likely you have already run-down your own personal catalog of lesions that won't heal, wishing I hadn't brought the subject up.

Instead of seeking a cure, searching for an escape from our desolate island of pain, we hold on to those memories. However dreadful, we embrace them as an explanation for who we are and how we got here. They become our defense, our excuse for why we haven't become something better; or, at the very least something different. I wish I could say I am unfamiliar with this topic, but sadly, am not.

Let it go! Forget the past and forgive those who have brought you to this place. Easy to say, not so easy to execute. How grim it must be to be an alcoholic and to be lectured by the temperate to forsake your addiction. Is our addiction to those scars we carry that much different?

Letters to Bizzy finds a man, John Tibbits, staring down the barrel of old age, having to come to grips with his mother's death and the regrettable fact that his dysfunctional youth has burdened him with a lifetime of unwelcome baggage. As he sorts through his mother's personal effects, he discovers boxes of unopened letters written some 50 years earlier from a man, Robert Guthrie, to his daughter, Bizzy. They tell the story of a life lived on a barrier island off the coast of North Carolina, Bogue Banks. There is nothing sensational in the telling, average by most accounts. However, through the eyes of Robert Guthrie we come to see beauty in the tragic, humor in the absurd, and sensitivity from the susceptible. It is in fact apologetic to the ordinary lives we live. Those of John Tibbits and Robert Guthrie are inexplicably intertwined and it is only until the end, do we learn how. For both it is a journey through their own private battles.

Bogue Banks is in fact a barrier island along the coast of North Carolina; and, like so many of the barrier islands along our eastern seaboard it has its own unique beauty and culture. Several of the characters in this book are based loosely on real people. I may be accused of stealing their personas to populate these chapters, but would argue their considerably embellished characters are in fact distinctly born from imagination and belong solely within confines of these pages. Set at a time when life moved at a somewhat slower pace, I have attempted to weave this elemental charm into the storyline and allow historic events to casually collide where appropriate.

This book is not intended to be a shrine to the melancholy, but in fact, begs for the spirit within all of us who strives to be free of former selves. If you can relate then hoorah! For those who have already made their getaway then this story should resonate; and, for those who have not, then let me tell you there is hope.

Acknowledgements

My mother was the master of the silent treatment and passive aggressive behavior was her forte. It didn't help she had a hair trigger temper. During my childhood, and through most of my adulthood, her treatment of family members, and me, caused great pain and disappointment. It was not a constant stream of torture, but it was frequent enough that one knew it wasn't an anomaly. These behaviors simmered just below the surface; and, her bearing was in fact the inspiration for the character Bizzy, a distinctly unhappy person. So, it is unfortunate that I learned, only after mother had passed, that she had an extremely difficult childhood. One that would be difficult to bear or forget. In her mind she would have characterized her childhood as a seamy past, an embarrassment, and would be certain not to share any of the sordid details with me. Consequently, she hid her regrettable beginnings, being a woman who was guarded, sparing her the discomfort and me the truth. It is most likely these early events contributed significantly to her dark mood.

Reflecting upon this revelation she probably did the best she could under the circumstances, and although one could hope she might have risen above the travails of her life, she was in fact only human. My own failings as a parent have not eluded me, and provide an uncomfortable perspective. It is, therefore, in the spirit of forgiveness that I give her a pass. It is regrettable that she would not live to appreciate this, which is sad. Perhaps, wherever she is, she now knows.

I am very grateful to *Dreaming Big Publications* and its Owner/Editor-in-Chief, Kristi Morgan, for accepting "Letters to Bizzy" for publication, and express my appreciation for all the editors of *Dreaming Big Publications* who assisted me in enhancing the content of this book.

And most sincerely, I want to thank my wife, Lisa, for reading this book many times, providing spelling and grammar checks, making suggestions for revisions, and putting up with my peevishness when frustrated by the effort. If she were my only fan, it would make the endeavor of writing all worthwhile.

A Recent Passing

It was a short obituary appearing in the Sunday edition of the Baltimore Sun, January 24th 2010. Not too much fanfare suiting mothers private inclinations; Elizabeth Tibbits died peacefully January 20th, "places of her residence, family who have predeceased her, and her closest next of kin, John Tibbits". Me. Just enough information to reassure their readers she was not a spinster, but discouraging any conjecture as to the sordid details for cause of death, or her lifestyle. While living she kept her nose out of other people's business and made sure they kept theirs out of hers. In death she wasn't about to change. That she made me promise.

At 88 no one could say it was an untimely death; and, although I was somewhat relieved she was no longer suffering, I wished we had more time together. Time to better understand elements of her life which defined who she was, and fundamentally who I was. A glimpse into her past and a little more information on those shadowy parcels which would explain uncomfortable silences during meals and reasons for changed subjects. Awkward exchanges at best, well intentioned, yet ultimately unproductive. But, at 63 I was now resigned to the immutable fact that I will never know any more than I already did.

Since turning middle age I have been forced to loosen my belt a notch or two with each successive year, Hair is thinning, making any attempt to do a come-over without being too obvious nearly impossible. Skin a little blotchy with broken blood vessels dancing across my cheeks reminds me of spider webs. Can't be absolutely sure, but the hump on my back could be from osteoporosis. I would like to say the years have been kind, but that would be untrue, and to be honest I haven't worked too hard at trying to improve my appearance.

I came down from Boston for the funeral, which was not well attended as the few friends she collected over the years managed to make their peace before her. Her pastor seemed somewhat annoyed at having to officiate this particular funeral, and I am sure it is in no small part due to irritations mother inflicted upon his rectory over the years. What a shame to piss-off the one man who was charged with honoring her life and putting a positive spin on the sinful existence of her humanity. Sitting in the front pew I made a feeble attempt to cry, but all I could conjure-up was acid reflux.

Would stay at mother's home for the next few days having the unenviable task of cleaning-out the house she lived in for more than 50 years. I was prepared it wasn't going to be much fun, but am somewhat surprised how painful it is to sort through the knick-knacks, keepsakes, and familiar items which only a month ago I would have taken no notice of, but now am forced to triage and determine what I will keep and what must be discarded. These are the sentimental reminders of a life lived all too quickly, leaving behind a not so subtle message that we all are just passing through. Unfortunately, most of it must go as I have little space in my loft in Back Bay.

I started with a plan, business records and legal documents first, items of value next, moving to furniture, and other personal effects. Room to room, I was disciplined for a time, only to be distracted by memories and distant ghosts. There were the doilies scattered about tables, arms of sofa and chairs, which father and I despised and frequently pleaded she remove to spare us from embarrassment of the all telling smirks from friends and visitors.; And as I now recall, there were very few real friends, mostly just visitors. "Now boys, you're just going to have to find something else to focus your energies on. I find them charming and that settles it." Over the years I absconded with a few, thinning out the herd so to speak, and pretty sure father did as well. Alas, to our chagrin a new, even gaudier, doily would replace the one missing in action, making the exercise pointless. Ironic isn't it. I would have been pleased as punch to throw every last one away when I was young; and now, I am struggling to drop the last few that are left into the trash bin.

On the mantle was the fancy platter which mother never used for serving. Food had no place soiling the lacquered floral scenery. No, it was decorative and would always remain so. A small chip reminded me of my time as a boy in a playful mishap I knocked her precious plate off its perch. I had been warned repeatedly not to play with my ball in the house, nevertheless, youthful exuberance got the better of me. As the ball left my hand I watched in slow motion, and in horror, as it grazed the plate sending it from the mantle to the floor. It should have shattered, but instead only lost a small bit of silver filigree at the edge. It wasn't the kind of thing that could be hidden forever as mother doted over the plate cooing to it as if it possessed a life of its own. Once my crime was discovered I would spend better part of a week in contrition, repenting of my wayward and careless act, wondering if she cherished the stupid ceramic plate more than me. Promised myself I would never own a plate I wasn't willing to eat off, or break.

Father's pipe rack remained as it did, now going on 20 years after his death. Mother claimed she could still smell the faint aroma of father's tobacco which reminded her of pleasant evenings in each other's company. I think she sometimes repainted pictures in her mind to portray a more civil domestic existence, as I am dubious as to their validity, at least on the whole.

No man should be forced to rummage through their mother's underwear drawer or items found in the nightstand next to their bed. Nevertheless, there I was half expecting she would burst in on me at any moment demanding an explanation for my voyeuristic philandering and wishing I would be struck blind from the realization that mother was, after all a woman.

Photographs littered dressers, coffee table and other corners of the house; pictures of mother and father as a young couple, my baby pictures some without teeth some with and those of me for every year of school, each of their wedding anniversaries revealing the progressive distance that grew between mother and father over the years, and summer vacations at the beach hotel three blocks from the ocean. Black and whites, colored too, silently reminding me of the evolution of our family and irrepressible forward march of time. Evidence that there had been a family and proof, albeit thin, that the family had at times learned to coexist. It wasn't long before my plan for a structured reconnaissance degenerated and I migrated from one stunning image of our past to another. My chest was tight and palms sweaty. It was exhausting.

*****

Nevertheless, despite the unexpected diversions and reposes, I managed to box all the items I felt I couldn't bring myself to part with. There weren't many, and the artifacts I did keep even surprised me, some correspondence between mother and a distant relative, which I guess in some ways humanized and filled in the gaps of a family that always teetered on the edge. Tagged jewelry to be gifted to her only niece from her half-sister, contacted local homeless shelter for kitchen utensils, and Goodwill to pick-up clothing and furniture, the rest went to the curb in a massive heap advertising the ignominious callous insensitivity of her only son. What amounted to a lifetime of toil, scrimping, and saving I managed to reduce to a small mountain of rubble. I made every effort not to make eye contact with her neighbors during this painful ordeal and prayed there might be an early trash pick-up, or at the very least garage sale scavengers to remove the evidence. I was to be disappointed. Along with the real estate for-sale sign plunged into the heart of her front yard, the picture was complete; "mother dies, son dismantles her dissipated life in the course of only a few short days." With headlines like this it isn't any wonder neighbors would

13

think the worse of me, or at the very best totally insensitive to the hallowed ground of the past.

Was ready to lock the front door and skedaddle before I brought any more shame down upon myself, when I thought better of it. I hadn't checked the attic, well not really an attic, more like a crawl space. There might be something hidden in its recesses. But mother never went up there. Does it make any sense to make the effort? It's most likely layered in decades of dust and festooned with cobwebs. I hate spiders! Locked the door, unlocked the door, stood pondering pros and cons wishing I could convince myself it wasn't worth the trouble. Standing there mumbling, I was guilted by my indecision and finally concluded I would regret not peeking to convince myself it was futile.

Rummaged through the garage and found the step ladder stacked behind garden tools; skinned my knuckles dragging the obdurate steps through hallways and up the stairs to the landing. Extended and locked, it was a lame and wobbly example of safety in the home. Contemplated how long it would take someone to find my body should I fall, but more importantly how many months would my cable bill pile-up before it was cancelled.

Tentatively I climbed the first two rungs swaying as my weight shifted from leg to leg. Seemed too late to go on a diet now. Should have known better, but in spite of that inner voice, looked down past the landing to the stairs and was immediately overcome by vertigo. Grasping the ladder in a death grip it required every ounce of conviction to inch my way higher. I dared not let go. At the top I used my head banging against the trap door to first dislodge and then shove it aside. Nervously reached-up to find the string dangling from the attic light, hoping it might save me should the ladder collapse beneath me.

Swaying back and forth from my determined tug, the light illuminated portions of its space and as it receded shadows reclaimed the dark. Back and forth casting an eerie countenance, wouldn't have been surprised if I found decaying remains of despised members of mother's bridge parties disposed of in a most inconvenient manner. Instead what I found is what I expected... dust, cobwebs, and what looked like mouse turds.

"I'm done! There is nothing else in this damn house for me to salvage and I'm getting out of here before it claims me." Reached to switch-off the light and in the process saw in the corner shoe boxes camouflaged with the same detritus of time. I don't know how I knew, but in that moment I realized I had found something, something out of the ordinary. I am not inclined to hear voices, but I swear I heard a voice from within these boxes, a voice from the past calling out to me.

Cross-legged I settled into layers of dust unacquainted by human presence and pulled the boxes towards me. Blew dust of the lid of the first, which was a huge mistake as the plume went in all directions including my eyes, up my nose, and down my windpipe. Choked and gagged, eyes watering, I spat and coughed up dirt for a good 5 minutes. Spent, breathless, spit and drool running out of the corners of my mouth where it mingled in clumps of dirt. I did my best to recover my composure, thinking there better be something worthwhile in those boxes.

What I found in the first box was a stack of unopened letters. Yellowed with age, glue dried and cracking it was obvious they had been neglected for some many years. Return address on the letters was Guthrie, no street number, no street name, no town, no state, just Guthrie. And they were all addressed to Bizzy of 102 Margate Lane, Charlotte, NC. Pretty sure grandmother had lived in Charlotte. Carefully I swept the dust off the remaining boxes and discovered all contained the same unopened letters, all from Guthrie, and all to Bizzy. Postmarks were Bogue Banks dating from late 1940's to late 1950's.

Seemed I had me a mystery. What would prompt mother to keep letters addressed to a character named Bizzy from some person, maybe a relative, unopened and uncared for all these years? Was tempted to discard the letters not wishing to somehow disregard feelings of the recently deceased and the privacy of why they remained unread; but, thought better of it. Perhaps if she had kept them there must be a good reason.

Managed to find the top rung of the ladder with my foot and pulled each box to the brink where they teetered. With judicious balancing I made my way down bringing one box at a time. In the end, congratulated myself that I hadn't been killed, and promised I would never pull a stunt like this ever again.

Sat at the kitchen table staring at the dusty coffers of my newfound enigma. Was curious but was spent from the ordeal of the last few days. At that moment all I really wanted to do was to take a hot shower and relax. The idea of diving into unknown territory and digging up potentially unpleasant secrets, especially with mother's passing being a current affair, did not appeal to me. If there were vexing confidences hidden on the pages of these letters I would prefer to face them in a different state of mind, so I packed them into the back seat of my BMW, along with other saved relics, and headed back to Boston. There I would wait upon an occasion when I was more predisposed; then, and only then, would I open the letters to Bizzy. For now, I had to focus on driving the interstate without getting killed.

My Dear Bizzy

A deep gloom has crept uninvited into my subconscious, taking up residence as an unwelcome guest. Winter weather hasn't been helpful. Dreary, damp, and cold, Boston has set a chill deep into your bones like no other place. I am sorry mother is gone, probably always will be; but there is nothing I could do about it and all the lamenting in the world won't change her condition. Must stay strong and run the course, spring can't be too far away.

I need to keep my work front and center. What do they say, an idle man is a miserable creature? We can't have that, I'll do what I'm paid to do. Read. Don't want to brag, but I've achieved a respectable position as a literary agent. One of the few independents that can claim they command attention of publishers and film emissaries alike, and am fortunate to represent several well-known authors. Sadly, there are too few of us left, each year less people read preferring to be entertained by sound bites from their smart phones. Right now, however, I have stacks of manuscripts from wannabes, unaware of this contemporary trend, piled next to my desk 3 deep and 3 feet high. Good! Keeps me busy and takes my mind off worthless crap. Who knows maybe I'll discover a new talent or maybe not.

*****

Work and demands of daily life, getting from sunup to sunset soon, consumed me. Yet winter won't let go. Now early March I'm imprisoned in my loft by an unexpected nor'easter, can barely make out the street below, snow blowing sideways and traffic paralyzed. It is only 4:00 but street lights are already on, struggling to penetrate the curtain drawn over the city by the storm. If I could get out, where would I go? Anything worth going to is closed and there is a curfew for early evening discouraging would be tipsters finding solace at corner pubs. To make matters worse I'm sick to death of reading paltry attempts of amateurs claiming their creative writing class has molded them into the next Hemingway. Their writing is mechanical, it has no feeling. Not an ounce of soul can be squeezed from the letters and words linked together in a chain of drivel. And if that wasn't bad enough, I'm forced to respond to their unsolicited submissions with words of encouragement, lying that their masterpiece doesn't match my current needs, but they should not be discouraged, and wish them best of luck. What I really wish is they would leave me alone.

Microwaved some meal in a pouch claiming to be lean, could afford to lose a few pounds. Grabbed the first plate in reach, which turned out to be mother's fancy platter, you know the one over the mantle. Flopped gruel onto the plate obscuring its ornate floral pattern, set up the TV tray, poured a glass of wine, and positioned myself in front of my flat screen television. Turned on Bruins game and watched as they took a shellacking from the Penguins. Had to switch, not that I am a hockey fan, but I am loyal to Boston. Flipped through a few nonsense sitcoms, started an old movie on one of the classic movie stations, ended-up at the cooking channel watching some attractive model, thinner than a toothpick, cooking a veal dish with a heavy cream sauce. Scene appeared somewhat disingenuous and the contrast to what I was eating was more than I could take...click.

"Testy", Ok I admit it. I wouldn't find anything entertaining, even if a marching band came crashing through my front door; and just think of the mess they would make tracking their dirty boots all over my carpet. Better put the chain on the door, just in case. Then something came over me, something to fill the void of the stubborn winter and disappointing evening, a meanspirited dark thought. It shocked me, not that I haven't had a few in my lifetime, but this was truly wicked.

In addition to primates, opossum, panda, and koala, I have been gifted with an opposable thumb, and would use this digit as an instrument for executing a crime of passion. In my mind I was already concocting my defense. Ever so lightly I pressed my thumb against mother's platter, it slid effortlessly across the tray. I pressed a little harder, it slid a litter further. I wondered how close to the edge could I get without it falling? Dangling with what looked like the lion's share hanging over oblivion, I was surprised it still clung to the table, a minor miracle of physics. My game reminded me of Russian roulette, except every chamber of the gun was loaded. I have to admit testing new frontiers was exhilarating. Just a little bit further. Oops. As it crashed to the floor I was reminded of a similar incident, traveling in time to face the angry countenance of mother demanding I explain my actions. "It was an accident", I pleaded, but we both know this was not true.

Bizarre as it may seem, broken pieces of the platter scattered across the floor and under furniture articulated feelings I had suppressed for many years. Pieces of a broken past. I wished for something different, but the truth of the matter was our family wasn't exactly happy. Looking from the outside in, no one would be the wiser; polite, albeit quiet, dinners. Followed by polite evenings and a polite goodnight. But our familial bonds were tethered by morays, cultural expectations, and obligations. Not love. To the same or lesser extent, perhaps all families suffer similarly. But I wasn't from other families.

As an aging man I shouldn't have to face these ugly truths. Truth? The truth is that no one is immune. Life deals us but one set of cards, those we may not have chosen for ourselves. And although I would like to think I was somehow special and free from this decree, I am in fact not. We certainly can't choose our parents. Nonetheless, it is up to us to make something of ourselves, and that includes our own happiness and so I would. But first, I need to search for what happy means.

Platter was now shattered and the spell was broken. I felt a little better.

*****

It continued to snow over the next two days entombing the good citizens of Boston in their domiciles, but more importantly me. I set aside the manuscripts for now knowing a couple of days more or less would make little difference in the outcome of those pathetic writers waiting on good news. Instead I settled into my recliner in front of my fake fireplace, bolstered by Irish whiskey, and the letters to Bizzy. I was ready to read one or two and see how the past would inform me, what would I learn, who would I meet?

First order of business was to determine what I could about Bogue Banks, at least where it was located. I think back to when I was a school boy, if I wanted to research a particular topic I would first have to go to the library, then to the card catalog where I would find suitable book titles, and write down their respective Dewey Decimal numbers. Sometimes numbers were clustered and books, should they not be checked-out, could be found in the same part of the library. However, I was never blessed with luck and more often than not books of interest were scattered from one end to the other forcing me to ascend stair cases to top floors, then descend to basement levels. It took nearly Herculean strength to collect and carry the many books I wished to plumb and my scrawny little arms burned from unavoidable accretion of lactic acid. Seated at an expansive table with good lighting, books scattered about me, I pressed open one at a time, bindings cracking from forced entry, endeavoring to find specific references of interest. Process could be facilitated if the table of contents were sufficiently detailed, but if not, I would triangulate finding chapter titles which best matched the topic, and skimming paragraphs for some indication I was getting close. Book after book was interrogated, process might take several hours, sometimes walking away with nothing to show for my efforts. Or only a piece of what I was looking for. By high school father had invested in an unabridged version of Encyclopedia Britannica which made my life considerably easier. Yet there was no perfect solution as it was impossible to condense all our world's knowledge and secrets into those few books starting with A and ending with Z. What I was searching might be found in the encyclopedia or might not.

Now there is internet and Wikipedia. Punch-in the topic, press enter, and out other end falls the most elaborate details you ever wanted to know. As a consequence, libraries now represent an anathema, and entering one for any reason other than nostalgia seems pointless. Imagine if as a schoolboy I had Wikipedia? I might have been able to skip primary and secondary education, college, and gone straight to my doctorate degree. But I wouldn't have read books, lots of them, and never fallen in love with the printed word. Who knows, might never have become a literary agent.

Anyway, I've digressed...Bogue Banks. Wikipedia describes Bogue Banks as, "a 21 mile barrier island off the mainland of North Carolina in Carteret County. The island, separated from the mainland by Bogue Sound, runs east to west, with the ocean beaches facing due south. Bogue Banks is the only island on the Carteret County shore that has been developed with housing..." The description with historical details went on at length. My Rand McNally Atlas shows Outer Banks terminating at its southern most point at Cape Lookout, which is immediately due east of Bogue Banks being separated by Beaufort Inlet. To the southwest of Bogue Banks is Wilmington and Cape Fear River. I don't consider myself to be well schooled in geography, nevertheless, I certainly heard of the Outer Banks and Wilmington, regrettably I've never heard of Bogue Banks. The tiny island is contemporary home to five equally tiny communities: Atlantic Beach, Pine Knoll Shores, Salter Path, Indian Beach, and Emerald Isle. This island was the origin of letters which I now had in my possession and ready to dissect; and little did I know, would color every aspect of stories contained within.

I decided to commence my journey by starting at the beginning, a very good place. Based on postmark dates I found what I surmised was the oldest letter. It would have taken little effort to rip it from its decaying envelope, instead I took a damp sponge and caressed the seal gently prying with a letter opener, parting ancient spit and glue millimeter by millimeter. If for some reason I was to release Pandora's box of curses, or as in my case unwelcome knowledge, I would endeavor to contain my mishap and reseal the envelope, imprisoning unpleasantness, putting the matter behind me.

Unfolded in my lap I made no effort to read words, that would come. Instead, I ventured to absorb a sense of context, sniff the air so to speak, feel the vibe imparted by the writer some 60 years ago. Mystical divining revealed nothing other than the boxes were musty smelling, and handwriting was not good. Can't claim my own is without fault, but this was altogether different. It was very bad, showing signs of poor rhythm and inconsistencies. Scratchings meandered up and down across the page, writer obviously challenged to stay on one plane. Disconnected cursive appeared throughout and would require words be stitched together to make sense. Flagrant exaggerations of l's and y's ran amok obscuring the integrity of preceding and subsequent sentences. Nevertheless, it was individualistic, distinctive, and masculine in origin, as I would find. Been told ugly handwriting is a sign of emotional, and sometimes volatile, temperament. I have also heard it is indicative of independent thinkers and creative eccentrics. Regardless, it wouldn't be easy to read.

April 7, 1947

My Dear Bizzy

 I hope this letter finds you, as I am uncertain of your current address, and hope it finds you well. I must apologize as it has been some time since I've last written. I wish I could offer a legitimate excuse, but as is often the case, time has a way of getting away from me, days pass, months merge, and before I know it another year is gone. If you're not careful years will add up. Seems only yesterday your mother and I were celebrating your first birthday; a wonderful event which took you by surprise and provided many sources of entertainment for mother and me. Not certain we ever got all the cake and ice cream out that ole sofa. But sofas are meant for the living, and not the other way round.

 Hard to believe you're now a woman. If my ciphering is correct you celebrated your 26th birthday only a few weeks ago. Happy Birthday! If you haven't reached the age, it won't be too long when the thought of another birthday will only bring resentment; and, you will be forced to appear grateful for all the well-wishers and glad handers reminding you're only getting older. Take my advice, don't. They'll only come back at you again next year with the same cheerful rubbish.

 You got your father's looks...sorry for that. Got the Guthrie nose and high cheeks and strong chin. Good news is now I am near on my late forties still haven't got a lick of grey hair. Maybe you'll be lucky that way too. You are probably tall like your dad, which is a good thing, and if I am wrong you don't have to say so.

 Hope you won't mind if I barge in on your life and write to you now and then. Sharing a little of what's going on, and maybe a few stories to boot would do me good. Almost like we were sitting together on the wrap-around porch chatting about this and that, watching the surf crash onto the beach. Have no proof, but I believe the bond between folks is strengthened when they get-up to talking. It may be just prattle, yet sometimes it isn't what you say, but how you say it, and that you had a mind to say something. Never had the gift of gab, don't mean I don't have a hankering to hear from you, and listening to your sweet voice would please me to no end. If you would write I would be most happy, if not it's alright, I'll understand.

For now, your loving,

Father

Don't know what I expected, but one thing is for sure a letter from a father to his daughter seems pretty tame, nothing to be alarmed about, but it might not hold my attention either. I'll reserve judgment until I read another.

A Beginning

May 9, 1947

My Dear Bizzy

Barely a month has gone by, and you must forgive me for writing so soon, but it is now start of vacation season here on the island which gets folks heart's pumping. Merchants are preparing for a flood of out-of-towners poking at their wares some, buying a souvenir or two, cottages are being spruced-up to welcome guests, swimming pavilion is hiring staff and cleaning and stacking towels, heard the Palace has already booked bands and is waxing the wood floors in preparation for those brave souls willing to embarrass themselves and step-out. What was shuttered is now getting un-shuttered and the good people of Bogue Banks are coming alive again after a long off-season hibernation. I'm sure at the other end of this thing we'll all be happy to see everyone go back to where they came from so we can get on with our own lives, a slower pace to be sure. This cycle has been going on since I can remember, or at least since they built the toll bridge to the mainland in 1928. But for now excitement is palpable and there is no reason to ruin anyone's fun. Anyway, got me thinking which is why I'm putting pen to paper.

When you left you were too young to remember much of the island so I thought this might be my opportunity to share something of your heritage. Heritage is the only thing we can claim is truly ours, can't be taken from you, and it would be a shame not knowing yours, or at worst that part where your blood runs thickest. All grown-up

can't expect you to embrace my values such as they are, but I don't suppose
you'll make a fuss about history.
It were the decline of whaling…

…which brought our family to Bogue Banks. The decline started in late 1700's and by 1851, when Guthries finally threw in the towel, there weren't enough whales to make a living for our community. Today some would say it was a senseless depletion of a majestic animal. But our folks simply didn't know what was around the bend, driven by a need to survive they had no idea they were contributing to extinction of a species. Anyway, times were bleak, but thought of pulling-up stakes and heading inland was abhorrent for those who spent their life on the water and whose forefathers knew no different.

God must have seen our plight, for word came there was good fishing on Bogue Banks, carried by a few adventurous men figuring our luck wouldn't last if we held-out where we were. Schools of mullet ran thick near the shores of Bogue, attracted by an abundance of bait fish, where a man could stand waist deep and collect all the fish he and his family could eat for a week with a simple casting net. Cooked fresh or in a stew it was mighty tasty. Salted and dried, mullet would provide sustenance during colder months of winter when fishing was sparse. During some months, loggerhead turtles were also plentiful and along with their eggs were considered a delicacy. Now days no one dares disturb their nests.

Before we made our move to Bogue Banks the Guthries' were originally scattered along Shackleford Banks and Cape Lookout Island. Spitting distance from each other if you got a strong wind to your back. Our kind were called Bankers, not because we lent money or managed financial institutions, but because of where we lived. Can claim we were hard working decent folk cause everyone, at that time, on Outer Banks were hard working and decent.

Not much will grow in sandy soil battered by wind and salt. Made our living off a few chickens, pigs, and milking cows, but mostly we were watermen, fishing, oystering, and whaling. Whale by-products were only reliable commodity us Bankers could use as currency for trade. Oils boiled down from blubber were used in lamps and to lubricate machinery; waxy spermaceti found in their skulls was fashioned into fine candles; and, ambergris from intestine was used by them French perfumers to make expensive scents. It was messy and smelly business, but it was ours, and there weren't no waste…couldn't afford any.

During season, sentries placed high on dunes would scan where water meets sky in search of whale pods. Spouts of water shooting skywards were telltale affirmation of what they were looking for. When sighted, our vigilant sentry would discharge his rifle announcing their discovery and calling to arms men of the island to drop what they were doing and muster at the beach where they would drag long boats out past heavy surf into open water. Massive muscles in their backs and arms developed from years of toiling upon seas pulled their vessels away from shore to intercept their prey. Battle between man and beast was won or lost by the balance between stamina and fatigue. Exhaustion could overtake both hunter and quarry alike, and who would die was not preordained. Fight would go on for hours traversing many miles of ocean; and at the end, should whalers be victorious their labors were not done. For they would have to drag their prize back from points beyond the horizon to shore where it had to be beached through treacherous waves and currents, all the while fending off pesky sharks inclined to steal a convenient morsel.

Once on shore, over the course of several days, community of men, women, children, the old and young would divide various tasks of converting the massive mammal into saleable products, and it was this community that would share in what profits were earned. As a nation today, especially since Stalin, we aren't much inclined to communism. Dirty Reds will pollute world politics and their form of socialism and redistribution of wealth will propagate a world of lazy beggars expecting the other guy to pay their way. Makes me sick just thinking about it. Yet Bankers lived a life of sharing both in work and wealth. Guess you'd have to say they were socialists too. Only difference is they were routed in capitalism and wouldn't tolerate slothful and shiftless laggards. It sounds complicated, but in fact it were simple to those who realized that working together wasn't just a way of life, it was essential for our existence. And Bizzy, there was something very satisfying about making ends meet and knowing at the end of the day your plenty wasn't at the expense of your neighbors.

Occasionally hurricanes, consorting with our perilous Diamond Shoals, would deliver a wrecked ship upon their beaches. After burying the dead, Bankers would salvage what goods that weren't spoiled and recover usable hardware to supplement their meager trade. During the heyday of sailing ships, wrecks were more common, but with advent of steamships and installation of light houses the proclivity of nature driven mayhem dwindled, and with it benefits of salvage.

Our good days were seemingly behind us and so the Guthries, Salters, and few other families packed their belongings and loaded their boats for the short journey that would solidify their future and that of Bogue Banks. Seasoned wood was hard to come by along the shore so homes were disassembled and packed along with kids, and livestock for the trek.

It weren't that our grandfathers were the first settlers. Algonquians, Tuscarora, and maybe even Cherokee tribes had made landfall and camped on Bogue Banks during resettlement as European invaders trampled their native lands; and, Nathaniel Macon completed construction of his fort at the eastern tip of the island by 1834. Just the same, it was our families who made the island their lifelong address and were first to create permanent settlements. My grandfather, your great grandfather, was among those few who resettled to Bogue Banks, and created a new beginning.

Most of our clan put down stakes in the heart of the island, and a few to western reaches, where the island is narrow and one can walk from sound to ocean side in a few minutes. If mullet weren't running on the ocean, chances are we could scare up flounder in the sound. Grandfather warned old-man Salter not to put his house where he did, he would never have a moments piece, but stubborn as he was nobody was going to tell him nothing. And as a consequence, over the years fisherman tramping past his house, from ocean to sound and from sound to ocean, day-in day-out wore a path in Salter's front yard. It was our highway, unobstructed by stop signs or those silly traffic lights which people seem to need to avoid running into each other, and which are popping-up everywhere nowadays on the mainland. Rustling and clanking of men past their window at all times of day couldn't have been conducive to a peaceful life, even on an island like Bogue Banks. Funny though…when folks finally got around to naming townships they thought it fitting to call our tiny spec of land, Salter Path.

There's a whole lot more of history associated with your birthplace I haven't shared, but I won't bore you with it now, and will save it for another day. On the other hand, you might be inclined to what I can recall of impressions of my early years.

*****

All I have to do is look around and see all the tourists scrambling to pack as much as they can into their time by the shore, buildings going-up, electricity, and now a road, to be reminded of all the changes that have occurred during my lifetime and how primitive our existence was when I was a boy.

Been told I was born on New Year's Eve some minutes before or after midnight which would have put me either in 1899 or 1900. Found complaining does little to change hard facts, but think I got me a legitimate beef when my parents don't know which century I came into. Being born didn't seem to make much of an impression, cause I don't remember the event, suppose most folk don't. Somewhere near abouts a year afterwards had me my first birthday, don't remember that either; yet when I stopped messing my pants on a regular basis and took to counting on fingers I started having some awareness of being a human, with associated senses. Have to say I'm fond of all my senses and glad they had a chance to develop as they did. In a world which has got itself in real hurry, it is a blessing to have spent my life on an island where over stimulation is not the norm. As a boy I was free to explore anything and everything within the distance I was willing to walk. Parents had no fear of external threats and there were very few natural threats to be concerned about. Maybe a sneaky

25

snake or gator; but, they figured I'd learn what I could touch and what to leave alone soon enough.

Island life ain't real complicated and if you have a mind there is a piece of this earth to appreciate, which many mainlanders will never know. All kinds of sights and sound, but there is one constant, the sun. Islanders can't get away from it, and perhaps take it for granted, for I've overheard untold number of tourists claiming we are truly fortunate for it.

South facing as we are, it rises on our left. Often I've greeted it at the edge betwixt and between land and water, as it peeks over the ocean, chasing away dew and remnants of a previous night, promising today may offer new hopes. In summer it feels like you could be standing only feet from center of our solar system, sun beating down on your skin pricking like tiny needles. Cicadas get to singing when it gets that hot. They get all wound-up, and at some point, when they've said their peace, wind back down. It don't take long, usually mid morning, before sweat starts pouring freely, oozing from brow, back, and every other pore as well. Ocean breezes dry you off pretty quick leaving gritty patches. Must be medicinal, cause I've never known a dog won't lick you clean if they get's the chance; and, who hasn't explored their upper lip tasting like the sea. As day wanes sun starts its slow descent on our right waving goodbye with a spectacular display of swirling reds, oranges, yellows, greens mixed in Carolina blue. Painted in ways makes you think the artist was a lunatic, or a genius. You can't look away until it sinks well into the sea, leaving you a little sad the day is gone and wondering if it will ever return. Heat stays with you well into night before it calms down a notch or two, and by morning process is renewed. Might think you'd become prostrate with all the sweltering incandescence, but our bodies have a way of acclimating, discovering a way to adjust to our surroundings; and, with it find a new speed. Isn't that we don't know the difference between hot and cold, but it's all relative don't you think. Personally wouldn't know how to cope in the Arctic, but them Eskimos seem to do OK.

On cloudy days, which are few and far between, we're thinking about the sun. Sometimes I feel bad for those folk who scraped and saved all year long so they could spend a few days by the sea, only to find their hopes dashed by inclement weather. For us islanders, a reprieve is nice as long as it doesn't drag on, and we are all too happy when the sun reappears.

Winter brings cooler days and it is a blessing to sit on the porch with a good book rocking and baking in its luster. Might have a mind to get off your behind and get on with business at hand, but you just can't bring yourself to break the spell and move. Being shortest season, one doesn't have to wait long for winter to change to spring, and spring is really beginning of summer. Truth be known, most of us natives prefer shoulder months where we have all the pleasures of island life, good weather, warm days, and none of the hassles of entertaining.

Most don't know Bogue Banks has got itself a woodland smack-dab in the middle, what college types call a maritime forest. Being that it is on an island takes some people by surprise. Some cedar and oak, a few dogwood, but predominantly pine densely packed hugging the sound-side, surrounded by sand and water, it looks for all purposes to be a mistake. But I don't think God makes mistakes, and by degrees I haven't found any yet. As a boy, sure was grand walking barefoot through shady trees, pine needles cool and soft beneath my feet, smell of pine tar clinging heavy in the air. Meandering with no particular purpose I'd eventually find a clearing, opening up to the panoramic vast ocean. It was like walking from one dimension of space and time to another. Greeted by ocean breezes bringing aroma of the sea, crisp, briny, expectant; same waters sound-side smelling brackish and faintly acrid, probably due to stewing of decayed leaves and such in calmer waters. I'd step out onto the hot sandy beach, burning the soles of my feet, making a mad dash to water's edge where cooling ocean waves would extinguish the fire, and pondering vastly different sensations experienced in the span measured only in yards. Reversing my steps was equally astounding.

If I live to 100, which seems unlikely, I will never tire of the sight and sounds of the ocean. In the course of 6 hours, tides and waves will change the complexion of the beach from a narrow patch of loose sand, squeezed between ocean and cottages, steep and hard to walk through, to a broad hard packed highway flat as anything you've ever seen. Staring out across water past limits of my vision I imagine there is another world, but there is no proof. Expectant explorers from another time believed should they travel too far they would come to the very brink and would disappear over the edge. What idiots! Long before I had any schooling, I knew our earth couldn't be flat, or have sharp corners either. Call it natural discernment, insight, common sense, or whatever but I knew as I stared across the sea our planet could not be broken.

Bringing my vision closer to shore I've watched ocean swells topped by whitecaps delivering waters from distant lands, sent by whom? As they near coalescing, gaining strength, rising-up, poised to unleash their power, frozen but for a second. Then wham, shattered upon an unyielding beach! You can't blame those who would think the waters had been destroyed. That is until you step into the surf and feel the power of undertow delivering that which once was, back again to distant lands, and to whom? Wave after wave after wave, Bizzy can you imagine how many waves have made landfall on Bogue Banks since the beginning of time, or for that matter since you were born? No two alike. Well, if that don't make an impression, likely not much will.

Sometimes flat as a mirror, sometimes a boiling cauldron, or crinkly with chaotic chop catching reflections of the sun like shattered glass, there are as many complexions of the sea as there are days in the year. Different moods, for the most part serene, however, at times that serenity is torn apart and the ocean is prepared to rip the very soul from your body. Black billowing clouds moving across the sky, squatting low on the horizon, at speeds that defy logic, winds coming out of nowhere threatening to tear clothes from your back. Neighbor's roofs, unguarded garden tools, favorite rockers, flying willy-nilly, as if gathered up by magic of a witch. Frantic howling swallows all other sound, eardrums thumping and popping as pressure drops into the danger zone. Waves rising into giant comers, 15, 20, 25 feet high, an unending phalanx from beyond sight marching as an army to invade our very shore, destroying everything in their path, bringing flood waters breaching breadth of our island, cascading torrents ripping houses from their foundations. And, as terrible as it is, there is something wondrous and majestic in demonstration of God's power unleashed. There will be those where temptation is too great, who can't avert their eyes, but will step into oblivion never to be seen again. Ocean in one moment is ready to consume all humanity and in the next, just that quickly, is supremely tranquil. Danger has past, but not the warning, leaving behind devastation that rips at the hearts of those who have lost everything. If unheeded, will it come again?

But man's resilience is impressive, and their will to recoup what is lost makes them either damn fools or damn brave. Had my own fair share of ups and downs on that rollercoaster and, can tell you there is an inherent desire to see beyond the pain to a point in time in the future where one can bask again in serenity of island life.

Now that I am older, eyes a little dimmer, skin stained by sun and wrinkled from ins and outs of a life lived on shores of Bogue Banks, same senses of sight, sound, smell, taste and feeling still thrill me and seem as new as they did when I experienced them when I was counting on fingers and toes.

Those, but a few impressions, I hope give you some idea of what our island speaks to me. Wish I had me more words to express what my heart knows. Maybe they'll come to me...

...and if they do I'll be certain to put them in a letter.

Well that's it for now. I've got plenty on my plate to attend to if we're going to meet summer on our own terms.

Will write again when I can,

Father

Fred

Milked my last drops of whiskey hoping to conclude Bizzy's second letter without having to get up; and having accomplished that, now needed a refill. Learned somewhere in my mid 40's that a drop or two of the brown stuff would take the edge off and put me in a more receptive mind for reading. Seems my definition of a drop or two has evolved over time and now I get a little antsy if there isn't a minimum of two fingers at the bottom, but who's counting? Reading becomes a somewhat loosely defined word, as often I find myself, without warning, slouched and eyes resting. Nevertheless, from the bottom of my glass emanates a prodigious amount of wisdom, for which I freely share. No one is impressed by a cheap drunk, and if you're going to the bother to lubricate the bearings, might as well do it in style. Buy single malt, and buy Irish.

Shifted my weight, scooting my butt close to the edge, started rocking, and heaved my hulk up from the recliner, which is now closest thing I got to a friend. Oh, I know people, and I guess I have had a close relationship with one or two of these people over the years, but I am not one to collect friends, or even cultivate friendships…too much work. Besides I despise those who fallaciously claim they have lots and lots of close friends. They are either lying or delusional. I don't even want to get into story of a so-called friend who stole my girl, at least not now.

Anyway, back to my recliner. Years of assimilation left imprints of my posterior on the seat cushion, which allows me to take aim and find my mark when conventional methods of sitting fail me. Stumbled a couple of feet finding my balance and was immediately reminded of arthritic joints and how this incessant cold was wreaking havoc with those systems which constitute the sum total of my questionable physique. Thought of life on Bogue Banks at this moment was appealing. I have on occasion contemplated moving south to Florida to escape winters, but the idea of having to associate with people my own age is revolting. Most smell like mildew and the rest like embalming fluid, and everyone is waiting for the other shoe to drop.

Filled my glass and drifted to the window. Pulled blinds apart, specter of old man winter glaring back. Blew hot breath on the pane fogging and obscuring truth of what was outdoors; and uncharacteristically, was grateful I lived in an age where I could remain warm and dry, protected from the elements. Wondered how many others across the city were staring out their windows at this very same moment and struggling with how to entertain them self.

And what say you of the letters, you ask? Not ready to make any definitive conclusions, having learned that premature assessments of writers are usually wrong. Despite the scratchings, there is something very natural in style and discourse of the man who calls himself Father. If I were to say what I've read was not compelling no one could fault me. Should we be surprised, for if we're honest, how many personal letters would ever fall into that category. No, tone is more relaxed, yet sincerity is deceptively alluring, and if patient, I may find more than bargained for. I certainly haven't reached the point where I've tired of exploration.

Even if the snow lets up, don't think I'll be going anywhere anytime soon. Made my way back to my friend, found a comfy position, pulled another letter from the box and...

September 19, 1947

My Dear Bizzy

> *Uncommon of me to complain, and I hope this doesn't portend of future trends wearing emotions on my sleeve, especially when writing to you; but, I've found myself bothered and perplexed by the ole ladies squawking.*
> *This morning I was summoned by Miss Alice to the big house...*

...nestled back in the Isle of Pines. It is a massive structure built to Miss Alice's exacting specifications, ornate, yet not gawdy, nestled in the pine away from curious eyes. Could hear her clucking as I came up the path and knew whatever bug had found its way up her nose, I was likely to be on the receiving end. Can't say I'm her only step-and-fetch-it on the island, but when she's worked herself up into a tizzy seems I'm her go-to for venting, and I've learned the hard way its best when she finds herself in one of these moods to come at her at an angle.

"Mornin Miss Alice, beautiful day out there today, don't you think? Nice breeze, not a cloud to be seen. Would you be wanting me to bring you up to Atlantic Beach, or drive you over to the mainland? Mrs. Waters says she'll

30

have fresh oysters by noon. We could stop along the way and get a couple dozen, or maybe on the return trip, whatever your pleasure."

"I'm not interested in the weather and you don't fool me with stupid errands! I didn't send for you to do any shopping and if I wanted oysters I'd send Gabrielle on her bicycle! Now you listen to me Johnny-Joe, you don't fool me. You cursed well know why I called you!" Ole lady called my Johnny-Joe, sometimes Johnny, sometimes Joe, and never knew why, cause they aren't my names, but that never deterred her.

"Well now Miss Alice that's not fair. I actually don't know why..."

"Don't interrupt me you idiot! I'll let you know when it's your turn to speak! Its' Fred! He won't budge and I want to know what are you going to do about him?"

Oh my! Somehow I've become responsible for Fred, and I can tell you it is a burden that can squash a man's spirit. There was a time when Fred was reliable and could be counted on to perform his duties without complaint. But now, his better days are behind him and chinks in the armor are showing all too clearly. Fred makes no effort to disguise his temperament and behavior; and, when he gets in one of these frames of mind, well, let us just say Miss Alice and him don't see eye-to-eye. To be fair, ole lady's patience has thinned, as I can recall in the past when she cherished Fred and would turn a blind eye to some, or all of his predilections. But now her hair has turned completely gray, lines on her face disguise her previous beauty, and she simply doesn't stand as straight as she did as a younger woman. Fred, well he wheezes a lot. Guess their relationship has advanced like other couples, and the saying, "familiarity breeds contempt", is all too true. Now seems they get's to fussing with each other at the drop of a hat, and, regrettably, I get caught in the middle.

*****

Miss Alice was born into money. Her mother died when she was only 10 and maternal grandparents, who were gazillionaires, raised her along with sisters, Grace and Mary. Destined for rarified air, she was sent to Miss Porter's School for Girls in Farmington, Connecticut, one of the finest finishing schools available to gentry and took singing lessons in Paris from Madame Machessi...imagine! Sadly her father also passed young leaving her an heiress to the family estate with significant holdings including a department store chain and numerous properties from here to Timbuktu. Yes, you'd have to say Miss Alice was loaded.

Miss Alice is not a native Banker which may explain why she gets on likes she does. Alice Green Hoffman came to Bogue Banks in 1915 when she was 53, I was just a boy. She were a puzzle to be sure. A woman of some means, she lived the high life in her penthouse in New York City and at her exclusive residence in Paris along Champ Elysees. Although she must have had her reasons, no one could figure why she'd want to put down roots on our shores. But that she did, bought pretty much all the island from John Royall, built her Shore House, and commenced to dairy farming. Not long after, she went to war with the good folks of Salter Path, taking them to court over a few cows wandering on to her estate. Well the whole thing got out of hand over nothing and lickety-split we'd learned that not only were our cows breaking the law, but we were squatters. All those years, generations before us, our families had lived on Bogue Banks without deeds to their property and thought nothing of it; and now, well we were squatters. Have to say that stung a bit. It weren't clear if she wasn't going to run us off, and islanders walked around on egg shells pretty near on a year. Court finally ruled we could stay, but it was made clear it was only by the good graces of Alice Green Hoffman. She's never let us forget, and is quick to reminding we're all beholding. So, you can see Miss Alice has always been a little prickly, at least since her days on the island.

It don't seem fair ole lady got herself like this. Can't believe anyone who is as cranky as her is truly happy. Portrait of her over the fireplace in the big house got her all fancied-up in an attractive chiffon dress wearing a faint smile, maybe a frown, but there is no indication she is anything but demure. She was a beautiful young lady. Hair was long and done up in a bun, as was the custom then. She had delicate features and skin as smooth as ivory. She wasn't what you would call athletic, but she had a thin waste and shapely legs, what you could see of them. I can only imagine the young men of Paris were smitten. She hosted and attended lavish parties, where all the la-ti-das and do-re-me's of Europe attended. Swirling to music of Strauss on marble floors under gilded ceilings decorated with crystal chandeliers, probably had a dozen or so bos chasing her all over town, sniffing like dogs on a scent. And with good reason, Miss Alice was not only pretty, she was sophisticated and cultured. Fluent in French, which I've heard her speaking to herself when she don't know I'm around, but she can get on in German and Italian too. At least that is what I am told by those who know. Royalty, likes of King Edward VII and his nephew, the weasel Kaiser William II, along with their respective courts and entourage were real cozy with Miss Alice. She was on familiar terms with the two, calling them Bertie and Willie, and was entertained on their respective yachts as they vied for her attention, making sure they would drop her name in certain circles to impress other swells.

Traveling back and forth from New York to Paris like a ping pong, she was the delight of every fancy ocean liner plying waters of Atlantic and was guaranteed the best first-class accommodations on every ship without as much as a by-your-leave. When she wasn't entertaining in Paris, she would be in New York, giving dinner parties at the Ritz-Carlton to nouveau-riche, Monday through Saturday. Sunday was reserved for planning more parties and writing letters to courtiers, her surreptitious code for gentlemen friends.

In formative years, Miss Alice was seen in the constant company of her niece, Eleanor Roosevelt, who she doted on like a puppy, reminding would be callers that she was after all a lady and they should mind their manners in the presence of kin. Eleanor, bless her heart, was homely by comparison which worked to Miss Alice's advantage on more than one occasion. Best way for a rose to stand-out in a crowd is to be surrounded by thorns. Notwithstanding, Eleanor would eventually win the affection of the son of our President of these United States, Teddy Roosevelt II, and they were wed, although it is rumored not always happily. I suppose that isn't too odd, marriages start off on the right track and sooner or later, usually by neglect, get derailed.

Now that I think on it, maybe it isn't any wonder ole lady got her nose turned-up, believing she is a tad better than our lot. But being nasty don't do her no favors and certainly don't put me in a mind to bend over backwards.

Yet, mama said there is usually a reason for people's nature, if you're willing to scratch the surface. It may have something to do with those summer vacations she took in the Hamptons. There she met the ne'er-do-well playboy, John Ellis Hoffman. His reputation preceded him, but funny thing about infatuations, they simply don't care. Lust, or love, got the better of her and, despite advice from family and friends, married the stinker. No surprise, when John continued to gamble, now with Alice's money, and was seen in the same company, women of lesser virtues, which had earned him the distinction of being a cad. Marriage lasted longer than their love, ending, 5 years to the day in divorce. It didn't matter that John was rotten to the core, the stigma of being a divorced woman clung to her like a crown of thorns. Those who couldn't get enough of Miss Alice before, now steered paths further than if she had leprosy. No men callers, no social invitations, the divorcee was left to stew over the inequities of this world, knowing it is impossible to go back in time and start fresh.

Speculating a little, but maybe it was bitterness, maybe World War I, but something drove her to Bogue Banks, turning her back on New York City and Paris. Only she knows. Living on this island can be a lonely thing even for those who aren't ostracized. Miss Alice wouldn't die alone, Gabrielle, her maid from Paris, moved to the island with her, and their relationship migrated from employer-employee to life-long companions. No small blessing for both.

Have to admit she's got a few surprises up her sleeve. Wouldn't expect her to stoop to working class, but don't you know Miss Alice was Bogue Banks first postmaster, sorting mail from her Shore House for watermen, some of the very same she sued. Feisty too, drove her Indian motorcycle all the way from New York City to Bogue Banks when she turned 71, makes me tired just thinking about it.

In spite of all the ups and downs, you'd have to say she's had a full life, and I doubt she has any plans on leaving this world for the next anytime soon.

"Alright Miss Alice, I'll go have a talk with Fred."

Now the thing you need to know about Fred is he isn't actually going to answer any of your questions, in fact, he isn't actually human...he's Miss Alice's motorboat. Long before they built the bridge to the mainland, Miss Alice would fire-up Fred and chug across the sound to conduct her business and acquire those provisions which could not be purchased on the island. In all kinds of weather and seasons Miss Alice could be seen sitting in the stern right hand on the tiller, left on the gunwale balancing the boat. One would have to say an air of contentment surrounded her and Fred. Both pleased to be out on the water inching their way from point A to point B. I think the tiny craft gave Miss Alice a sense of independence and ability to control her coming and going. It's the same feelings folks get nowadays owning an automobile. This kind of power is heady, and I'm sure it engendered a deep fondness for Fred. And now, long after the bridge has been built, Miss Alice still prefers the company of Fred over that of 4-wheeled vehicles.

Fred was as reliable as most motorized contraptions, but when it comes to moving parts they all reach a point in time when things start to fall apart. First it's the spark plug that gives out, like your ticker; then gaskets begin to leak, kind of like your bladder; and finally clogged fuel lines from decades of sludge, pretty much the same as your arteries. It all adds up, the consequence being Miss Alice is stuck somewhere between where she started and where she wanted to go. You can be certain she had no intent when beginning the journey to be let down by Fred and forced to row to the closest shore. To say the least, the conversation between the two would be hard on sensitive ears.

Fail me once, shame on you, fail me twice, shame on me. Miss Alice isn't the kind of person to let people take advantage of her...and that included Fred. I've seen the same thing happen with folks as they get older. When they begin to get around the bend a bit, forget appointments, need a little more help with everyday life, becoming a bother to younger family and friends; well, that's when patience runs thin and hurtful words replace kindness. I do believe if Miss Alice could, she would divorce ole Fred, and maybe she associates Fred with her ex.

Anyway, routine was familiar. I would lug my tools down to the dock, take Fred's temperature, feel his pulse, then commence to operating. Patched him up more times than I care to remember, but that's what doctors do, and I sense he was always grateful.

Stepped down into the boat, he rolled a little as he always does, his way of saying hey, then settled-down to let me work. Fred was sparking, no obvious electrical problems; pull cord had compression, can't be blown gasket, had to check for fuel. "Well I'll be darn, Miss Alice hadn't opened the fuel cock to the tank. Fred wasn't sick, he was thirsty." Problem rectified, it took only one pull and Fred got real chatty...ring da ding, ring, ring, rummm, rummm. Fred's verbosity caught Miss Alice's attention, cause she came down the pier quick-step trying her best to disguise a grin, holding onto her anger just a might longer, at any rate while I was around.

Now I could've told the ole lady it weren't Fred's fault, could've told her that her negligence got him parched and feeling low. But some people won't, or can't, hear what others are saying, and there is just no point jawing. Figured this was one of those times to let it go. Helped Miss Alice down into the boat and with head held high, right hand on the tiller, left on gunwale, she and Fred motored out into the sound, hard feelings had past, and they were as content as ever had been. Reconciled, was pretty sure I wouldn't hear from Miss Alice until she and Fred got to fighting all over again.

*****

Time marches on, there is only so much life left in his planks and spars; and, one of these days we're going to have to lay Fred to rest. When we do, I won't be surprised if Miss Alice isn't too far behind.

Thomas

All the carrying-on about Fred, got my nerves jangled, which as I get older seems to occur on a more frequent basis. With most of the tourists having now returned to the burgs and towns from which they came I had free time on my hands and thought a little fishing might be the tonic needed to bring me back to earth.

Fishing is God's gift to man. It allows us to stand at the crest of his altar, humbled by the magnificence of His seas where we may come face-to-face with the Almighty and chat about this and that, sort through those troubling affairs stuck in the back of our brains, and even ask for forgiveness, which is a healthy thing for mortals that know their place in the scheme of things. Countless times I've walked down the beach with fishing tackle as one man, and returned a different person. It's certainly cheaper than them psychologists and a whole lot less embarrassing. If you got the right kind of bait might even catch a fish.

Fishing also provides a not so insignificant excuse for middle-aged men to be standing knee deep in the ocean half-dressed. After reaching a certain age when physical attributes are called into question and motives are unclear, men look a little peculiar alone on the beach, especially now women have taken to swimming in mixed company in outfits which could only be described as lurid. Kind of like those creepy guys you see once in a while at the amusement parks ogling kids...they just don't belong. But you put a rod and reel in their hands and the very same man looks right at home, almost respectable and if two or three fishermen stand shoulder to shoulder then you have verifiable proof of their virtuous character.

So there I was knee deep jigging with a fancy new lure, for which I overpaid, thinking I was onto the secret no other man was privy to, when Thomas sauntered his way towards me. Now as friends go, Thomas was one of my closest and dearest, but, when it came to fishing Thomas could make the very best angler look stupid. There is nothing more degrading and challenging to your manhood when you can't get a bite and the guy only a few feet away is landing one fish after another. Well, that was Thomas. Didn't matter if I was fishing with fresh cut bait or Hardy's guaranteed plugs from London, Thomas would always put me to shame. Heck, he could catch more on a bare hook.

"Oh, hello Thomas, wasn't expecting you."

"Now Robert, don't sound so excited to see me. Heard you was up to Miss Alice's and thought you might find your way here after the smoke settled. Figured you would appreciate a little company. If I was wrong, I can scoot down a ways and let you be."

"No Thomas, I'm just frazzled. Stay as long as you please."

I met Thomas in 1922 when he moved to the coast to work at Asbury Beach. These were intoxicating times for our little island. In the late 1890's Atlantic Hotel was constructed at the terminus of the Atlantic and North Carolina Railroad in Morehead City bringing the outside world to our doorstep and with it the jingle of change in their pockets. John Royal being an enterprising and clever man seized on the opportunity to entertain patrons of the hotel by opening Money Island Beach pavilion on Bogue Shores, ferrying eager devotees from sun-up to all points on the clock after sun down. Not long after, Asbury Beach was opened and the island became a destination for would be sunbathers and gadabouts. The Asbury was a bathing and ballroom pavilion reserved exclusively for colored folk. Some white people thought it was awful generous to let coloreds have their own pavilion, and I thought the coloreds were awful generous to let us have ours, but in truth I was jealous as they seemed to have more fun. They were always dancing, playing cards, sipping bootleg, and dressed to the nines. Made me want to join-in but in those days you had to be a little cautious about being seen fraternizing with folks of a different shade.

First time I saw Thomas I instantly knew this was a man who could be trusted. Lanky and tall, he had a look of confidence and his smile weren't painted on, it was the real deal. You could tell folks gravitated to him. He was selling tickets, 50 cents for use of showers and dressing facilities for the day, $1.00 included dancing with refreshments. Saw me loitering with a couple of pals and called me over.

"Hey buddy, do me a favor. Watch my window for a few minutes while I go take a pee."

To say that I was a little nervous would be an understatement, "I don't know, don't want to get in any kind of trouble. I mean you realize I'm white?"

"What you worried about? Ain't nobody goin to bite!"

I figured if he could trust me than I sure could trust him and so, there I stood selling tickets to Asbury Beach getting some of the strangest looks a man on this side of heaven has ever received. From that point on Thomas and I became inseparable and I would become the only white man to be employed by the Asbury.

Thomas must have seen the fragile, almost vulnerable side of me, which a man may try to hide from the outside, but eyes don't lie. Now I'm not sharing this Bizzy to gain your sympathy, for sympathy is worse than a disease. In point of fact as a boy I was inflicted with all sorts of deadly ailments. At 5 I got the mumps. My mother and father being concerned and loving parents took me straight-off to Dr. Dietrich who pronounced as nonchalantly as if he was ordering a sandwich, "your boy is goin ta die." This was followed by large doses of some nasty elixir which he seemed to have cornered the market. At 7 it was chicken pox, and the good doctor once again proclaimed, "your boy is goin ta die." Measles, at 9, "your boy is goin ta die," broken arm, hay fever, poison ivy, it was always the same. At 14 I went in for my annual check-up as fit as a fiddle. The doctor didn't even bother to look up and declared, "your boy is goin ta die." Word eventually got around from the eastern to western tips of our little island. On more than one occasion I overheard local busy-bodies tisk-tisking, "poor little Robert, that boy is goin ta die." The fact that I wasn't dead already didn't seem to register, so I was forced to walk amongst the living as a ghost.

I can't be sure, but I think Dr. Dietrich was setting low expectations, so in the event one of his patients did actually die well then, he had warned them hadn't he? On the other hand, if they lived then it was a miracle of modern medicine for which he was bound to be praised.

Thinking I was always on the verge of dying left two profound impressions; one, I was always looking over my shoulder for the grim reaper and two, I seemed to appreciate the little things most others took for granted, which is a good reminder to be on the look-out for a silver lining. I imagine when I do finally get around to dying it will come as no surprise.

At 17 I received word Dr. Dietrich had passed away from some unspecified concern, but chances are it was liver disease which took him. When he wasn't prognosticating my future, he was pickled. And when I mean pickled, he was stewed to the gills. Funny thing, as sorry as I was of his passing, my health improved demonstrably overnight! Due in no small part to the fact I was no longer expected somewhere else. Anyway, all the drama of having one foot in the grave scarred me in a way I thought was a secret only to me, that is until I met Thomas. We've never spoke of it, but he could see things only a friend could discern, and I've always known he'd look out for me no matter what, which time has only proven true.

*****

Business was lively in those days and there was an undeniable vitality that was palpable from infusion of money. After a day of lying on the beach, wading only waist deep as most mainlanders couldn't swim a lick, they would get all dolled-up and retire to the dance halls to kick-up their heels doing fox trots, shimmy, black bottom, and the newest swing dance, called the lindy. Bands banged out jazz rhythms while sweaty men and women spun in the humid night air. Blaring horn sections could be heard drifting down the beach for miles. Even though it was prohibition anyone with a mind and a few dollars could always find a drink, Sheriff Stone pretended not to see. Couples would drift outside to inhale the breeze coming off the ocean and could be seen wandering off behind pavilions to smooch a little. Single young ladies were more often than not chaperoned by an aunt or matronly friend of the family. Being watched like a hawk, they were never out of arms reach. And should a male approach too close their chaperones would throw a blocking tackle and repel cads like bug repellent, squishing them if they could.

Wasn't long before investors from Down East got in on the action, building a toll bridge in 1928, bankrolling what would become the Circle, one of the grandest pavilions ever built, and constructing a boardwalk for strolling. Atlantic Beach caught fire with excitement rolling from the east like a locomotive. There was plenty to go around, but not everyone was excited to see their island invaded by mainlanders, talking their smart talk, and spending easy money. But like a boulder rolling down hill, once it gets going not much is going to stop it, that is until October 29, 1929, the day the earth stood still. Great depression took everyone by surprise sweeping the nation like a cancer eating us alive and stealing the wealth from richest to poorest citizen, and us Bankers included.

Tourists became a thing of the past, a faint notion which stirred fond memories. It was like someone flicked a switch and all the colors of our world were replaced with grays and black. One-by-one hotels, pavilions, cottages, and dining establishments boarded-up with for sale placards pronouncing all reasonable offers would be considered. And, as they closed so did the chapter on growth of Bogue Banks, putting many working men out to the curb like rubbish.

There is something pathetic and painful in the sight of men out of work. How quickly do we find, when tossed on ends, that we were after all defined by what we do. With time some would recover their dignity and learn they were more than just a job, they were men and women defined by their character; and others, were not so lucky, aimlessly lost.

Routine was familiar, men gathered usually early in the morning as if they were going to their jobs. Sometimes over coffee, sometimes a soup line, but always asking the same question, "what are you going to do now?" Hoping someone might have an answer, but knowing everyone was in the same boat, and it was sinking. Crowds thinned out by mid-day when the realization sunk-in there was no miracle, there simply was no employment.

Thomas and I caught-up with Newman Willis. Newman had been the caretaker at the new beach hotel on the Circle, with a wife and new baby he was suffering from the same anxiety all Bankers were experiencing. Before I could even ask he knew the question, "well boys, I'm going to do the only thing a man can do when he can't find legitimate employment. I'm going into politics. I'll start local, but after I'm elected as governor of North Carolina, I've got my sights set on the white house."

I have to say those were mighty tall words for a man who just lost his job and didn't have two nickels to rub together, but don't you know he said it with such confidence Thomas and I took the hook, line, and sinker. Alas, Newman never did make it to the white house, however, he was Atlantic Beach's first mayor and a good one too.

Newman having chosen politics, there were only two other occupations left for Thomas and me, preacher and undertaker. You may ask yourself what do politicians, preachers, and undertakers have in common? Fact is, we all know preachers and undertakers deal with those matters in the here and hereafter; and, if it weren't for all the dead registered to vote, it is unlikely most politicians would get elected. So there we were, preaching or undertaking. I can't speak for Thomas, but I wasn't good enough for one and the other simply wasn't appealing. I'll let you guess which. Nevertheless, Thomas and I were out on our ears scrounging for odd jobs to keep hearth and home intact. In a way it was good we were squatters, as we had no mortgages, and with no land ownership we paid no taxes and they can't kick you off what you don't already own.

Thomas and I hung around the harbor in Morehead, sniffing out opportunities. Kicked around the idea of becoming merchant seamen, we'd put to sea where work was steady and in spite of poor pay, you had a bunk and 3 squares a day. But only way to land a berth during these hard times was if one of the crew died. Neither of us could wait.

Nevertheless, we were destined to be salty dogs and when Cap'n Chisholm lost two of his men to unreasonable vicissitude encountered by inappropriate exchanges with law officers, Thomas and I didn't hesitate. We joined the Cap'n and would set sail from early summer through early winter as part of the mosquito fleet dragging nets in search of prawns. Now I'm actually partial to blue points, but crabbing season is too short and no one was buying, so shrimping it was.

Off the coast of North Carolina we got three types of shrimp; browns, whites, and pinks. Browns are more plentiful and can grow up to 9 inches in one season. When hatched they feed in the estuaries, sounds, and rivers doubling in size every couple weeks. When full grown they swim out into the ocean, which is where shrimping boats, and their crew, work waters using trawl nets passing back and forth like furrows in a field, scooping as much wealth as their boats and backs can handle. Little known fact is the size of the seasonal catch is dependent on weather. Cold rainy winters yields smaller catches, whereas, warmer dry winters produce exceptional harvests.

Cap'n Chisholm was a patient man and lord knows he needed to be with his two new rookies tripping over tackle, tangling nets, and either running the boat at the wrong speed or coming about too fast chopping our nets into tiny pieces. Although he'd grimace at our blunders, never was there a harsh word nor any indication we were on a short leash. Guess he took the good book to heart where it said count it all joy when you meet trials, storing up works of faith for that day when you would meet your maker. In some peculiar way I felt good, perhaps a little holier, knowing we were helping the Cap'n earn his rewards in the heavenly realms. It was unlikely there were two slower learners than Thomas and me, but we had desire and were motivated by lack of other options, so we would stick with it as long as Cap'n was willing.

We put to sea not long after we'd signed-on. It was early June and the morning was already stinking hot. Without a breeze the sun reflected off the water and threatened to melt the skin off our bodies. First two hours seemed worse, getting acclimated and knowing before there was any relief it was going to get hotter. Thomas and I swung the giant booms over the rails lowering nets till the ocean grabbed at em' pulling them taught beneath the surface. Filling nets with shrimp is not complicated. They're either there or they're not. Can't call them, can't attract them, it is hit or miss. Fortunately, Bogue Banks is rich with the crustacean making the effort worth-the-while. First one side then the other, pulley and blocks were attached and hauling commenced. It took the combined strength of Thomas and me, squaring off with legs leveraged against bulkheads, to pull weight of the net and shrimp from the water. I could feel the muscles and tendons stretched to the limit as we worked together pulling on the count of three. One, two, three...pull...one, two, three...pull! Dripping nets strained to their limit inched their way from the depths and onto our decks where squirming masses of shrimp did their best to find a way back into the sea. Cap'n could tell we were suffering and offered words of encouragement and a bottle of coke. "You boys are doing fine, don't worry, a breeze is bound to pick-up by early afternoon." He was wrong. Not a quiver, not a hint of any air movement, it was dead still. Thomas and I had been working stripped to the waist, but as the sun continued to beat down we were forced to put on long shirts and pull the collars high up over our necks.

Sweat pouring off like Niagara Falls, I prayed for rain to quench the inferno which we were forced to endure, but there wasn't a cloud in the sky, and any hope of it breaking evaporated as fast as the sweat on our brows. Nevertheless, I prayed that much harder, "dear lord, I knows you created the heavens and earth, and granting one little rain shower is a simple thing for you to do. If it is your will we sure would appreciate a couple of drops right about now. Thanks and amen."

Wouldn't you know our Lord heard my prayers for before I could get the words out of my mouth the sky turned. Great billowing clouds rolled across the heavens like chariots unto battle, sun swallowed by titans of the firmament. Wasn't so much scared as in awe, and maybe a little prideful I could call down the angels from on high. As Thomas and I stared, gawking at the spectacle, Cap'n put the boat in neutral and made his intentions known, "Thomas, Robert this ain't no time to be taking a break. We got a squall coming-in and its coming fast. Get those nets in the boat pronto!"

Wind shifted and as it did the patter of drops began. They were monstrous, each one large enough to fill a thimble. Patter changed to drumming and drumming quickly turned to torrential downpour. Rain quickly washed salt from my scalp into my eyes, stinging unmercifully. Deluge ripped at the surface of the ocean confusing the limits between sea and air. Thomas and I felt our way like blind men to the nets screaming orders at each other as if we were ordained with powers from above; but all we did was manage to jam the pulleys with lose hemp into a knotted mess. If we couldn't get the nets aboard, we risked getting caught sideways into the storm. Rain was so intense I couldn't see beyond arms-length and if I couldn't see then Cap'n couldn't either.

Cap'n Chisholm's patience had reached the breaking point, "you two dummies get in here! Robert you take the helm while Thomas and I try to cut ourselves free." Language like this could only mean he was pretty upset with the both of us.

"But Cap'n I can't even see the bow!"

"You just keep us on an easterly compass heading. When I scream come-about, turn due west. If we stay far enough off-shore we should avoid running aground. We'll zig-zag until the storm lets-up. Robert, I'm depending on you.Don't screw-up!"

Cap'n and Thomas escaped the bridge into the cockpit and instantly were consumed by a flood of water; and even though I couldn't see them, I knew they were out there, cause I could hear them screaming at each other. Only minutes before, I thought it couldn't get any hotter; and now, I had a chill running down my back, standing at the wheel soaking wet, shaking, staring through the windscreen at the shroud of darkness that had swallowed our tiny vessel. Disoriented by a world consumed in water, it was easy to let the boat tack off its intended heading, and I was forced to focus on the compass to maintain our course. Heck it wasn't like I could see anything anyway.

It was nerve wracking, hollering going on in the cockpit, alone at the helm with boat and our lives in my hands not knowing if I was going to ram another vessel or run aground. I was hoping Cap'n was keeping track of when we should come about, but my wait on his orders seemed interminable. All I could remember was his admonition, "don't screw-up!"

"Come-on Cap'n, don't leave me hanging!" I recalled as a kid it was the anticipation of something unpleasant that made suffering 10-times worse, whether it was mama's medicine, final exam at school, or having to hold Thelma's sweaty hands in Sunday school when it was time to pray. Thinking on it always made me nearly sick and here I was nearly sick waiting on orders I wasn't sure I was up-to.

Garbled screaming sounding like men drowning, banging, and then after I thought it would never come. "Robert come-about...now!" I couldn't have been more alarmed than if I was struck by a bolt of lightning, and my response matched my fright. I spun the wheel hard to starboard, pushing the throttle as far as it would go. Boat fought opposing impulses, waves putting her on beams, and the force of the turn threatened to dash loose objects to port. I watched the compass as it slowly moved on its journey turning east-south-east, then south, then west-south-west, and finally west and with it a semblance of equanimity regained. Triumphant in my execution, I throttled back the engine and expected to hear some kind of acknowledgement from our Cap'n...nothing.

Was surprised, when I felt Thomas's hand on my shoulder. He had the look of a man whose stared the devil in the eye. "What's wrong Thomas?"

"He's gone."

"Who's gone?"

"Cap'n."

"What you mean Cap'n is gone?"

"When you came-about the violence of the turn took the Cap'n off his feet and he went overboard. Would've took me as well if I hadn't been tangled in netting." In the heat of the moment I had committed a rookie's blunder, one I would not soon forget.

Thomas and I searched for nearly two hours screaming out into oblivion till we were hoarse, squinting to see through a maelstrom of machine gun rain looking for any sign of our master. There was no response, it was hopeless, Cap'n Chisholm had crossed the Jordan and was now beyond the veil. At times like these all of your pride flees in an attempt to evade repercussions. Meek, remorseful, you come face-to-face with the real you and recognize that the other guy was propped-up by egotism, a self-regard unwarranted by merit. It is unfortunate that it takes events like these to strip away the façade we all wear. I shed tears to be sure, but wasn't certain if they were for the Cap'n, or for me.

In that moment all I could think about was how am I goin to explain this to Mrs. Chisholm. Then I realized I'd have to report his death to the police, and my role as a murderer. I'll go to prison for sure. Maybe I'll rot in Odom or Pasquotank, maybe I'll get the death sentence. Either way, I've brought shame on the good name of Guthrie and will be vilified by those who I once counted as friends. It hadn't sunk-in, but I would soon realize that I was not only going to the gas chamber, but now without an employer, I was also without a job.

For the next 6 hours Thomas and I would have to ride-out the storm. It was impossible to find Beaufort inlet in muddled darkness so we kept off-shore running east, running west, hoping we hadn't made any terminal navigational errors. Thomas did his best to cheer me up, but I was inconsolable and could find no joy in my present life, or the prospect of its future. Contemplated ending it by joining the Cap'n, but recalled my father's admonition that only a coward takes his own life and the badge of a courageous man is realized when he is willing to face the truth despite how unpleasant it may be.

As dawn broke I could just begin to see the flashing light from Cape Lookout Lighthouse and eastern limits of Bogue Banks, those markers for which most mariners take hope guiding them to protected waters and port, but for me they were the physical manifestation reminding me soon I was going to be answering a lot of questions.

Chugging past the piers lined with fishing boats I imagined the incriminating stares from other crews as we were forced to parade, captain-less, in our ignominious march. Seldom have I felt more ashamed. We made our berth and completed the retinue of securing our ship as if nothing was amiss, not to obscure the facts, but more to prevent any further recriminations for incompetence or neglect.

I knew what I had to do. Stiffly I walked with an awkward gate down the pier with my head held as high as I could muster. My destination, Shepards Point Café. I was certain to find our sheriff gathered over early morning coffee, and there I would turn myself in for incarceration. Practiced my admission of guilt in my head, but as I neared the cafe my mouth dried to sawdust and I feared I would, in addition to my crimes, make a fool of myself. A picture of police and patrons laughing at me as I attempted to spit-out those heinous actions which cost Cap'n Chisholm's life.

I stood at the front door of the café and tentatively reached for the doorknob expecting it might shock me. Almost fell through the doorway when it opened. Worked myself into a tizzy, temples bounding, beset with tunnel vision, it was hard to make-out anything in the room but the table where Sheriff Stone sat with his cronies. Sheriff was an easygoing kind of guy, never seen him flustered, but I don't suppose he ever had to face-off with a murderer before.

"Sheriff, I got to tell you something."

"Sure Robert. Pull-up a chair and you can tell me what you had on your mind."

"No thanks, I'd feel better if I stood."

"OK Robert, suit yourself I can listen from where I'm sitting. But get on with it so us working gents aren't late to work." This got an appreciative chuckle from his buddies, who for the most of them, didn't have jobs and would reposition their posteriors only if they went to sleep.

"Well sir, I'm here to tell you I've gone and killed Cap'n Chisholm."

"Hmmm, that's some serious news Robert." Everyone in the café commenced to laughing as if I had cracked a joke. Must have found myself in an asylum, cause only lunatics would find the pronouncement of a capital offense from a murderer funny. I didn't find the laughter respectful of poor ole Cap'n Chisholm either. I turned ten shades of red and was on the verge of cracking the nearest guy in the jaw. "Robert, don't you suppose you ought tell the Cap'n you've gone and killed him before making your confession."

"What kind of nonsense is being perpetrated Sheriff Stone? I just got done telling you Cap'n Chisholm is dead. You all should be ashamed of yourself!"

"Well you may be right, but…" At which point Sheriff Stone pointed to the corner booth where Cap'n Chisholm sat pretty as you please, definitely a jaw dropping moment.

"Hallelujah, jeepers creepers, bless my soul if this don't take the biscuits! Cap'n I thought you was a dead man!"

"Now Robert calm down, you're going to give yourself a coronary. I can see how you might come to that conclusion, but as you can see, I'm fine as a fresh coat of paint. When I went overboard I had me a pretty good idea which direction was shore, so I commenced to swimming which I did until I crawls out of the ocean. Wandered down the road towards Atlantic Beach where I hitched a ride home. While you boys were trying to thread the needle, got me a bath and a good night sleep. Came to Shepards Point this morning figuring you and Thomas would eventually materialize. And here you are."

Over coffee Cap'n, Thomas, and I sorted through some of the deficiencies in our training and promised to double-down our efforts to become better seamen. Cap'n Chisholm wouldn't hold a grudge and we would sail with him for many more years.

When I think about it I learned two valuable lessons from our crusade. First, weather can change in a heart-beat along Bogue Shores and it is best to keep this in mind when you cast-off. And two, prayer is mighty powerful in the hands of believers. Be careful what you ask for.

*****

My rod bent nearly double. I yanked it hard to set the hook reeling in my catch as fast as I could to be sure it wouldn't escape. It was a monster and I covertly glanced out of the corner of my eye in Thomas's direction to be sure he was a witness to this sporting wonder. Leaning back and forth I embellished the fight adding drama to the battle between man and aquatic goliath. It had fight and wouldn't be landed without a challenge, drag of my reel whined as it made its way to deep water threatening to take all I had. There was no other way, I'd have to wear him down. Back and forth we fought, and as we did in the back of mind a selfish notion took seed. When I am victorious I'll have bragging rights over Thomas and he'll have to admit I'm the better fisherman. Could already see my picture with my prize catch in the local paper. Thomas, of course, was in the background looking like a whipped dog. Only yards from shore I nearly had him, but once again he fought seaward. Oh no, he turned and ran to shore! I couldn't reel-in the slack fast enough, turning sharply the line snapped and with it my hope for fame. There is nothing worse than a broken heart, unless it's a fish that got away. Rod returned to its normal canter, line limp laying on the water, I faced Thomas. Now I wouldn't say he had a smirk, cause he ain't the vindictive kind, but he wasn't frowning either.

"Well Robert, at very least you'll be able to say, you should have seen the one that got away. Better luck next time. Got to go now, but I'll see you tomorrow."

Not absolutely sure, but I think Thomas fishes sometimes just to get under my skin. Nevertheless, fishing is what brought my forefathers to these shores, and no matter how bad I am at it, it's in my blood. As long as I have breath in my body I'll figure some way to make it to the water and dangle a line and who knows, maybe I'll catch a fish or two. But if I don't, I got Thomas as a friend and I'm sure he'll share some of his catch with me.

My Hat

There's been something on my mind for a while, puzzling to the point I am willing to share with you Bizzy and hopefully get your opinion, should you be so inclined. Now there is no way to say this delicately, so I'll come right-out with it. There is a fundamental difference between men and women. Not so much in the way we eat, air we breathe, or certain bodily functions, for after all both genders are part of the human race. But there are distinctive personality differences I am sure most would acknowledge. For instance, men are inclined to offer advice when women simply want us to shut-up and listen. Women tend to gush and get all sentimental when it comes to loving, men don't know how to be either; men are likely to overestimate their abilities and in doing so brag wherever there is an ear, women don't care. The list is long, but for the most part men and women can work-out these differences finding some acceptable middle ground upon which they can reach a truce. This ain't what's bothering me. No, I'm referring to the level of intolerance women show towards men when it comes to integrity of their chapeaus.

Every salty dog who puts his bow to sea in search of shrimp knows that a hat is a fundamental piece of equipment. Without one it wouldn't take long for the sun to roast your noodle. Sun can blister your scalp in no time. Even men endowed with a full head of hair are susceptible. Selection of a cap is of course a personal choice; and, despite women's view on the matter, men in fact do exercise a modicum of fashion when picking a lid. Some will make their selection based on utilitarian criteria, broad brim covering the skull, ears, and nose. Others will choose a hat because it dons their favorite logo, tractor supplies or diesel engine, for example. In either event, they wear their hat proudly because it says something about themselves, advertising to the world what faith they hold in commercial comings and goings, sportin matters too. When new, no one will protest texture of fabric, colors, or style. On the other hand, as they age and take on a character of their own, it is likely they will illicit approbation from the fairer sex.

I can recall numerous instances where I have been accosted by uninvited female critics expressing the most disagreeable judgments against the cleanliness, rectitude, and appropriateness of my hat for public exposure. Of course, being out in the sun for hours of the day, day-in day-out, is bound to leave a residue of salt and stains literally from the sweat of your brow. Heading shrimp is a messy business, covering your hands in acid and shrimp brains, which I don't care how careful you are is bound to find its way to the brim of your cap. Over time the bill frays and along with stains, guts, and other discolorations your head piece reaches a state where a man can be satisfied. It has attained the laudable condition of being "broken-in". Parting with a hat that has been "broken-in" is unthinkable. Yet that is exactly what women propose we do, "throw that disgusting cap away!" Nay! The familial bond attained between a man and his hat is not to be tested. Why I've seen grown men jump overboard, disregarding life and limb, to rescue from certain destruction their beloved covers snatched by gusts of wind. Most men would rather die than casually discard a hat in deference to women's urgings.

Wasn't too long ago I was patronizing Mrs. Waters emporium on the quest to replenish a favorite marmalade, which I indulge on a frequent basis. Minding my own business, which can be a difficult thing to do on a small island, I had collected a few items and was reaching for the aforementioned condiment, the last one on the shelf, when a hand was extended for the very same. Coincidently Miss Alice and Gabrielle had elected to do some shopping as well. The hand belonged to Miss Alice. Somewhat startled by the near collision I stepped back and our eyes met. Well actually my eyes looked at hers, her eyes, on the other hand, were focused 2 inches above mine.

"Good gracious me alive! What in the world is that on your head Johnny Joe?" Miss Alice again forgetting my name was Robert.

"Ma'am?"

"Don't you ma'am me you revolting reprobate of a man. Get that horrid article out of this store immediately."

Turned-out I was wearing one of my favorite broken-ins I had kept from my shrimping days, probably near-on twelve years old. To say it had personality would be an understatement.

"Oh my word, it smells to high heaven!"

Gabrielle, who normally remains impartial, was standing behind Miss Alice with pursed lips pinching her nose, "tu pues".

"Mrs. Waters, oh Mrs. Waters, would you please ask this man to leave your premises. There is food which could be contaminated by the perversity of his very presence!"

48

Now it might have had a faint odor, but the likelihood of compromising any produce was simply ridiculous. Although there was a time when leaning over the pickle barrel it kind of got away from me. Some said the pickles tasted better, but I wasn't about to take credit.

"Hang-on Miss Alice, there is no call getting in a twist over my hat. It is perfectly safe. If it were dangerous a lot of Bankers would already be dead. Let me finish my shopping and I'll be out of here quicker than Ex-Lax." Suppose I should've used a different reference cause Miss Alice went to swooning.

"Oh! Oh! Gabrielle, help me I'm fainting."

As Miss Alice slid into Gabrielle's arms I decided to nab the last marmalade and skedaddle. Normally I would have done the gentlemanly thing and offer the marmalade to Miss Alice. But under the circumstances, insulting my cap and fainting, I opted to provision my larder instead.

A few days later Sheriff Stone paid me a visit.

"Howdy Robert."

"Sheriff, what can I do for you?"

"Seems there was an incident the other day at Mrs. Waters involving Miss Alice, and your hat. The plaintiff, that would be Miss Alice, has issued a criminal complaint and has asked me to make an arrest. As unpleasant as it is for me Robert, I have no choice. If I don't cater to her inclinations she could make it difficult for me come next election. Hate to do this Robert, but I'm goin to have to take the hat and the marmalade too."

"Are you kidding? Are you really arresting my hat and marmalade?"

"No, just the hat, the marmalade is being detained as material evidence."

"Has the world gone and lost its ever-loving mind! Sheriff you realize what you're saying?"

"Now Robert, I know it sounds loonier than a fruitcake, but when Miss Alice gets like this it's best to humor her. Be a good fellow and hand them over and I'll be on my way and out of your hair."

Reluctantly I complied, but I wasn't done with this nonsense and would fight it in court if necessary. Heck, I'd take it all the way to the Supreme Court.

Very next day I petitioned Carteret County court for a hearing to make a defense. I was hoping Miss Alice might back-down if she thought of having to appear in front of the Honorable Judge Peebles over the absurdity of a miscreant hat. A date was fixed and subpoenas were issued. Apparently, I misjudged Miss Alice's conviction, for she readily accepted. She would be represented by one of her flashy expensive lawyers from up north, a Mr. Weasley, whom she kept on a retainer, and probably a leash. I don't mean to speak ill behind the poor fellas back, but after all he was a lawyer. No doubt this would be a new experience for Mr. Weasley.

I have many talents, but elocution and debate are not among them. I was at a loss of who could represent my defense in court. Wasn't like I could afford a silvery tongued practitioner; or hope for a pro bono solicitor aspiring to make a name for himself. After some consideration I concluded I had but one option, Newman Willis, mayor of Atlantic Beach. Newman wasn't a lawyer, just the same, he was a politician practiced in the arts of winning votes from his constituency on the promises of unattainable fluff. In addition, he was a man and, therefore, had a vested interest in the outcome of this case. Having sufficient intellect and skills to get elected I figured we'd have a fighting chance.

On the date of the hearing we appeared at the courthouse in Beaufort. In the court room were Miss Alice, Gabrielle, Mrs. Waters, Mr. Weasley, Sheriff Stone, Newman, myself, and an assorted array of bench warmers who had nothing better to do than satisfy their deviant curiosity into other people's sordid business.

"Hear ye, hear ye, hear ye, all rise for the Right Honorable Judge Peebles presiding this day in the County of Carteret." Judge Peebles sauntered up to the bench, found his chair, and glared over his spectacles at the assembly for which he now governed. "You may be seated." We were off and running.

Newman and I had discussed the particulars, and I certainly made my plea as to the injustice of the misdirected power of our legal system. Yet, I had no idea what defense Newman had planned, and as proceedings commenced wasn't too worried, believing truth would carry the day. However, my confidence began to sag as one witness after another was called by Mr. Weasley and were delicately and skillfully guided through the intricacies of modern tort law, each testifying to the wretchedness of their personal trauma having been exposed to the aforementioned incarcerated hat, which was currently sitting in all its inglorious nakedness front and center on the judge's dais. Newman sat speechless, making not one objection, and picking his fingernails with a file.

Mr. Weasley summarized, "your honor, in-conclusion you have heard consistent and verifiable evidence as to the indecency of the article which now resides in your possession. I have had very few cases in the course of my career as egregious as the one before you today and it is my sincerest hope the good citizens of Bogue Banks can recover from the injury and suffering they have endured. Therefore, I would humbly ask you to render the harshest sentence consistent with the crime. The hat must be destroyed immediately, and marmalade returned to Miss Alice Hoffman."

"Thank you Mr. Weasley. I will now call on the defense to state their case. Newman, if you please."

It was Newman's turn. As he stood he gave me a wink and a thumbs-up. "Your honor, I would like to introduce new evidence." Grumbling and fidgeting in the crowd spread like poison ivy.

"I object your honor! Mr. Willis has had more than sufficient time to disclose his evidence to this court and my office. If you permit new evidence at this time the process of fairness of discovery will be damaged and an outcome of bias will be implied. Certainly you can not tolerate this precedence." From where I was sitting I could tell Judge Peebles didn't like being challenged in his own court, nor did he like this highfalutin pompous Mr. Weasley any more than the rest of us.

"Overruled! Mr. Weasley, I can appreciate the long trip you had to make to be here today, and you must be very tired, which must be the explanation of why you think it is appropriate to lecture me in my own courtroom. I'm not inclined to permit such liberties from our local boys, but especially not from a damn Yankee! Understand, Mr. Weasley?"

"Yes, your honor."

"Good. Newman you may proceed with your evidence."

Newman called on the bailiff to wheel a cart to front of the courtroom. It was covered with two sheets.

"Ladies and gentlemen, but mostly you ladies, before you I would like to present exhibit A."

Upon which Newman removed the first sheet revealing four hats that would appeal to women of cultured sensibilities. There was a simple, but tasteful, pink felt pillbox; a Gatsby with purple bow; a black beaded veil hat; and best of all, a French beret with a jaunty peacock feather. Women of the courtroom were oohing and aahing, taken by the spectacle of feminine couture. I have to admit, if I were a woman I also would have been salivating over the pageantry.

"Your honor, I would like to call but one witness, Miss Alice Hoffman."

Miss Alice seemed somewhat reluctant to take the stand uncertain as to the "what" Newman had planned.

"Now Miss Alice, can you see before you these women's hats?"

"Of course, I do Newman, don't be a dolt."

"Yes of course. Miss Alice can you share with the courtroom your impressions of these hats?"

"Well, I'd have to say they are all very very attractive. Clearly, they have been acquired from a boutique catering to contemporary fashion. I like all of them, but am particularly attracted to the beret."

"Thank you Miss Alice, you clearly have demonstrated esthetic good breeding." Miss Alice seemed to appreciate the complement as she smiled and her shoulders relaxed under the glow of admiration. "Miss Alice, would you venture to say other women would also find these hats attractive, let us confine ourselves for the moment to those within this courtroom?"

Miss Alice looked to the ladies sitting on benches straining to absorb the magnificent headwear and was rewarded with demonstrable nods of approval, "yes, yes I believe I can speak for the other ladies here in this courtroom and say they are of mind to agree with me."

"Excellent! Your honor, I put to you, and to other members of this courtroom, the general premise that women can, and do, form a bond with hats which appeal to their personal fashion sense. This bond from all appearances seems to be sincere, and by degrees from my impression is consistent with those of men and their caps. But, let us not be too hasty, for I would now like to present exhibit B."

Newman lifted the edge of the second sheet and paused for effect, you could of heard a pin drop. Then with a flare of a matador taunting the bull with his red cape, Newman pulled the sheet revealing four hats, identical in all regards except they were tattered, dirty, and torn. Oohing and aahing was replaced by tittering of whispers and tut tuts of women disgusted by the drama of contrasting exposition.

"Quiet! Silence in the court! I will not allow my courtroom to degenerate into some cheap vaudevillian melodrama! Next person who makes a peep will be found in contempt of this court and booted into Sheriff Stone's jail!"

"Again Miss Alice, may I have your impressions of the hats in exhibit B?"

Sensing the trap had been set, Miss Alice unsure of what she should say sat silent.

"Miss Hoffman, you will please answer the question put to you by the defense."

"Yes, your honor, I would have to say these hats are unattractive."

Newman was ready for the kill, "thank you Miss Alice. And may I conclude that you would be disinclined to don any of these hats?"

Squirming, which is unusual for Miss Alice, "yes, I would not want to wear any of those hats."

"Thank you again, and would you think the other women of this courtroom would share your same feelings?"

Miss Alice didn't have to look, "yes, they would."

Bizzy, thing you need to keep in mind is our country had just suffered through one of the worst financial depressions in its history, and was now slowly recovering, thanks in-part to a war-time economy. But no one had forgotten deprivations experienced and sacrifices both men and women were forced to make. Many had to wear tattered clothing, including hats, and were happy to do so. Newman was counting on this collective memory, especially from men who would lend their support to his legal suppositions.

"Your honor, based on the testimony of Miss Alice Hoffman, and I might remind you the plaintiff in this case, I am bound to conclude my associations of general principles. Women will formulate a bond of convenience with a hat that suits their whimsy, cooing and glowing in the sparkle of contemporary vogue. But let this same hat get a little tarnished, a little old, a smite out of fashion and they are all too quick to discard their once beloved in a most capricious and callous act of abandonment. Is it any wonder this same woman would set upon the defendant to curse and abuse the poor man for what? I will tell you what! For being loyal, for holding dear that which was once new and shiny, but now, due to no fault of its own, has seen better days! This man, and his hat; no, let me say all men and their hats, show the unfailing consistent allegiance through thick or thin, in good times and bad, sticking together until death do us part! Are we to allow the injustice perpetrated against this defendant for being loyal and honorable go unchallenged? Your honor, I put to you it is the predispositions of women that are on trial!"

The courtroom erupted with shouts for "justice" from the men, and "destroy the hat" from the women. It was an ugly business.

"Order! Order in the courtroom!" Judge Peebles hammered his gavel, banging repeatedly until it broke, continuing to demand order until he was hoarse. But there was no controlling the unruly masses. Men were pulling women's hair, women were kicking men's shins, there was scratching, clothes were ripped, curses and oaths exchanged. Tables and benches were turned-over, papers were tossed into the air. Newspaper men were frantically penciling copy for the evening paper, photographers snapping pictures. And Newman, he was grinning from ear to ear.

In all the confusion no one noticed I had casually sauntered over to the judge's bench, Sheriff Stone was trying to put handcuffs on a fairly large women, bailiff was attempting to revive the judge, and I without as much as an "excuse me" retrieved my hat and marmalade.

Funny thing about a small island Bizzy, no one was likely to forget or forgive an incident like the one I described. But they also weren't going to disrupt the decorum of island life and make any fuss. In days to come people went about their business as if nothing had occurred; and, if any mention was made of the topic they would act innocent feigning ignorance on the subject. To do otherwise would implicate them in the frightful and horrid affair, which, for most, was worse than living with the bitterness they now harbored. Yes, to women folk I was no longer welcome in their company, but as soon as they needed a favor or a handy bit of work they could always count on me. However, I knew better than to try to visit Miss Alice at Shore House until I made my peace.

I let a fashionable number of days pass before Miss Alice received the package from me. Inside was the jar of marmalade, the beret decorated with a jaunty peacock feather she favored, and a note:

"Dear Miss Alice, hope you are doing well. I thought you might enjoy the enclosed marmalade; and, I believe no other woman on the island can do better justice to the beret than you. Yours truly, Johnny Joe."

I knew I was forgiven because Miss Alice was seen proudly displaying her new hat all over the island. With time it became a favorite of hers, and she happily wore it for many years, long after the blush of crisp folds and color faded.

Newman was reelected to public office and I was seen in mixed company wearing the hat which had been responsible for a riot, now conveniently forgotten. It eventually would disintegrate and I was forced to lay it rest, but I will always hold dear the memory of my hat which was at the center of the island's most controversial moral turpitude between genders.

A World War At War

Listening to me go on about petty disagreements and social inconveniences one might get the impression the good citizens of Bogue Banks were immune or ignorant to real world conflicts. The kind which pits one nation against another, where the balance of power can be tipped, destroying the very fabric of democracy and freedom, and where men's lives are lost or gained. But I am here to tell you we may be backwater, but we are neither immune nor ignorant. Unfortunately, I've seen my fair share of young men from the island pack their bags, shake their father's hands, kiss their mamas goodbye, and walk down a path never to be seen again, at any rate not alive. Sons of Bogue Banks have fought in every conflict since the island was settled. There was the war between the North and South, Spanish American conflict, World War I, and not too long ago World War II. We even had a Guthrie go all the way to China with his regiment to suppress the Boxer Rebellion in 19 and naught. My uncle fought in Cuba during the Banana Wars of 1912, and after years of torment would eventually succumb to malaria he picked-up in the jungle. Bankers don't have war on their minds and are usually the last to look for a fight, but when a fight is unavoidable, they will be there to answer the rollcall.

Noteworthy is the conflict between the North and South. In our early days, not too long after we settled on Bogue Banks, our country got itself in a real mess, emotions bubbled over resulting in the bloodiest fighting on native soil in our history. Some saw it coming a country mile away, but despite its evidence, the Civil War would not be averted. On the surface it appeared as if the conflict was generated by moral issues of slavery. Simplistic reasoning was that southern states were embedded in the belief that some men and women could be held as property and as such, owners could do what they wanted with that property, disposing of it as they might a parcel of land or an old nag which, sadly, was true. Northern states found the notion of slavery abhorrent. Taking any man's freedom is a sin against God Bizzy and there is no question it is a moral dilemma. However, peeling back layers, it is evident that it was the economics of slavery that was the real problem. It had insidiously seeped into the financial vitality of the South making them as dependent on their habit as a junkie is on heroin. What really got their hackles-up, was their inability to control a federal political system which could impose laws abolishing the rights of property owners, forcing them to go cold-turkey abandoning lucrative incomes, dictated by those who from all appearances had no skin in the game. In retrospect, it is sad that men felt compelled to take up arms, brothers fighting brothers, tearing at the framework of our nation, a fragile constitution of states at best. But this is what they did and had they not there is no telling if our darker brothers would ever have been emancipated.

North Carolina was, geographically and politically speaking, on middle ground between Southern and Northern sentiments and they resisted as long as they could, holding-out for a better outcome. In no rush to secede from the Union, they hoped a resolution could be achieved without drawing a line in the sand and resorting to bloodshed. But they were surrounded and pressured by those states that had joined the Confederate States of America, South Carolina being the first, and pressured to do likewise.

It was only one week after Fort Sumter fell to Rebel forces that President Lincoln called on all states to dedicate troops and suppress the southern insurrection. North Carolina's governor, John Ellis, could no longer maintain his posture of neutrality. He had finally reached a point where he was forced to either lend the state's allegiance to those who would wage war to protect their way of life, or to those who would threaten it. North Carolina held-on as long as possible, finally Governor Ellis refused to support Lincoln's proclamation and the state seceded from the Union, May 20, 1861.

Federal forces rushed to blockade southern ports recognizing the balance of war would be waged by control of trade routes. Marginalizing men and materials would place a strangle hold on coastal communities where fighting was most intense. This was no more true than in North Carolina, where command of navigable waters meant supremacy over those counties pushing inland all the way to western borders. As a consequence, in the Tar Heel State the Civil War would be, for the most part, a coastal conflict.

Protected only by wind swept barrier islands, the state was vulnerable to Federal forces from the sea. Breach of any of the limited deep-water inlets would give Union Navy access to Albemarle and Pamlico Sounds and from there they could steam into Roanoke, Tar, Neuse, Chowan, and Pasquotank rivers threatening to sever Confederate blood flow at the jugular. Governor Ellis keenly aware of the menace ordered the coastline darkened. Fresnel lens from Cape Lookout Lighthouse, range lights from Bogue Banks, and smaller lenses from buoys were ordered removed. They would remain unlit for the balance of the war. No sense making it easier for the Union Navy to locate critical arteries. Nevertheless, them Yankees poked around probing defenses until they found soft spots; and, once they made their way through inlets the game was up. In early months of 1862 coastal waters of North Carolina fell to the control of Federalists. Meager resistance from the Confederate Navy, a hodgepodge of river steamers and tugboats converted to lamentable warships, was dashed by overpowering ironclads and gunboats flying Northern colors. Southern sailors suffered one embarrassing defeat after another at the hands of the superior Union Navy. A hopeless cause, first Roanoke Island fell giving the Union dominance over the upper Outer Banks, then General Burnsides army landed on Bogue Banks and quickly seized Fort Macon giving them control now over the lower Banks as well. Humiliation seemed complete, but the South would rise again for one last hoorah.

Late to the game, the South mounted hastily constructed river ironclads of their own, CSS Albemarle, CSS North Carolina, and CSS Raleigh. Striking back with ferocious perseverance, a rallying cry was heard shaking the confidence of Union sailors to the quick. Some foretold of a turn of events which would place the North beneath the heel of Southern boots; but as it would turn-out it was wishful thinking. Sherman's march to the sea conquering major cities of Georgia leaving behind only scorched earth brought the Confederate States to their knees. Soon other southern cities were desecrated by the North. When Wilmington fell a mortal blow had been delivered and North Carolina was doomed.

Throughout the Civil War bankers remained loyal to the Confederacy, yet they were fiercely independent and resisted all attempts to be marched off to parts unknown. They would enlist but only if they were assured they would be stationed in their own communities. Arguments waged back and forth until Confederate Generals turned purple with rage, and while they did, organized Union forces trod the shore-line cleaning-up poorly led and equipped native militia. It is not clear the outcome would have been any different had bankers been willing to integrate and accept those precepts and inconveniences required by all armies. Nevertheless, it begs the question.

Aside from Gettysburg and few other monuments, you would expect there would be very few remaining artifacts from the Civil War to be found. But, that is where you'd be wrong. Musket balls, bayonets, and even articles of clothing are still being found by sides of roads, in fields, and woods, just about most places where soldiers tromped getting from one place to another. Thomas and I have, on many occasions, stood on the shoreline, just east of Salter Path, at one of our favorite fishing holes. It is the last resting place of the SS Pevensey, which now provides shelter and food to our scaly friends and at low tide exposes her smoke stack as if peering to see if the Union navy continues to threaten our shore line.

SS Pevensey was an ironclad side-wheeler employed by the Confederates for only one purpose, to penetrate Union blockades strategically placed at entrances to critical shipping ports. She had left her home in Bermuda early in June of 1864 loaded with blankets, shoes, clothing, and bacon. She also contained muzzle loading rifles and canons intended for rebel soldiers at Fort Fisher on the Cape Fear River, near Wilmington. In the dead of night of June 9th she somehow missed the mouth of the river and steamed northeast to Bogue Banks, now occupied by Federal soldiers. Her fate would be sealed by a Union gun boat, USS New Berne, which patrolled the coast of North Carolina vigilantly looking for Southern gun runners. Stealthily approaching from out of the mist, New Berne sprayed Pevensey with shot severely damaging the ship. Her captain was forced to turn her bow north and run her aground where they were greeted by Yankee soldiers as they made their way ashore. The crew would remain guests of the Union Army at Fort Macon for the balance of the war. No attempt has been made to raise the Pevensey and she is now so deeply buried into the sand that some say her keel sticks-out along the banks of the Yellow River in China.

As a boy it was not uncommon for me see veterans of the Civil War dressed in ragged Confederate uniforms parading under rebel colors, some missing an arm, others a leg but all pretending they had been the victor, promising the fight was not over and they would be marching north to give them Yankees a thrashing. But as I grew older their numbers thinned-out with each successive year until the beginning of World War II when only one or two old-timers remained alive, still fighting in their minds the war between the states. Progress, sometimes, is achieved one funeral at a time. But don't you know, even today, the war between the North and South seems to continue, long after those combatants have passed and probably always will. Makes you wonder.

*****

I'm not here to tell you a world at war is a good thing. Lord No! But there are some undeniable benefits which have been manifested only because men have gone to fighting. If it hadn't been for World War II it is likely we would never have widened and paved the road from Fort Macon through Atlantic Beach all the way west to Salter Path. Having to move military equipment on our sandy rutted roads probably would've been near-on impossible. That road now makes coming and going a whole lot easier and is a subtle reminder we came from somewhere and got some place to go. And that's not all, the war brought electricity to Shore House which kept me pretty busy wiring Miss Alice's parlor and kitchen so she could entertain without stinking up the house with kerosene lamps. She got herself one of those modern electric refrigerators, which meant fewer trips to the grocery.

Along with the war came an influx of thousands of soldiers, marines, sailors, and coasties billeted from one end of Bogue Banks to the other. It would be a lie to tell you that with all the servicemen stationed on the island spending their hard-earned money that businesses didn't prosper; and, the financial vigor enjoyed by our little island was a salve for the pain and injuries from that depression, which remains all too clear in our memories.

Not unlike the Union Navy, Germany's strategy was to harass US merchant ships hoping to weaken Europe which was supplied along shipping lanes in the Atlantic. During World War II German submarine warfare had reached its peak of efficiency. Unterseeboots, or U-boats, patrolling east and gulf coasts systematically destroyed military and merchant vessels. North Carolina was particularly hard hit with more than 50 ships being destroyed within spitting distance in the first 8 months of 1942, early into the war. In addition, U-boats were landing German infiltrators on US soil to gain access to military secrets and commit acts of sabotage. The very idea that Germans could penetrate our defenses and bring the war to our shores was disheartening and our morale was in jeopardy of being broken.

With considerable wisdom our government considered Bogue Banks to be the linchpin in our defenses and it was to be protected at all costs. Military presence on the island served two main purposes. One, to protect Morehead City and Beaufort harbors, critical as distribution ports. And two, for coastal anti-submarine defense. Within weeks of formal declaration of war, two Army artillery units were positioned on the island. Battery A was secreted to sand dunes west of Atlantic Beach and battery B at Fort Macon. Both were equipped with 155 mm howitzers, which could accurately deliver deadly shells over 9 miles out to sea. Marines established a training outpost west of Army Battery A where recruits from Camp Lejeune practiced firing at offshore moving targets. Not too long after the Coast Guard expanded their presence on the island. Supplementing naval destroyers in search of elusive U-boats, they manned observation towers along the beach keeping an eye peeled for unfriendly visitors. Morehead City hosted the Navy, which by mid-war, had leased the entire port facilities and that of nearby Radio Island. To say the least, the place was hopping.

Well intentioned to serve my country with other patriots, I had contemplated joining-up at the start of the war. Unfortunately, at 42 years of age, with permanently damaged vertebrae from decades of wrestling shrimping nets, I wasn't considered a prime candidate. Marching was out of the question, which eliminated the Army and Marines. Navy politely declined my services, and the recruiter for the Coast Guard was less delicate, "sure old man, we'll take you, as long as you don't mind being our anchor." As silly as it sounds, I couldn't buy my way into the war, but seeing how the Nazis were sniffing around our front porch I wasn't about to wait until they knocked on the door. Only thing left for me was the Civil Defense.

Civil Defense was a non-military endeavor organized at state and federal levels to prepare American citizens in the event of a military attack. In spite of the intended central role of the Office of Civil Defense, its design was for the most part a grass roots effort driven by the needs of each community. What was needed in the Piedmont area of North Carolina wasn't needed on the coast and vice versa. From New York City to New Orleans, from North Dakota to California, I'm sure there had to be as many flavors as there are grains of sand. Bogue Banks didn't have air-raid shelters, and with limited number of motor vehicles there was no point organizing drives to collect tires for direly needed rubber. My job was pretty simple. I'd patrol the island on my bicycle after dark imposing the mandate for black-out, for once again a war turned the lights out on Bouge Shores. Pedaling from one lane to another, hoping my pant leg wouldn't get caught in the chain, I'd make sure every house and business had covered their windows with dark curtains, and no light was peeping. Even headlights on cars were required to be blackened, which in the dead of night made for interesting driving. Couldn't take any chances, as U-boats had been known to navigate by the outline of distinctively lit communities along the coast and would lay-off busy harbors waiting for shipping to emerge from behind the protection of submarine nets laid across the mouth of channels. Once out in the open they would stalk their prey until they could get a clean shot with bow or stern torpedoes, retreating to the bottom to hide after they had made their kills.

I would do my best to stem the flow of bleeding as long as I had the cooperation of our Bankers. Took my job seriously and everyone knew there was zero tolerance for unzipped slackards illuminating our island and exposing our country to foreign threats. I didn't like to do it, but I had the power to issue tickets to those who neglected to comply, and warrants for them belligerent repeat offenders. Now I know the difference between those self-important people who have a mind to lord it over others because they've been given a little power, and those folks who have a job to do. No matter how small and unimportant it seemed to others I believed my efforts could make the difference between some sailors living and dying and I wasn't afraid to say so. Got to wear a helmet and arm patch with letters "CD" proudly displayed. Not everyone respected the job and there were even a few mean spirited that said "CD" stood for "completely defenseless", which I did my best to ignore.

Moving amongst shadows of night I couldn't help but become a spectator to all kinds of transactions. There were the usual things, like raccoons getting into folks trash, Mr. Cavendish our local drunk crawling home at odd hours, and if I timed my route right, I'd spy old man Talbot rushing to the outdoor privy three or four times a night on account of a weak bladder. But most titillating of all events was held in the back room of Jack's Bait and Hardware, not much bigger than a closet, lit by one incandescent bulb hanging from a wire. It was the meeting place for the Optimists Club which was code for local boys getting together to play poker. Every Wednesday and Sunday night I was sure to find an assembly of our finest Optimists, and now the war was on a few off-duty servicemen as well. All were welcome. Slouched behind their cards, self-described sharks peered at the men across the table trying to discern their tells and anteing-up a nickel or two if they felt bold. Usual gang included Jack, Newman, Thomas, Sheriff Stone, Judge Peebles, Cap'n Chisholm, Doc Stevens, and when I wasn't on patrol I was known to sit for a hand or two. Most the time there was so much cigar smoke I could hardly recognize people I'd lived my whole life with.

Well it was the beginning of May 1942 and the war was just heating-up. The coast was in a frenzy due to Nazi wolfpacks sinking everything afloat, putting saboteurs ashore, and by now Bankers had gotten use to me yelling at them to turn their lights out. One U-boat, U-352, had been particularly annoying to shipping. Her captain, Kapitanleutnant Hellmut Rathke, was obsessed with earning the Iron Cross for sinking 100,000 tons of enemy ships. Seemed he was in a powerful hurry to get his medal. Fortunately, his aim wasn't very good; but it didn't stop him from scaring the bejeepers out of allied vessels. Rathke evidently found the waters off Bogue Banks to be quite fertile and decided to camp-out, which put our island on high alert.

With the risk being so close to home, Optimists felt an urgent need to meet more frequently. Newman, our lodge's president, reminded us it was our responsibility to maintain our club's namesake for good of our community and he could think of no better way of accomplishing our goal than playing poker. So, poker we played.

I can't remember if it was a Wednesday or Sunday night two men in uniform showed up to try their luck. Don't recall ever seeing them before, but then I wasn't familiar with every man in uniform stationed on the island. They seemed friendly enough, yet there was something different about them I couldn't put my finger-on. Their uniforms looked a little odd, and I thought they had a funny accent. Maybe they were from Boston.

Being a little suspicious I thought I should get Sheriff Stone's opinion. Nonchalantly I leaned to my left to whisper in Stone's ear. "Sheriff, what do you make of those two fellas?"

I guess Sheriff Stone thought I was trying to peek at his cards, "never you mind Robert, they ain't hurting anyone, and at least they ain't trying to cheat, unlike someone else at the table!"

Being properly chastised you might think I would let it be. Nope, I had me a question and someone was going to answer. I leaned to my right and whispered to Thomas, "Thomas, I got me a funny feeling about those two. You know, like they don't belong."

"Robert you got a funny feeling cause they just fleeced you the last two hands. Maybe if you do a little less talking and focus on the game they wouldn't seem so strange."

Seemed I played my cards wrong, in more ways than one and over the next few weeks, those two boys kept coming back every night we had a game, winning more than they lost. Like I said they seemed friendly enough, so I let it be.

While the Optimists did what they could to support the morale of our community, Kapitanleutnant Rathke and the U-352 stirred up waters. Chasing ship after ship from Frying Pan to Diamond Shoals. Wasn't hardly anything with a hull they wouldn't shoot at. It all came to head when a Swedish freighter, Freden, on her way from Aruba to New York was hounded by the U-boat as she made waters off North Carolina. Time after time U-352 attacked. Freden's captain fearing she was doomed ordered abandon-ship twice. Both times, however, Freden evaded death. United States Coast Guard cutter, Icarus, hearing Freden's captain radio a plea for help sped to the scene. At 16 knots Icarus quickly closed the distance. Instead of turning tail or lying low, foolishly Rathke launched two torpedoes at Icarus, but his aim hadn't improved with time. Now it was Icarus's turn to go on the offense. Mercilessly she pounded U-352 with depth charges delivering deadly blows to the submarine's internal organs. Hemorrhaging out of control, U-352 was forced to surface. Icarus was ready. She hammered the submarine with her 3-inch gun and raked the decks with machine gun fire killing 17 of the 60 submariners. Rathke ordered U-352 scuttled and less time that it takes to tell, she slid below the surface to join those souls of other lost ships in the graveyard of the Atlantic. Rathke, and the remaining crew of U-352, would spend rest of the war imprisoned at Charleston's military stockade.

Odd, might be a coincidence, or not, but after the sinking of U-352 those two boys didn't show for poker. Maybe they had their fill, and maybe they were preoccupied somewhere else. One thing's for sure, with the Optimist's shrewd discernment and nose for sniffing out trouble it would be nigh on impossible for anyone to pull the wool over our eyes.

Spies at Shore House

Change is the inconvenient truth by which all folks are forced to live. Changes in our bodies, in our health, and in our landscape imposed by greedy developers. Family members moving on, or dying; and, so on. If we're honest we would admit our contempt for change. And despite the flux constantly swirling in our worlds we grasp at those tenuous threads of stability, an illusion at best. Clinging to the belief we are secure in the constancy of the familiar and denying what is patently obvious, we become incensed when confronted by reality. If you think this is an axiom for the world at large Bizzy, then you can only imagine how islanders hate those differences imposed by time, most won't even talk about it.

World War II not only threatened our democracy and freedom, but also forced everyone to endure a litany of burdens. Wartime rationing, separation of family, loss of bread-winners, and maybe most important, abandoned sweet indulgences. Unpleasant changes to be sure. As uncomfortable as it is to admit, people forced to endure these deprivations wanted somebody to blame. If they couldn't find the guilty, they would choose someone near at hand to be their proxy. Hitler was too far away to be of any good for people of Bogue Banks, so they would nominate a local target, a scapegoat, perhaps someone innocent. Not absolutely sure, but I think this how Miss Alice found herself looking down the barrel of hateful accusations and a near treasonous outcome.

To say Miss Alice had not endeared herself to the close-knit society of Bogue Banks would be an understatement. As you may recall, she made her entrance as one of the apocalyptic horsemen, purchasing large sections of acreage that had stood open and free to those original settlers for over half a century. Miss Alice made her home on our island, but she came from New York via Paris and lest we not forget, the war between North and South was still being waged by those Bankers who consider themselves chosen to wave the confederate colors. No question, she was a Yankee. Flaunting her wealth in the face of those who had little, she built Shore House, an enormous mansion, hidden amongst pines away from the community of natives. Large "No Trespassing" signs were posted clearly advertising her disdain for wandering islanders. Litigious by nature, she preferred to resolve issues of land ownership in court, bullying common folk with high paid lawyers from prestigious firms and after she won, wouldn't let people forget. Given Miss Alice's qualities, Bankers wouldn't have to exert themselves to find that someone to focus their anger on.

I suppose every town has someone like Miss Alice. A little eccentric, no doubt introverted, crotchety and rude to the point where there is no question it's intentional. There is usually a reason for their deportment, and if we're generous we'd realize most likely they have been damaged by events somewhere during their strained existence. Real doozies which would knock the wind out of the sails of the most stalwart. They behave the way they do because it's the only defense mechanism they can call upon from their repertoire; and, you have to admit it's pretty effective. Engineered by their own bitterness, they at times seem surprised by the reaction they illicit, not fully comprehending the impression they lend. Forgiveness and forbearance goes a long way under these circumstances and, in some cases, can even bring a change of heart, softening hard exteriors to reveal good people inside. After nearly 30 years, I imagine Bankers were on their way to warming-up to Miss Alice. Yet, she wouldn't make it easy for them to arrive there. Inconveniently, she was fluent in German and had a two-way radio with an enormous antennae pointing towards the Rhineland. Inopportune coincidences, juxtaposed at a time when citizens were on edge and fearful the far-reaching Teutonic tentacles of the Hun could reach them in the hamlets and towns in which they lived.

I'm no expert, but a mob takes some time to develop, fermenting so to speak, gaining strength and boldness as they win converts to their way of thinking. For example, them agitators in that little village of Reigelberg, Switzerland didn't storm Frankenstein's castle first night they got wind there was a monster. No, probably started with a few smart alecks throwing a stone or two at the castle windows as they rode by on their bicycles. Followed by big talkers in well-lit taverns bolstered by the safety of numbers bragging how they weren't going to tolerate the noble crazy doctor tinkering with life. Anyone who objected to their hysteria was made to feel like an outsider, maybe even an ally of Frankenstein, which was the quickest way to create disciples. And of course, a mob wouldn't be a mob if we didn't throw in liquor. Alcohol is fuel required for the engine of discontent, and once ignited races out of control. Well, the rest is history and I suppose we'll never know if the monster, if he had any say, was completely content in the design and results of the experiment.

*****

Bullet holes in the "No Trespassing" sign on the sandy lane leading down to Shore House were unmistakable, but like others I chocked it-up to a bunch of unruly kids looking to punch as many holes with their 22 rifles in anything that wasn't moving. Wouldn't be the first time. Didn't even need to ask Miss Alice, went straight to Jack's Bait and Hardware, got a new sign and had it up before she was the wiser. However, I found it a bit odd to see the very next day the new sign riddled with bullets and the presence of shell casings scattered on the ground as a calling card. A little too disconcerting for my taste and I was beginning to think this was the work of people sending a message. Beginning of mob madness.

Next morning found myself at the entrance of Shepards Point Café, thinking a Danish and coffee would taste pretty good right about then. Had the door half-way open when a disturbance nearly took it off its hinges. Sheriff Stone was standing one leg forward, shoulders back, arms spread wide, breathing heavy, Jim Williams was on the diner floor wondering how he got there, Jason Slaughter was sprawled across a table, everyone was red-faced. Appeared there had been a scuffle and Jim and Jason were at the receiving-end.

"Alright boys, you have had enough. You get on home before I reconsider and lock you up for disturbing the peace. Go on! I ain't kidding!

Jim and Jason slowly collected themselves, with a look that was both embarrassment and indignation. As they made their way out of the café, they weren't alone. Four of their buddies joined them in an act of solidarity, all of them within a hair of losing their temper.

Jason turned and left a parting shot, "we ain't done here Sheriff!"

"You better hope we are Jason! If we meet again on the same terms it's going to end a whole lot different! And, I don't want to hear you, or any of your pals, spreading that seditious garbage about Miss Alice around town ever again!"

Have a knack for being late to a party, most times I'm disappointed, but not this day. Something very disturbing about seeing grown men fight, especially when its folks you know. I don't ever recall Sheriff Stone having to get physical, it isn't in his nature, but seems as if he can take care of himself if needed. Good to know.

After Sheriff Stone calmed down he told me Jim and Jason had been mouthing-off about Miss Alice being a spy for Nazis. They fabricated an elaborate tale of how she was radioing specifics on ships anchored in Morehead harbor to offshore U-boats. Tonnage, vessel names, flag they were flying, bill of laden, and schedules for departure were coded and tapped-out on her wireless in the dead of night. Those boys made it sound believable, claiming she was responsible for all the ships being sunk off-shore, resulting in some of our local sailors meeting an untimely end, and embellished with how she always signed-off, "Heil Hitler!" Radical half-wits they hung-out with started getting real agitated. Sheriff Stone told them to zip it and cool-off, which is when Jim and Jason decided they would try to push the sheriff around. The rest of the story you're familiar with.

Now if those fellas would have taken a moment to think about the facts, they would have realized how silly they sound. Cause there is no way their story holds water. First, Miss Alice was forced to forfeit her property in Paris at the beginning of World War I as requested by the French Government because of hostilities perpetrated by her loony acquaintance Kaiser Willy and his German army. Second, all residual real estate she held in France prior to beginning of World War II was now confiscated by the Third Reich. Holdings estimated to be equivalent in value to her current residence on Bogue Banks. Why would anyone who has lost as much as she at the hands of Germans, want to work for those thieves. Third, anyone getting close enough to the harbor to steal critical shipping information would be shot dead, no questions asked. Or at the very least, thrown in prison faster than a jack rabbit, never to be seen again. Fourth, she doesn't know how to use her 2-way radio. It's always on receive, and is employed for entertainment purposes, listening to crooners she fancies from around the globe. It is doubtful she even knows which switch to throw in order to transmit and, even if she did, at her age with arthritis there is no way she could tap-out an SOS, let alone elaborate coded messages. The story of treasonous acts by Miss Alice is pure fancy crafted by men who prefer fiction, which gets to another proposition. Mobs aren't interested in the truth. All that was needed now was a liberal dose of liquor.

A week or so went by and what appeared as tranquility returning to Bogue Shores was simply the quiet before the storm. I didn't take any mind to what was stewing, which is a natural condition I'm afflicted with, tending to focus on more important issues at hand, like fishing and napping. I just march-on smiling at myself for the good fortunes God has bestowed upon me, no lofty aspirations, thinking the best of folks, knowing no matter how bad today is, tomorrow will only get better. For it isn't what you take out of this world that enriches you, it's what you put back.

Saturday came and Atlantic Beach had rolled-out the red carpet for the King Mackerel fishing competition, one of the few events not cancelled by war. Newman officiated handing out the trophy for the biggest catch. This year it went to the Cooper brothers for landing a 65 pounder on light tackle. Spirits were high, beer was flowing, and everyone seemed to enjoy a reprieve from world hostilities. Hated to be a Debbie Downer, but I reminded everyone of lights-out at sundown. "If you all want to continue with the party take it indoors and keep your shades pulled." A few grumbles, but by the time the sun set streets were clear and the town was dark. Content our little island was tucked-in for the night I proceeded on my nightly patrol naively believing all was well.

Pedaling with my head-down preoccupied by spinning spokes, wouldn't have seen the conflagration if it hadn't been for a skunk I nearly ran over. Veering wildly hoping to avoid a collision, I sped away trying to outrun pungent vapors chasing me down the road. Almost made it. I covered a distance in minutes which normally takes me near-on an hour. Clearly distracted by my new cologne I was taken back when I approached Shore House to see the night sky glowing. Having clearly articulated my position as to the application of incandescent lighting after dark, I was sorely vexated at the spectacle before me. Was reaching for my ticket book when it dawned on me the sky was lit like a torch because Shore House was on fire.

"Fire! Oh my goodness gracious alive, fire!" Screaming like a little girl I ran down the sandy lane towards Shore House hoping Miss Alice and Gabrielle were safe. Smoke was pouring out the windows and front door. I tried to poke my head in but it was too intense, stinging my eyes, I choked and spat out black tar. Rounded the back, thinking there might be an easier entrance, where I nearly ran into Jim Williams, Jason Slaughter, and the rest of their gang sitting on the ground. Sheriff Stone, Miss Alice, and Gabrielle were standing over them looking more than a little peevish.

"Robert, glad to see you, got to go inside and help Thomas put that fire out! Take my revolver and if any of these boneheads move, you plug'em."

I'm sure Sheriff Stone wanted to put the fear of God into those boys, but the fact is I wasn't going to shoot anybody and they knew it. And I'd be lying to say I wasn't nervous knowing if the rabble wanted they could have disarmed me anytime they wanted and used the gun against me. Fortunately, smelling not too pretty none of them wanted any part of me.

We weren't from the big cities, where crime is a constant companion. Closest we got to misdemeanors and miscreants was in the local newspaper. I always believed islanders were bred from better stock, trustworthy and honest; a community where women, children, and elderly were free to go about their business in the knowledge nothing was going to bite them, where Bankers didn't have to lock their doors, at any rate not until now. It was disappointing, what these boys had perpetrated damaged my faith in humanity, in the belief of fair play and that innocent people were safe in their own homes at night. That was all undone. If they would set Shore House on fire what else would they do? Our world was more fragile than I thought, and at that moment the likelihood of getting it back anytime soon was as remote as the moon. Insidious and sneaky, change had snuck-up on me when I wasn't looking and was now forced to see my world differently.

Thank goodness Sheriff Stone had considered the possibility of Jim and Jason creating a disturbance and threatening Miss Alice at her home. He deputized Thomas and the two of them staked-out Shore House for the last week, catching them boys red-handed.

Fire extinguished, the sheriff was ready to end the ugly affair and take his captives off to jail. "Miss Alice if you and Gabrielle are alright, we'll be off."

"Hold-on sheriff I have a few questions I'd like to pose to my tormentors, if it's alright with you."

"Be my guest ma'am."

"Jason, if I'm not mistaken you lost your boy, David, at Bastogne? Rumor is his platoon was pinned-down for two days straight. German artillery punished the American line without mercy. When it was over there wasn't enough of David to ship home."

"Yes ma'am, I lost my David."

"How very sad, I'm sure it has been difficult for you and your wife to come to grips with his loss. I remember David as fine young man, quick with a smile, generous with his time, and courteous. But mostly I remember him as one who would fearlessly defend his friends against bullies. I wonder what David would think of how you have been getting on lately?"

"And Jim, didn't I read how your little brother, Matthew, was the hero of Omaha Beach? When all seemed lost, and where many others had failed and died, he climbed a bluff destroying heavily defended German pillboxes, and in the process sacrificed his own life. But his sacrifice rallied the troops and by the end of the day the beach belonged to Allied Forces facilitating assaults on weaker defenses further inland. The tide of war was determined by young men like Matthew. Do you think he went to war so you could pull his good name into the gutter?"

"For the rest of you, which of you hasn't had a family member or close friend who has laid their life at the altar of freedom? When it is your turn to meet them in the hereafter how will you account for your behavior here tonight?"

"I suppose I haven't been the best neighbor. I know my tongue is sharp and have done things I'm not proud of. But do you believe that I deserve to be accused as a spy for the Nazis? Do you believe I deserve to have my house burnt to the ground? For if you do, I won't stop you and I won't let Sheriff Stone stop you either. But how does that make you any different than the Nazis we're defending our country from?"

Mighty powerful words, as sharp as a sword cutting to the quick. Not one of them could look Miss Alice in the eye. Heck, I even felt guilty. Heads bent low from shame, she had convicted them for their dishonesty, and her words would echo in the recesses of their brains for some time. I'm not prophetic, yet I knew their punishment would last as long as they had breath.

In spite of the fact the mob had been caught in the act of arson attempting to burn Shore House, and perhaps killing Miss Alice and Gabrielle in the process, at their trial Miss Alice pleaded with Judge Peebles to be lenient.

"For no man who has been confronted with the pain of their loss should have to endure the indignity of prison. How will this help them to heal? They have suffered enough and I will not have this on my conscious!"

Judge Peebles, moved by Miss Alice's entreaties sentenced each man to only 1 year work release. Restitution for damages to Shore House would be repaid by their sweat. As they worked to repair the fire damage, most of them got to know Miss Alice for who she really is, at times proud, at times vulnerable, and susceptible to the same insults life brings to all of us.

Many years later a reporter for the local paper wanted to do an article on the "spy at Shore House." He had promised his publisher he would finally get to the truth behind the covert espionage during World War II. One can only imagine his disappointment when he interviewed Gabrielle, "why yes, I recall the war years vividly. Miss Alice knew all too well what fate our sailors and soldiers would have to meet and she did everything within her power to give those boys a few minutes of comfort. During those years she fed and entertained many. She never turned anyone away. Some of the younger boys who were home sick and scared were welcome as overnight guests. Miss Alice helped each one with their letters home and made them promise they would write their mamas no matter where they were stationed. For those we lost, she would make sure to visit their parents comforting them as best she could. Not everyone could go to war, but she served her county the best way she knew. Miss Alice was a true patriot."

*****

Sometimes Bizzy it takes a heap of trouble to bring the good out of people, maybe even a war. Unyielding, we resist with all the stubbornness of a mule. Holding back, iron-willed, we guard ourselves cloaked in anonymity so no one will know who we really are. Only until we have been marched to the very brink, where we stand poised above the chasm, are we forced to decide. We have a choice, we can step into oblivion never to be found or we can free our inner voice. Some only get one chance.

On that day I saw a side of Miss Alice I'd never seen before. Admittedly it was a surprising change.

A good change. Took a lot of years in the coming, but was well worth the wait. Don't mean she doesn't have her moments, still gets grouchy and a little full of herself, but knowing there is a nugget of thoughtfulness and tenderness inside makes it easy to forgive and forget the rest.

Life is too short to let insults and slights mar you. Smile when you don't feel like it, laugh when you want to cry. Be a shining light to others so they see your beauty from the inside. Sometimes it takes only a kind word to make a difference. My advice to you Bizzy is don't hide yourself from the world.

Suppose I should get off my high horse and stop preaching, will write when I can.

Father

Candy Buttons

Streets clogged with snow, guarded by cars consumed by mounds of white fluffy stuff, indistinguishable as motor vehicles. Muted sentries waiting for someone to rescue them with a snow brush. From my window they look like sugary lumps, lines of white candy buttons on paper strips father use to buy me when I was a boy. Admittedly the scene is beautiful and it takes me back to a more innocent time in my life. Unfortunately, in a day or two the luster from virgin snow will have turned to dirty slush and prospects of slogging through frozen thoroughfares, mounting barricaded sidewalks, and stepping into icy puddles is far from appealing. It is likely the DOT will take weeks to remove mountains of snow accumulated over the last few days and return our city back to some semblance of normalcy, a loosely defined term.

Hunkered in my cocoon, protected from the blustering assailant, I've spent my time engrossed in those curious ramblings of a man whose voice is exercised by pen to paper. My prurient interests have brought me to an end of the first box of letters to Bizzy. His writing is honest, and no doubt he is a storyteller, but it is unclear to me the relationship between father and daughter. Recognizing I live in a different era, but who would, or why, write so many elaborate treatises on the subject of his life and times in which he lived to a daughter, over the span of years. From all appearances it looks to be he was working very hard to communicate, when others would just pick-up the phone. If you've been knocking on the door and no one answers, it's probably time to stop. Maybe I've spent too many years behind the desk reading failed attempts by eager hopefuls. Playing amateur psychologist, analyzing their motives as to what drove them to write in the first place. And of course, having completed my post-mortem examination, dissecting and laying their intent bare on the mortuary slab, I resolve in my own smug way that their pathology is terminal. I once asked, after rejecting a third manuscript from an aspiring writer, "why do you write?" Without hesitation the young lady responded, "because it gives me joy." There was a time when I would have understood and appreciated her answer, but now I'm not so sure. Because it gives me joy. What does that mean?

Experience and years have conspired to mold me into that perfect machine. Insert the manuscript, pull-back on the crank, and watch the wheels spin. Without the slightest modicum of emotion both story and style are digested moving through mechanical small and large intestine leaving behind the fecal remnants of someone's ambitions. Occasionally I find the meal satisfying, but more often than not, I am left with a disagreeable taste and discomfited by bloating. If I could but reprogram the engineering marvel to take smaller bites, or consume palliatives, perhaps the effort wouldn't sound so wretched.

Was there a time when I wasn't jaded? I think so.

*****

I loved reading when I was young, consuming all the literary greats, Steinbeck, Faulkner, Joyce, London, Conrad, James, Wilde, Brontë, the list is endless. Curled in my little world safe from the chiding of parents and cruel taunts from presumed playmates, I found solace in the theater of caricatures and scenery crafted by authors who knew me all too well. Yet, had it not been for my imagination could their words have come to life, could they have created such drama? Perhaps, but the partnership between purveyor and consumer is undeniable.

Illness plagued me in my early years, suffering from nothing as melodramatic as an incurable disease, but suffering none-the-less. Forcing me to retire to my bed for weeks, my mind naturally retreated with me, inquisitive, thoughtful, fruitful soil for authors to plant their seed. No one wishes to be sick, but had I not been forced to the solitude of my room I may never have found the therapeutic effect of literature.

My first love, you ask? Timidly, with only the slightest hint of embarrassment...Dracula! Father snuck a copy into my room when mother was preoccupied, and I kept it secreted in my bed covers. Spellbound, I devoured pages of Bram Stoker's novel unable to withdraw. The picture was painfully vivid. I was mortified at the very idea that Jonathan Harker, an English solicitor, had been summoned, then imprisoned by Count Dracula in his castle in the Carpathian Mountains. His torment upon realizing his captor was a vampire nearly drove him insane, nevertheless, despite his almost certain ruin at the hands of demons, he bravely designed his own escape. Gloom and dread shrouded the existence of Dracula in his fortification in Transylvania, which he eventually was forced to abandon. Mystically his un-dead corpse was transported to Whitby England, the home of Jonathan Harker. There he would slowly drain the vital force from the fragile and enchanting Lucy, close friend of Jonathan's fiancé, Mina. Lucy will succumb and enter the realm of those once living to be Dracula's concubine. Confronted by the tragic tale, my child's mind struggles to accept the soliloquy painted by Stoker. Mina becomes the next victim drawn by Dracula's seductive power. All seems lost. Can there be no salvation for mere mortals as long as blood-sucking creatures are free to roam our planet? Fortunately, the unassuming, but sage, Professor Van Helsing arrives none too soon. Professor Helsing and Dracula engage in a duel of wills. Parrying and thrusting with emblems of Christian faith, Van Helsing endeavors to expel the fiendish presence. It would be easy to dismiss the story as one of many age-old sagas between good and evil, but there is more, for Stoker captures the depths of despair trapped in the shadowy corners of our own minds. Is it too much of a stretch to believe such events could occur, is it too much to believe you could be caught in this very same despondent web of terror? I for one, was impressed by the harrowing tale, but more so by the images Stoker crafted inside my head, leaving a lasting effect of how creative juices pressed to parchment could unleash the power of my own fanciful wit. This was the first book, of what would become many, where I couldn't put it down. Magnetic forces were overpowering, drawing me back to digest words, sentences, and paragraphs, absorbing chapters and to dog-ear favorite passages. What an experience!

Fascinated by portraits imagined by verse, I was inspired by those who so cleverly connected simple words into masterpieces of art. A passion for reading soon bled into my curiosity for writing, and I wondered was the act of composition limited to only a few select creatures blessed by talents others only dream of. Motivation wasn't my problem, but what if my skill didn't match my desire. Could I live in the knowledge that what I cherished most, was out of reach?

I tinkered with creative writing as one might with a 2-stroke engine, assembling and disassembling short stories for purpose of learning how they work. I had but one topic, the vacant and hidden world mother concealed from me. Propositions of what was obscured behind the veil were played-out on paper, versions rewritten with different beginnings and different endings. Plausible scenarios, implausible, I meticulously wrapped the English language in form around the plot of my life. Each rendering chronicled some hopeful parody, each was discarded and although I was never to uncover the truth through writing, I did manage to find my own style.

Uniquely singular, an author's style is his signature, unmistakably it marks transcripts and letters birthed in the course of his, or her, transactions. Have you read Faulkner, could he be mistaken for Poe? Style may be dressed-up, or down, it may be disguised by unfamiliar topics, yet a discerning eye will always see through deceptive pantomimes revealing cryptic hints leading the reader to uncover the truth behind the author's identity. My style would be my ticket to expression of ideas. It would give me speech, and with it, liberation only few have experienced.

In high school I wrote for the school paper, a serial about a dog named Skipper. Nothing particularly unusual about Skipper, he liked to chase squirrels, he drank from the toilet, scratched and licked unmentionable parts of his anatomy. And he could talk. Not that his owner had any clue. Skipper wasn't one to talk your ear off, not one of those verbose hounds who will corner you and wear you down with meaningless prattle. No, Skipper was a closet orator. His audience? Those lost souls, the downtrodden. People in need. Of course their initial reaction was shock and amazement, but after he talked them down from the ledge, he would leave them with some comforting nugget of wisdom giving them a reason to push forward with their lives, but always made them promise never to reveal the secret of his talent for speech.

Over the course of four semesters, I managed to crank-out 12 narratives staring Skipper. From reaction of students congregating around lockers between periods, they seemed to be well received and it would be a lie if I said I didn't thoroughly enjoy my own writing. However, I always wrote under my pen name, Oscar, fearing my work would not bear-up under scrutiny of scholarly reviews. As a nascent writer, the last thing I could tolerate was criticism. It would be like telling a mother her newborn was ugly. It's not the kind of thing you forget, or for that matter ever get over. So I cloaked myself in anonymity protecting my tenuous ego as I strode the hallways of learning.

Senior year I entered a short story, "September Tears", and did so bravely under my own name, into the schools writing competition. Melancholy seemed to be popular as it won grand prize for new authors from the Pen and Quill. It marked my first successful foray into the world of original literature, recognized as my own. My name was read in the school assembly, blood rushed to my head, choking back emotion, tears welling in the corner of my eyes. The newborn wasn't ugly, it was beautiful.

I received acceptance letters from Boston University and NYU, both recognized for their outstanding literary programs. From all appearances, my future as a writer seemed certain. Eager to begin my studies, I bragged to all my friends that someday they would be looking back and saying they knew me when. A little too soon to be writing my acceptance speech for a Pulitzer, but don't think it wasn't on my list of things to do. I couldn't have been happier, but it was to be short-lived. Instead of the limelight of ivy towers and cocktail parties held in my honor, I was to star as the central figure in my own tragic comedy.

Never outwardly critical, that would have been the honorable thing to do. No, mother had been fashionably supportive of my interests in writing, while encouraging me to be open to other doors of opportunity. However, subversively she had been planning to thwart my aspirations. Father opted to stay-out of the entire affair. I assumed that without explicit affirmation from either I was free to explore my passion, which in some perverse way was true. What I didn't realize was the impact of mother's passive aggressive resistance; that is until one night when lying in bed I overheard them discussing my future.

"Now Elizabeth, let the boy be. He has his heart set on being a writer and who knows he might be able to make a living from it."

"Make a living? You must be out of your mind! Have you read the crap he writes? That stupid story about Skipper would get him kicked out of backstreet bookstores, and his style is like finger nails on a chalk board! I've never been more disappointed to think my son would flitter away his talents on the impossible pursuit of writing! And you, you do nothing to discourage this nonsense! Mark my words, when John fails, which he most surely will, he'll be dragging his tail between his legs back to us where he'll spend the rest of his miserable days as a penniless burden!"

In spite of the less than inspiring endorsement, half-heartedly I would matriculate at Boston University as a student in the English Department. It seemed too late to consider alternate career paths. However, knowing I was a disappointment to mother killed the very thing which gave me life, and it was her enunciation of a few deliberate and unkind words that would silence my voice. But, mother never really had my back. She had declared war on father and me long before this incident and I chalked it up as another battle ground where she could draw blood and spoil the party. It was just her nature.

My studies didn't seem to suffer greatly from a knife wedged into my back, but there was little passion in its pursuit. Work resembled reflexive robotic movements, facts packaged onto an automated conveyor belt were delivered to my temporal lobe, where neurons imprinted knowledge for future regurgitation. All very efficient, professors loved me, but the process completely bypassed the heart.

Made a few friends during my years at college, mostly peers pursuing their own interests in literary arts. Douglas, my best friend by default, was less adept at academic achievement, however, he seemed to be one those few with an innate ability to express others secret emotions in a few terse sentence fragments, sometimes captured on back of an envelope. Grades weren't everything, for girls swooned over him. Blond with curly locks spilling over his forehead, handsome features, broad shoulders, and ready smile, I don't recall ever seeing him in the quad without a female companion on his arm, or one or two chasing after him. We studied together, had a beer or two on Friday nights, and occasionally would go down to the Charles to sail dories. We'd talk of this and that, mostly wondering how we hoped to make a living from literature. I kept my private life for the most part to myself, but he must of sensed a spark of creation had been smothered, for he would at times encourage, and at other times plead for me to write just a few lines. To dip a toe. Politely, but firmly I would decline, yet I appreciated the asking and privately contemplated there might come a day when I would relent.

*****

Not much of a lady's man, simply didn't have the attributes most coeds were attracted to. So, it came as somewhat of a surprise when I met a young lady during my junior year and oddly she liked me. Tall, slim brunette, attractive by any standard, Alicia came from blue-bloods and old money. By the expression of others as we strolled on campus, it was clear no one could figure how I was able to attract her. I was never preoccupied by social circles people kept, but I have to admit Alicia opened some fairly attractive doors. We were welcome at parties and private clubs that in my previous life I would never have been permitted to enter, and as indelicate as it may sound, as long as I was with Alicia money would not be a problem.

She doted on me in ways that were both endearing and comforting in the knowledge our relationship was not one sided. Alicia gave me confidence where others had failed me, and with it the ability to believe in myself once again. Before long, a few cold embers were reignited and fanned into a small flame, an old desire had been rekindled. I wanted to write again and she encouraged me to take a chance. Awkward at first, I poked a few holes in the ice looking for daylight. I resurrected Skipper, but added a little more flare and sophistication. He now had his own penthouse in Soho, one of the more fashionable addresses in Manhattan and rubbed elbows with nouveau elite. Skipper was the talk of town and his antics delighted Alicia. On Sundays she would stretch across the day bed in my apartment reading the Post, while I wrote silly stories, Simon and Garfunkel played softly in the background. Occasionally she wanted to take a peek, I always made her beg. We had found a comfortable world and there was no reason it shouldn't go on forever.

It is no cliché when I say she filled a void that had been empty my entire life. Proud to be her man, I was even prouder to be in love, and secretly I planned to ask for her hand at the end of my senior semester. But in the meantime I would write.

Douglas was both surprised and thrilled I took up the pen again, and before long the three of us were inseparable. Two of us writing everything that popped into our heads, and Alicia always sincerely eager to consume both garbage and the sublime. Accolade was generously offered, but when we solicited her opinion as to who was the better writer, she became coyly evasive. During this time I started a new work, when I could steal myself away, usually leaving the two of them to debate where we should reside once we had graduated. My style reemerged, and having found my groove

76

words flowed freely. It was good, it was better than good, it was my best, and it would be my gift to Alicia for our wedding.

Semester was drawing near an end and it was time to visit Shreve Crump and Low, finest jeweler in Boston. I didn't have a lot of money, but I'd made up my mind no matter the cost I was going to buy the best ring they had. Alicia was worth it, she had given me her heart and she helped me find my lost voice. What price can you put on that? Nervously I entered the rarified air of their shop, the doorbell clanged behind me. Suppose I looked like all young men buoyed by infatuation, naïve, indecisive...hell, scared out of my mind. They had seen it all before, and graciously guided me through the process. When I left I had drained my last nickel on a 1 carat nearly perfect diamond engagement ring. Overflowing with joy, I prayed I'd never forget that moment.

Narrative finished, a diamond burning a hole in my pocket, there was only one thing left to do, go find Alicia and make her my wife. I don't skip, it's not manly, but I did something nearly akin as I floated across campus to Alicia's dorm. Knowing she wouldn't be expecting me, I ran up the back stairs hoping to surprise her...which I mostly certainly did.

I flung open her door thinking I would find Alicia consumed in one of her erudite magazines, instead she and Douglas were in bed going at it like two bunnies. My heart stopped. As embarrassed as they must have been, it paled in comparison to the shame I felt for being duped and betrayed. Did I miss something, should I have seen this coming?

We exchanged no words, we just stared at each other in disbelief. Curious, for in that moment I thought what would've happened if I had been 30 minutes earlier, or 30 minutes later. Nothing for it now, there was no going back. I left the manuscript on her table, placed the diamond on top, and walked out of her room, and her life.

Some weeks later Alicia, had the courage to confront me. "John, I'm sorry. I know I hurt you and I can't tell you how it saddens me we aren't together. You can't forget the wonderful times we spent together! Is there any chance I could repair the damage, that you could forget this one indiscretion? Please don't throw it all away over one stupid mistake! Could we make a go of it again? Please, I'm begging!"

"No, Alicia you can't, and we won't. But I have one question. Why?"

My pointed interrogation seemed to engender more pain from the ugly truth of her liaison then the actual crime, she grimaced, "because I love his writing."
*****

Four more years to get my Ph.D., absolute verification I had attained the highest level of knowledge on literary subjects, and without question positioning me as far from creative thinking one can attain. I wrote not a lick. Nevertheless they were impressive credentials which attracted the attention of a number of well healed literary agencies on the east coast. It was an easy way out, they would get to parade their new employee with a bunch of letters behind his name and I would get a relatively benign job requiring only that I read. I made my way through the front door of Nathan and Kaplan of Beacon Street, found a cozy couch to spread manuscripts, set-up shop, and began the business of deciding who would get published and who would rot.

Our world is composed of those who can, and usually do; and it is composed of those who can not, who will frequently teach or sit on the sidelines as critics. I landed somewhere near the sidelines.

In my late 20's met another woman, Pamela, we dated on again off again for over a decade. When I look back on our relation, the only reason I stayed with her as long as I did was because she constantly threatened to leave me. And when I finally realized there was no attraction other than her threats, she was history.

Dating in my late 30's was like shopping at a second-hand store. Although the items were diverse they already had been picked over and were either a little worn-out or broken. By the time I went out on my own as an independent literary agent the thought of trying to meet women was too painful. It was easier to sit at home, and a lot less expensive.

*****

Not exactly the stellar beginning I'd hoped for, yet I'm in it for the long run. And despite how depressing I may sound, I believe there is one good book in every person. Finding it and writing takes a leap of faith, some will, others will not. I am certain I have that one good book, but sticking it out there so literary critics can chop it off has made me a little gun shy. Which is more than a little ironic, given my profession, don't you think. But I still have time, and where there is time there is hope.

Things Lost Along the Way

Painful truth is things for mother didn't start out as they ended. Photos of her as a girl reveal a happy carefree child, unfettered by sadness or despair. Those of her and father when they dated are of a young woman full of life on the verge of a sunny start. Although pictures can be deceiving, the camera lens has no vested interest. It only captures those candid images filtered through dilated apertures, sincere or insincere, it is what it is. I would, therefore, conclude there was a time when mother was content.

Portraits of thinly veiled disappointments, genesis of which I can only imagine occurred much earlier in her life, become obvious in more contemporary albums. As if life itself weighed heavy, slowly bending and pressing, squeezing what joy existed into tiny memories and ultimately eradicating any previous notion they ever existed. Pictures in the back of the anthology are of faint smiles, the product of an eager photographer beguiling his subject into an artificial pose. One can only imagine the effort it took to produce such remorseful depleted snapshots. We all have memory books to remind of us of where we came from; sadly, the story of mother's life, and of those she touched, is a progression of things lost along the way.

There are certain women, many of whom, are gifted with nurturing spirits. Their sole happiness is derived from taking care of loved ones and ensuring no one is needy. Imbued with the nature of saints they joyfully assume their appointed purpose, believing their role is to mother infants into children and children into young adults. They suffer when their offspring suffers and rejoice in the jubilation of their issue. Mothers are the glue which bind the family, and spirit which allows us to venture into the vast world beyond. Without them where would we be? Is it any wonder we dedicate a day annually to celebrate their contribution to humanity with flowers and ornamental greeting cards testifying to their virtues?

My mother was none of this. It wasn't like she didn't want to, which she didn't; this was not willful, it simply wasn't part of her constitution. Her preference would have been to remain the bell of the ball, being wooed by eligible young men while father was allowed to cool his heals in anticipation. However, living at a time where to abstain from the socially laudable responsibility of parenting could only be explained by anatomical or physiological defects, mother would agree to participate in the act of birthing me, for only one reason...it is what women did, and to appear unwomanly would've been too hard to bear. If I were to ascertain the tipping point for mother, where life's see-saw dropped from happy to unhappy, it would be when I came into the world After I was born her image was irreversibly changed to that of a matron, and there was no retrieving the enchanting bachelorette. Having been cheated by societal pressures she would resent her new role; and, if she thought she could have escaped recriminations of abandonment, she might have left father and me to fend for ourselves. Mother's only solace was now in tormenting the facilitator, father, and product, me, of this monumental disappointment.

As an infant I was not keenly aware of anything, however, the absence of maternal love, which is so critically important for imprinting, left an indelible mark upon my affinity for mother. I would not want to exaggerate the outcome, but I did not expect, nor did I look for, any warmth emanating from the woman who bore me. Not then, not later, and definitely not now.

As a small boy, when put to bed, if I had a choice of being tucked-in by mother or not, I preferred not, making my way into slumber on my own. For frankly the woman scared me, especially when my room was dimly lit, for then I could only see vague outlines of her face. Sharp contours of her countenance and strangely menacing voice could drive me from my covers to the sanctuary hidden beneath my bed, where I believed I was protected from evil, and where dreadful fears of mother were expelled from my impressionable mind.

My childhood wasn't a total wasteland of heartless matters. On the contrary, mother knew how to play the game, to solicit adoration we so eagerly were anxious to provide for kind gestures she metered in dribs and drabs. It sounds crazy, but if you think about it, there is a reason for the insanity. Measured out in small doses, just enough medicine to keep the patient alive, but not so much they make a full recovery, allowed mother to keep father and me exactly where she wanted. In limbo.

A pleasant afternoon at the park, a family in apparent perfect harmony, would illicit exuberant, you might say over-the-top, veneration for mother and wife. Father and I laid it on pretty thick, encouraging those pleasant interludes and hoping it would be rewarded. But mother knew exactly how far to let us go before she would yank the chain, finding, or fabricating, some minor infraction which deserved her cold shoulder. As I live and breathe, I swear screaming, and even corporeal punishment, would have been preferable to the silent treatment. The cacophonous refrains of mother's symphony had father and me walking on eggshells through the minefield of her ill humors waiting for the next explosion, wishing for a truce.

Holidays could be particularly discouraging. Mother was like a tigress on the prowl in search of some meaningless accident to hang her indignation, an excuse to be a beast. Father would try so hard to keep things in check, to keep a lid on her anger which could boil over at any minute. Tension was palpable and it was inevitable he'd goof-up. One Thanksgiving mother asked him to take the turkey out of the oven so it could be basted. Poor man was literally shaking as he bent low, slowly drawing the heavy pan toward him. Almost had it to the counter, but regrettably it got away from him and the pan, juices, and turkey spilled onto the kitchen floor. Had I not put my foot out to stall its momentum the turkey would have found the stairs to the basement. Father and I would eat that bird by ourselves that night.

How does the song go, "the hopes and fears of all the years are met in thee tonight." No truer words have been spoken. Days, and even weeks, before Christmas mother would pretend to be delighted in anticipation of the yuletide season. Decorations would appear, cookies would be baked, even carols sung. Spirits were high, and I always prayed it was for real, but it was just the trap being set on the eve of celebration. A broken bulb, a forgotten card, basically nonsense, and mother would retreat to her room fuming in exaggerated theatrics, while father and I were left to pick-up the broken fragments of our dreams.

There were times I could tell mother knew she had taken it too far; and, had that look she might relent. At the brink, almost ready to dissolve, she would recover her footing, her heart would freeze, and the all too familiar face of granite reappeared like magic. What she started had to be finished, for realizing should she give-in, just once, the game would be up. And so it would go, with each year letting another opportunity to be human fall between the cracks, her tender past evaporated leaving only the residue of disappointment.

As mother aged, she lost track of who she was. She had told one too many lies and was now forced to live in them. The façade became reality and she could no longer remember who she'd been, separating real from unreal. Gaps delineating manic depressive behavior disappeared leaving only the dark cold silence of who she had become. Surprisingly it was an improvement, for there was no false expectation lurking around the corner for anything different than what we had. A pattern emerged, acquaintances, people she counted as friends, and family, the participants in her life, pretended nothing was amiss. Our routines were expected, memorized, and automatic. She had formulated her own make believe Cinderella distortion and cast those she knew as profligates suspended in madness. For all of us had fallen down that rabbit hole contrived by my mother.

81

Death brings no relief. For the one you struggle with most while living is the one you struggle most with in death. Not a day goes by when I don't wish it had been different. And if wishes were dollars I'd be a millionaire.

And you say, "oh, boo hoo!"

Well, that's all I'll speak on that topic.

*****

Lights flickered, sound of transformers arching and popping clearly audible from my apartment, darkness was eminent as the storm dumped heavy wet snow on charged dynamos designed to remain dry. Squall should have abated by now, but its fury continues with a vengeance.

Where did I put those candles? I rummaged in the hall closet, under the sink, about everywhere I could think, and was reminded of the emergency plan I intended to put into place last summer when life was comfortable and safe. It had gone neglected. Other neglected items came to mind; copies of my passport; extra key to my apartment concealed in a place I would remember; telephone numbers of those few remaining next of kin pasted in my wallet, in the event something unexpected occurred and a will, should that unexpected event turn-out to be...well, unexpected.

Wham! Explosion of the electrical switching station on the corner shook the building, power was gone, and it was a little too late to worry about any of that now. My only recourse was to settle into my recliner and wait until service was restored. Waiting for things to return to normal was my preferential default and you might say it was my modus operandi for dealing with life's sharp turns. So far it has been a successful strategy, but it depends on others doing something I was unwilling to do for myself; and, although I should be ashamed by my lethargy, I am not.

Knocking on my front door brought me back from unproductive musing. Wasn't expecting anyone, especially with this weather. A thought came to me. Oh dear Lord, please don't let it be Peggy. Sweet as treacle, mildly nosy, I've managed to avoid the woman down the hall for over a month. However, it was not without great effort. Avoiding the elevator forced me to mount eight floors of steps in the moldy damp stairwell on more than one occasion. Grasping my chest on the verge of a coronary was worth it if I could remain concealed from Peggy. From darkened alcoves, stealthily I would peek down the hallway to make sure the coast was clear then tip-toe like Wiley Coyote past her lair, sprinting the last few steps to the protection of my apartment. It is not that she isn't attractive. In fact some would say she had a natural elegance. A woman I would guess in her early fifties. She was easy on the eyes, with light brown hair, pretty face, she obviously took care of herself, but something about the woman makes me uncomfortable, and I would rather gnaw my arm-off then be trapped in the same room. Just my luck she has decided to make me her personal project. She had been trying set a trap for me since she moved into the building. One where my lifestyle as a bachelor was threatened.

"Hello, who is it?"

"Its Peggy, from down the hall. I've brought some candles and soup; thought you might need a little company while we're snowed-in."

Good grief, I was right. Need to think fast, need an excuse. "Oh, hi Peggy, gee sure wish I could let you in, but I just got out of the shower and I'm naked."

"Good, me too!"

Looked through the peep hole, and despite the faint light, could see she wasn't naked; and, she knew I wasn't either. Now what? "Peggy, I've had a bad cold and wouldn't want to get you sick. Why don't you put the soup and candles outside the door and I'll get them after you've returned safely to your apartment."

"John, why don't you open this door and let me in, if you make me sick then you'll just have to take care of me."

I had lost. There was no point trying to contrive lame excuses, she could see through the holes of my lies faster than I could concoct them and she had no intention of going anywhere until I opened the door. "Come on in Peggy. Make yourself at home," which she did.

Over the next three hours I sipped her soup by candlelight, which honestly was pretty good, and listened as she droned on about how the building had gone downhill, lambasted the superintendent for being drunk all the time, and divulged torrid secrets of neighbors I'd never met. Had my sleeve rolled-up and was ready to start chewing when she spied the letters to Bizzy.

"My you must have quite an admirer to have so many letters."

By the light of candles she couldn't make-out they were old and crusty, and I saw an opportunity to affect my escape. "Why yes, they are from my wife."

"You have a wife? I had no idea! I don't recall ever seeing you in the company of another woman."

"That is true. She has been unfortunately detained, and unable to visit."

"And, why is that?"

"Well, I am embarrassed to have to tell you Peggy, but the woman is fiercely jealous and has a terrible temper. Last time I was seen in the presence of a female associate, she lost her mind and shot the poor soul full of lead. She was sent to Cedar Junction for 10 to 20, a maximum security for the mentally insane. Heard she's up for parole this week. Can I offer you something to drink?"

"No thank you, I appreciate the generosity, but really must go. Perhaps, some other time."

"Oh please, I was so enjoying our little chat. Must you?"

"Yes, yes, yes, I am sorry, but...oh my, look at the time. Really, bye, bye."

I have to admit, my ploy was low down, and I felt bad for deceiving the lovely lady in apartment 8D. There is no doubt I will receive my punishment when it is my time, but for now am grateful for those letters, and the man who wrote them, which, without, I would have been forced to gnaw off my own arm to escape the clutches of Peggy's advances.

Poured a dram of fortification into my glass, collected as many candles that would fit on the end table to illuminate a circle on my lap, and slid another box by the foot of my chair. My exercise for the balance of the day would be bending my elbow and occasionally bending down to recover a letter.

April 11, 1952

My Dear Bizzy

Life on the island seems to only get better with time, deprivation from depression and war years are now only vague memories. Blessings of plenty provided by land and sea are a reminder wealth and position aren't everything men should strive for. Body and soul are in fact enriched by those things money can't buy.

Why just this morning, Thomas and I, as part of Salter Path's fishing crew, brought in an enormous catch of mullet. Dawn broke with the sun exploding onto the ocean welcoming both men and boys...

...as they pulled long boats into the surf. Teams rowed no more than 50 yards offshore, dropping weighted nets parallel to the beach. As the school of fish entered the gauntlet their escape was drawn shut and the process of moving heavily laden nets onto shore began. Use to be it was all done by the sweat of our brow and the muscles in our back. Now we wait on the Massey Ferguson tractor to back into shallows where we attach the nets and let the wagon do our work.

This evening we'll have a fish fry with everyone invited. Dinner will be served family style with neighbor sitting next to neighbor. Women are already preparing corn bread, spoon pudding, taters, okra, kale, you know all the fixings which has my mouth salivating as I think on it. Platters and casserole dishes will be passed overhead, cross tables, behind backs, the movement of food orchestrated by generous hands resembles a ballet. Best come hungry cause there is no excuse for empty plates and the offense of denying a taste of every woman's hard efforts is likely to land you in the dog house till next year. Lots of sweet tea, so don't worry.

Conversation is lively, with our best storytellers positioned at the head of each table to ensure our evening is entertaining. Eat as much as you want as it is unlikely we'll make a dent in the banquet of food prepared by many hands, but make sure you leave a little room for desert. Strawberry short cake, apple crisp, cookies, cakes, and hot coffee fill-in holes left behind to make sure stomachs are stretched to bursting. By end of the evening the satisfied, reluctant to depart from company of good friends, will begin to stroll down the beach pushing their bellies ahead of them, making their way to home where they will lay their heads to dream on this dish or that, debating if they had it to do over what seconds would be piled higher.

I declare, life is good!

Times, They Are a-Changin

Just about everything has gone and got itself mechanized these days. When I was a boy, someone thought it was a good idea to put an electric motor on a washing tub, and not too long ago a fella figured if you put the coils to a toaster in a spinning barrel them clothes won't have to be hung-out to dry. And speaking of toasters, a simple timer prevents burning bread to ashes, as it pops-up perfect on cue. Miss Alice got one of those vacuum cleaners that sucks-up dust and dirt, not that she uses it herself. Some of them new contrivances aren't all that useful, but are just plain fun, like retractable ball point pens and electric can openers which don't work all that well.

All the modern gadgets are enough to make your head swim and ponder how many more can be invented. Engineers claim they were designed as time saving devices, but now what in the world are we going to do with all this free time once we've saved it? I suppose it's a slippery slope, cause once islanders get a taste for automation they'll be begging for more. They call it progress, but I wonder?

I guess this has been the way of life throughout the ages. A hundred fifty years ago someone invented the brass screw and you can be sure there were folks who were skeptical it would ever be successful. All this blabbering, well it's a round-about way to get to the topic of shrimpin and how Thomas and I were a day late and dollar short on all this technology.

*****

If you're going to shrimp, best be the captain. He stands at the helm, makes a few turns now and then, barks orders to his crew, and mops his neck with a kerchief to show how hard he's been working. Which is why Cap'n Chisholm is still able to shrimp after decades at sea, and why Thomas

86

and I are broken-down relics limping from one odd job to another. Not that I'm complaining, the man is practically a saint and gave me an opportunity to make a living when no one else would. But the business of crewing shrimp boats is mind numbingly hard and fraught with all kinds of hazards.

Working hours aren't ideal, nevertheless, if a man is to make a buck, sometimes you just have to get-up with the roosters. Actually, it was 3 am, way before roosters start their cock-a-doodle-doing, and one could argue closer to midnight than dawn. While Cap'n Chisholm was warming up the diesel and sorting through his charts by the glow of lights on the instrument panel, Thomas and I were relegated to filling fuel tanks, preparing nets, laying on ice, and checking trawl doors and winches to make sure nothing was hung-up. Long before most folk had their morning coffee the mosquito fleet had already put to sea and many would be pulling their mid-water nets on first or second runs. Spreaders inherently want to close by force of water pulling on the net and it was Thomas' and my job to make sure they didn't. One of us would throw our weight against the pulley inching the spreader into position, while other would hammer home chocks to lock doors into place. Timing was everything, and if you misjudged either the pull or the lock someone was likely to get hurt.

Pinching injuries were the worst. Threat of losing a digit or two over the course of a career was highly probable and while I crewed I don't think I ever kept an intact finger nail on either hand. Dropping tools, stepping into open holds, tripping over nets, diversity of injuries one could experience while shrimpin was endless. Most were treated on the spot, bandaged to stem bleeding, or splinted if broken, luxury of going to the hospital would have to wait and it was not uncommon to see an ambulance at the dock anticipating return of the fleet to pick-up a customer or two.

Longevity of those who shrimp is defined by accumulation of injuries or, in my case, the number of times I would slip a disc, and still recover. Sometimes I could feel it coming on, a nagging twinge or lower back ache, but more often than not, there was no warning. One minute I was reaching-up to pull a winch, and next finding myself on all fours unable to move. Usually it was so painful I couldn't even whimper. Thomas didn't need to ask, when he saw me like this he knew. There was only one thing they could do for me. Stand me up. It was an ordeal which resembled unfolding the legs on a card table, and felt like fire brands being slid under the skin on my back. A few weeks hobbling around, easing my way into and out of chairs, carefully stepping up, more carefully stepping down, and eventually I would recuperate, regaining sufficient strength to make my way back to the boat for light duty.

During my days with Cap'n Chisholm I injured my back six times, each leaving a little more scar tissue, not as strong as God's own, which made the next event that much more likely. It eventually caught-up with me and the risk of making me a permanent cripple was too great. I didn't have a choice, but had to retire, and on May 26, 1940, the day Allied soldiers began their evacuation from Dunkirk by "little ships", and beginning of World War II. I walked down the docks for the last time headed for my home on Bogue Shores. Could have chewed on my bad luck, but instead was moved by the bravery of common citizens who volunteered to take to whatever craft could float to aid the British Navy in evacuating over 330,000 service men trapped on French soil and thanked my lucky stars we'd never see that war grace our shores. I was, at any rate, right about the bravery part.

Thomas, a man of stronger constitution, and a few years younger, was able to hold-on a little longer, but he too was eventually forced to throw in the towel, simply unable to cope with the grind of physical complaints. Wouldn't you know it, after we got ourselves all beat-up, them time-saving folks decided to install hydraulic winches on shrimp boats. Probably would've prevented half the injuries us salty dogs were unfortunate to earn and just maybe, kept us in the game a few more seasons. However, there is no point crying over spilt milk, we had our run and were more fortunate than others who went to sea, never to return.

*****

Islanders take care of their own when they can and I wasn't ashore very long when Mrs. Cartwright offered me the honorable position of caretaker for her properties. She and her husband, God rest his soul, had accumulated a number of cottages over the years that she rented to tourists. Now that her husband was departed, she needed help in opening-up at beginning of the season, maintaining during season, and closing-up at end of the season.

Pretty good with a screwdriver and wrench, wasn't long before I found my calling, a jack of all trades, plumber, carpenter, electrician, you name it, I did it. In early spring, boards were removed from windows, musty and damp rooms were aired from being closed-up for months, new linen placed in closets, water turned on, ice boxes spruced up, even chased off vermin that had made their home in crawl spaces beneath foundations.

Seems folks who rent cottages expect to get the Taj Mahal. Problem is they've got 1000-dollar taste on a 10-dollar budget. Won't lift a finger to change a light bulb, turn a spigot, and will let their bratty kids run amok, usually clogging toilets with items that make your head spin. Aside from pounds of toilet paper, I've found beach towels, baby dolls, car keys, wigs, sand, dead fish, live eels, newspapers, underpants, undershirts, bow ties, an entire stamp collection, you name it, and I've found it.

In season I'm on call 24/7. When something gets broken, they want it fixed, and they wanted it fixed immediately. By the way they act, you would think the world has come to an end. Cranky and impatient, if I don't show up right away they'll throw a hissy fit. Not surprisingly, when I arrive they are amazed I can't resolve their petty problems instantaneously and practically pee themselves to get me out their hair so they can go back to whatever lame excuse they call living. Most of the time it is a minor inconvenience, and had they a mind to enjoy the reason why they came to the beach in the first place, probably wouldn't have even noticed. Nope, they load-up their cars inside and out with paraphernalia and junk they will never use, reminders of their miserable existence, and move from one household to another, bringing with them all the irritations and anxiety they should have been trying to leave at home. Catering to the urges of testy guests keeps me on my toes, and in-season I place a guard on my mouth to make sure I don't give them a piece of mind they deserve.

Miss Alice wasn't too keen on my new job which at times has kept me from being at her beck and call. You might say she lacks an understanding that she doesn't always get exactly what she wants exactly when she wants it. Which reminds me of those boorish tourists who show-up annually to drive me to distraction.

*****

Naturally curious, I've done a study on human nature, and in particular the nature of those people who spend their hard-earned money on vacations by the shore. Being what you might call a handy-man, I'm practically invisible to the self-absorbed sportin types who on a good day have a difficult time recognizing their own. It is especially useful for spying on those inobservant who can only focus on one thing at a time. Themselves. All I have to do is wear my tool belt and shuffle around like I'm engaged in fixin the whatchamacallit over by the thingamabob and they ignore me completely.

There are two general classes of beachgoers. There are outdoor types and there are indoor types. Indoor types are relatively easy to dispense with in my study as they rarely divert from their normative behaviors. After they arrive and unload their vehicles they settle-in to the somewhat primitive comforts beach cottages afford. Doors and windows closed, blinds pulled, over the course of their week-long stay, which I must assume they endure, are they rarely seen outdoors and never will they brave the perils of beach or ocean. Exercising extreme restraint, ne'er will they have to experience the trauma of finding sand in their shoes or between the sheets of their beds. Being indoor types, the opportunities I've had to observe their species is quite limited. Nevertheless, I am astounded by their nervous and furtive discomfort once they have revealed themselves and are exposed to nature. Panicked, they sprint between vehicle and domicile and if cornered by a neighborly hello or smile, are inclined to lose their minds. If I were the suspicious type, I might assume they are engaged in nefarious activities which they hide from prying eyes in the confines of their self-inflicted prisons, but reality is they just don't like the beach, and probably don't like people, as well. Indoor types will, at the end of their sojourn, return to their homes no shade darker then when they departed, but no doubt, will brag to colleagues, their minister, members of the PTA, aunts and uncles, and anyone else who will listen to their hogwash what a delightful time they had on their annual foray to the shore. Why, because a vacation to the ocean has somehow become an emblem of status for the post-war middle-class.

By now Bizzy, I am sure you're impressed by my intellect and powers of observation, which is in itself a miracle since I barely graduated from high school. But wait, we got the outdoor types to cover.

Outdoor types are far more complex and I will humbly submit the range of my study will be inadequate to cover all the curious varieties I have encountered during my treatise. Yet, mama didn't raise no quitters, so here goes.

For lack of better definition there are weak bladder types and strong bladder types. Both are determined to spend as much time on the beach as humanly possible, which is admirable given my own appreciation for wonders of our island. Weak bladder types will scurry down to the beach set-up their towels, then scurry back to their cottages to do what only God knows. No more than a few minutes and they once again reappear at the beach. Maybe they'll apply suntan lotion, or dip into the ocean, but just as quickly escape distractions of the shore to return double-time to the dwelling by the sea. All day long the ping pong between ocean and house continues unabated. Of course, I don't know if they have a weak bladder, but it is as likely an explanation as any other.

Strong bladder types will march purposefully from their residence, often equipped with trappings required for the attendance of children and the elderly. Ice chests, umbrellas, chairs, tables, beach toys, books, hats, and other crap. Resolute to make but one trip, they balance the armory of equipment in awkward contortions entangling legs, binding arms and threatening to gouge-out eyes. Being assailed by young and old they set their course and stumble forward. After several failed starts, and oaths that would make a sailor blush, they eventually arrive at their prearranged real estate and set-up shop. Most are obsessive compulsives by the detail of structure designed in staking and decorating their plots. However, eventually they find solace in their labors and land full-square into one of the beach chairs they have designated as their own, where they will remain for the entire day. Even under the threat of hail and brimstone they won't budge. Most will read, some will snooze, but none will move. Over the course of 8 hours most humans are obligated to evacuate their bladder no less than once. I find the frequency has become more regular as aging has become a constant adjective in my lexicon. So it is with some amazement that the object of my study, the strong bladder type, seems disinclined to natural urges other men cannot ignore.

Although doubtful, it is possible that during my observations I have been inadvertently neglecting measurements, which has provided opportunity for strong bladder types to sneak into the ocean, where waist deep they find relief. Despite those innocents who believe to the contrary, it is not an uncommon deceit for beachgoers. Just so you are aware, when you see two or more women in conversation at ocean depths sufficient to obscure, it is likely they are engaged in other activities. Nevertheless, even the most liberal of critics would have to agree these creatures who plant their posteriors in the sand for better part of the daylight hours border on being superhuman and have earned my utmost respect.

Then there are the distilled types, which figure the beach is as an good excuse to drink as any. Lushes in any environment, the shore affords a new opportunity for drinking under the somewhat protective cloak of anonymity. Most are effervescently cheerful, slapping you on the back greeting you as long-lost pals, but are vague as to where they hail from and rarely use anything but first names, usually not your own. That assumes you can understand anything they are saying. Generous to a fault they offer copious doses of rotgut grain alcohol they have been mixing in various noxious concoctions. Once poisoned they will party on verandas, on the beach, and in the ocean. Throughout the early morning, mid-day, late afternoon, early evening, and night they are never seen without a bottle or tumbler slopping contents on themselves and others. Evidently enough makes its way between the lips to cook the turkey.

One doesn't actually need to see them in action to know their coordinates. They leave their calling card at the curb for all to see. Barrels upon barrels full of cheap empty liquor bottles overflowing without even a slight trace of any food being consumed. Distilled types come in both male and female genders, and to be honest, I'm not sure which is worse.

Some beachgoers believe, because they have rented a cottage for a week, the entire beach is now their personal property. They arrive with an entourage of like-minded nincompoops, who relish nothing more than picking a fight with people they should endeavor to try and get along with and share in the beauty of the ocean. Instead of finding an area away from other sunbathers where they might be forced to turn their belligerence on themselves, they arrive to the beach late and intentionally plop within inches of another unassuming group. Immediately they will begin to snigger and critique their neighbors, first under their breath, but soon it escalates to clearly audible verbal abuses.

"I don't understand why your children have to run and play so close to our blankets?"

"Can't you see we are trying to read, why you loud mouths always have to scream and shout so loudly at the beach and disturb good folk?"

Their annoying jabs eventually erupt, with tempers flaring and everyone having a miserable day. Of course, they will feel vindicated in their anger. After all, it is their beach.

I call this group the egotist type. They are from my way of thinking the least desirable of all beachgoers, especially since they go out of their way to target innocent fishermen. A speck on the horizon, barely visible by the naked eye, but if the egotist discerns it is someone fishing they will walk miles out their way to stalk their prey. Obstinately placing their beach chair right on top of where unassuming anglers fish. They can't wait to begin their rude assaults on the sportsmen.

"How dare you threaten our peaceful repose with razor sharp lures and hooks being carelessly flung only inches from our blankets. You people have no right to fish where innocent sunbathers are gathered. I have a mind to call the police!"

To prove their point they wade into the ocean directly where fishermen cast their lines. Fuming, indignantly they churn the waters chasing away game fish, then slosh ashore to confront the poor devil who has lost his chance to have some fun. If the fishermen relent and move away, it is likely the egotist will follow, hopeful in sustaining their antagonism. Egotists don't come to the beach for fun and relaxation, they come to reinforce they are somehow better than others.

Let-us-burn-ourselves-to-death-the-first-day types, are destined to be removed from the gene pool. But until then, they merit a brief description. This type most likely has light features, blond, blue-eyed, and fair skin. It is probable, until their visit to the beach, many have never seen the orange orb which hangs in the sky. They come from towns like Schenectady, Sheboygan, Syracuse, Sacred Heart, Salem, and Saint Paul. Cities where the sun is something people read about, but rarely experience. Ignorant of the dangers, they descend upon the beach in outfits which can only be described as thin, including the newest fad, bikinis. Hopeful to acquire the glow of burnt umber, many of our brethren from Latin America proudly display, but, unaware they lack pigments to achieve their goals, they let it all hang-out.

Within an hour of being exposed to powerful rays of the sun, their pasty white skin begins to acquire a pinkish hue. Subtle, yet distinctively different then the way they arrived. It is not too late to escape, but they lack sufficient common sense to come in from the rain, so why would we expect them to protect themselves from atomic rays of the sun. So-called friends are either afraid to offend or, more likely, keen on seeing how far this calamity will progress. I will skip all intermediate phases in ascendency of colors as the day proceeds, that would be too painful to elaborate. Nevertheless, our catastrophe is inevitable. Sun-down produces the most excruciating and unexpected realization. They have been roasted alive and now resemble steamed lobsters. Any attempt to aid them with lotions or other topical medicinal remedies is passionately repelled fearing someone might actually touch them. They remain in a state of suspended animation, arms extended away from their bodies, eyes blinking with a curious expression of, "what now"? Sadly, for them the answer is "nothing". Only time will provide the relief they seek.

Some will transform into the phyla of indoor types, and will remain sequestered in dark rooms for remainder of their vacation. Others will bathe in ointments and tinctures donning the most outrageous outfits, long sleeve shirts, long pants, broad brim hats, and dark sunglasses. They arrive at the beach, usually after everyone has settled-in, with painted-on smiles. Greased bodies uncomfortably squirming under cotton fabrics, Noxzema caked in layers on what little skin is exposed, looking for all the world like Casper the Ghost. When offered to go for a swim, a walk, or even to sit, they politely decline explaining they actually prefer to stand motionless, as it is what they would do normally. Compassionate as we may be, there is nothing we can do for them. To ruin our own fun makes no sense, so they become persona non grata, and ignored by all they quickly blend into the scenery. Don't feel sorry for the let-us-burn-ourselves-to-death-the-first-day types, for mark my words, next year when they return they will have forgotten the trauma of the previous and will repeat their outrageous performance, achieving the same results. As I've said their kind is destined for extinction.

*****

Conclusions from my study on human nature are not particularly flattering, but I would be remiss Bizzy if I left you with the impression all renters who frequent our shores are idiots or jerks. For the truth is without miscreants of the world, psychologists would have little to talk about; and therefore, it is their lot in life that they should get the lion's share of our attention. I can only imagine what kind of world we would live in if, instead, normal folks were the focus of our regard.

I have been fortunate to meet some renters who are fine people, respectful of our island community and natives who call it home. They come from all parts of our United States because they understand the beauty of a beach vacation on Bogue Banks. If something breaks and they need my assistance they are patient and even apologetic to be such a burden. I've made friends with a few of these gentle people and even kept in touch over the years. And to be honest, they are the reason I get-up in the morning with pliers and plunger to do battle with time saving devices that we've all come to expect as part of our normal lives, and despise when they don't work.

Have to admit I miss those simpler times, when a window and screen brought fresh air inside, folks sought the solace of cool sheets on hot nights, and entertainment was watching the moon rise. To be sure they're still available, it's just we've gone and got ourselves all confused with gadgets.

Teach, etc., etc., etc.

Rumors are a funny thing, most intelligent people understand they rarely constitute factual information, and on the whole misrepresent the truth leading those inclined to listen down the primrose path. Nevertheless, these very same will press their ear to the ground in hopes of overhearing the goings-on within their community, rationalizing it is their duty to stay informed, even if it is a falsehood, and the trail of he said, she said, enhances the credibility of even the most incredulous of tales.

Rumors spread like the flu and if we aren't careful can make you just as sick. Some, drawn by the allure of exaggerated tales over the lack of uninteresting facts, can't help themselves and may even participate infecting others.

Those who start rumors obviously have an ulterior motive. It may be for entertainment value, to see how many they can fool, or to destroy another's reputation, maybe it is for financial gain, but there is always a reason and it is rarely innocent. Keep this in mind as I share with you the story of a pirate's treasure.

*****

Edward Teach is not well known outside of our little community of Bogue Shores. However, if you ask the world at large who is Blackbeard most will recognize the scoundrel immediately as the ruthless pirate who terrorized islands of the West Indies and North American colonies of our eastern seaboard. Blackbeard and Teach are indeed one in the same. His lifelong associations with wealthy merchants and new American nobility indicate he was probably born into a respectable family. That would change.

John M. Tabor

At an early age he left his home of Bristol England and traveled to the Caribbean arriving sometime in the late 1600's, where many English ex-patriots joined in the business of privateers. Not what you would call, in the purest sense, criminals. For in fact they were sponsored by their government as reservists in the British Navy, but left to their own devices to recover, through force, spoils from foreign antagonists, primarily the French and Spaniards; and, in doing so lined their own pockets. A portion of those riches were returned to the crown, which insured their good standings with those who would eventually grant pardons.

Their comfortable laissez-faire relation in the business of international trade would ultimately succumb to the tide of political alliances, and once the enemy became the collaborator, privateers no longer had a license to kill. Many would find legitimate venues for their lives in the New World, but some, either because they lacked skills or because they had a taste for blood, would tip-toe into the domain of piracy, stealing from anyone and all, regardless of national allegiance. Little doubt, young Edward became a villainous thief through his associations with these vagabonds.

Our story becomes more interesting as Blackbeard and his rabble crew made his way to the Carolinas. He sailed in the Queen Anne's Revenge, a gun sloop, fast, and maneuverable few could escape. Tall with broad shoulders Teach wore knee-length boots and clothing to match his long black beard, which he braided into knots. Adorned with bandoliers of pistols over his shoulders and cutlasses from his sides there was no mistaking what business he intended. Under an enormous hat was a mass of black hair in which he lit candles. Smoke curling from under the brim gave him an otherworldly appearance, likely the spawn of Hades. Menacing looks and fearsome reputation was often all it took for those he fell upon to throw their money and valuables at his feet in hopes of escaping death.

Amassing his wealth as he pillaged one seaside town after another, he would eventually make his way to Topsail Inlet, what today we call Beaufort. It is here Queen Anne's Revenge sank on shifting sands, and Blackbeard claimed his treasure was lost in the sinking. A fabrication which William Howard, former quartermaster, vehemently denied during his testimony at his own trial as a pirate before the Court of Admiralty.

Edward Teach quickly integrated into the social fabric of our charming southern city and now frequented the company of gentlemen and gentle ladies, feigning the innocence of a misdirected youth. His charisma attracted and won the hearts of those he beguiled, including Judge Tobias Knight and Governor Charles Eden of North Carolina. Although, he was careful to maintain a polite distance for appearance sake, both were enriched by gifts, the source of which doesn't take much imagination, lavishly proffered by the pirate gentleman.

Edward would remain in the general vicinity of Ocracoke Island and Bath establishing himself as a humble neighbor and would marry the daughter of a wealthy landowner. His guise was nearly perfect, the ruse intended to cover his end-game. It was during this period, those who knew him well, claimed he buried his treasure in the vicinity of islands which we now call home. It has fueled controversy for several centuries.

Blackbeard eventually won his prize, a pardon from Eden and title to those remaining ships which constituted his personal armada. Under the cloak of respectability, he could once again return to the business of piracy, guarded by impunity from a government edict.

Incensed by obvious immoral transgressions perpetrated by those bribed by ill-gotten goods, governor of Virginia and Head of the Crown colonies, Alexander Spotswood, would not tolerate their larceny. Teach also was practiced at disrupting the commerce of Virginians and had earned the ire of its governor, and so Spotswood ordered Lieutenant Robert Maynard of HMS Pearl to apprehend the scoundrel and his aides de camp, and bring them to justice.

Particulars of who was out-gunned during the ensuing battle off the beach of Ocracoke Island are vague. What is clear is Maynard employed subterfuge to attract Teach into hand-to-hand combat. As the smoke cleared from the blasts of opposing canons, Blackbeard's vessel grappled bulwarks of the Pearl and a swarm of pirates boarded the Lieutenant's ship to find only a small contingent of sailors. Bolstered by the sight of a nearly empty ship Blackbeard threw caution to the wind and rushed upon Maynard and a handful of defendants. Just as quickly an onslaught of Maynard's men, kept hidden below decks, rushed upon the unsuspecting pirates killing and wounding many. Decks were awash in the blood of those defeated. Maynard and Teach squared-off in an epic confrontation. In the end, Maynard would be victorious and Blackbeard would be bested. But it is noteworthy that Blackbeard died only after being shot five times and cut more than twenty by sword and saber. Maynard removed Teach's head and placed it upon the bowsprit of the Pearl to remind those who might be tempted that piracy would not be tolerated in these colonies.

Eden and Knight would face the embarrassment of indictment and trial. However, insufficient evidence could be brought to convict either. Both were free to consider their own questionable character, and undeniably poor judgment in personal associations with the murderous pirate.

Legacy of Edward Teach endures, in part because of the notoriety he left behind, and in part because his hidden treasure has never been found. Things lost have a way of bothering us Bankers. Especially in-light of things found, things like Tom Veal's pirate treasure in Dungeon Rock Massachusetts and Thomas Tew's treasure chest valued at over $100 million.

Over the years I don't know how many pocket knives I've misplaced, maybe as many as 15 or 20. Don't have them now, but because they didn't disappear or evaporate they are out there somewhere and if I had a mind and looked long enough I might find them. There is a picture being painted here for you Bizzy, and it is likely you are clever enough to figure out where we're going.

Now there is only one other piece of information you need to know. Blackbeard still haunts islands in around Ocracoke, including our very own. They say the pirate roams inlets and beaches along the coast of North Carolina in search of his head, hopeful one day he might be recognized again by those he called friends, Devils own if you ask me. Others say he doesn't give a hoot about his head but paces from secreted landmarks to where he buried his treasure to relish in recounting pieces of eight, bejeweled scabbards, and tiaras which remain hidden to all but him.

*****

It was the winter of 1938, as I recall it was unseasonably warm. Shrimpin season was over and Thomas and I were what you might say furloughed, which meant we could be found either on the beach with fishing rods or at the Optimists club with a deck of cards. Having free time on our hands, and being men, we fell into our routine as quickly as a drunk falls off his stool. Up with the dawn patrol, all business-like, Thomas would pound on my front door, "get your lazy bones out of bed, there's fish to be caught and you can't do it hiding under your covers!" Down to the beach we'd march quick step, sometimes to the cadence of a ditty Thomas was fond of:

"Heidi-hi, Heidi-ho,
we's gots to go down,
we's gots to go down.

Down to go fishin,
down to go fishin.

Heidi-hi, heidi-ho,
we's got to fishin,
 we's got to fishin."

Hot coffee and bait, sliver of sun peeping over the horizon wondering who was making all the racket. Finding our rhythm, casting, waiting, we fell into our own thoughts, occasionally setting the hook; distracted by the whine of our reels as fish found deep water disrupting our reverie, taking with it as much line as we were willing. Sometimes our ice chest was full, sometimes not, but we never left empty handed for those who fish are always enriched by the company they keep and the beauty of God's creation.

By mid-day it was time to pack it in and head on up to the house. Thomas would clean a fish or two, fried in bacon grease, slathered with mayonnaise and wedged between bread, with maybe a pickle depending on your druthers, made for some mighty tasty sandwiches. On those days when I was overcome with vigor, I'd shuck a couple dozen oysters. Flavor of the sea would burst in your mouth, as the meaty muscle and briny juice slipped down your gullet. I have to admit, once you start slurping them dainties it's hard to stop.

After lunch Thomas and I would kick back in rockers, feet propped on the porch railing, hands resting on our bellies, sun baking us like we was bricks. If we was careless and got to chattin, it was possible we'd miss our naps, but usually not.

Somewhere later in the afternoon one of us would kick the other's feet from the railing and remind him of the serious enterprise being neglected at the Optimists club. As sworn members, and fearful of our tardiness, we'd rush as fast as our legs would carry us. Breathless, hooting our hellos without missing a step as we ran past fellow Bankers, down sandy paths past the emporium to the back door of Jack's Bait and Hardware, bursting into the midst of either the pledge of allegiance, which always preceded serious club functions, or the vocation upon which we attended. Poker.

"...with liberty and justice for all. Amen."

Newman stared down his nose at Thomas and me looking more than a little peeved, "you boys are late again. If you keep this up I am going to fine both of you what amounts to double your dues." It really wasn't much of a threat as I don't recall last time any member paid dues. "Now if you're here to play poker then sit your sorry behinds in them chairs and commence to start losing." Newman always took the business of the Optimists very seriously.

Conversation got around to this and that, some of it intended on keeping the members informed as to current affairs, some of it intended as a ploy to sidetrack the other's game.

Judge Peebles usually said little, unless he had a good hand, and was ready to ante. "You boys hear about that fellow staying at Mrs. Cartwright's? Came all the way from Richmond, says he's an archeologist, friendly sort as their type goes. I'll raise you a nickel. Name is TJ Wolf. Yep, claims he's got verifiable proof for whereabouts of Teach's treasure." Now that's the kind of news that'll raise an eyebrow or two, and it was a damn sly way to take our minds off the game. And while we were distracted, the Judge slammed his cards on the table, face-up, "full house!"

It was always a good idea to keep on the good side of Judge Peebles, but at times he could get under your skin, usually when he was taking your money, "thank you boys for being good sports, but mostly thank you for your nickels." Scooping his loot into his Stetson and snickering at the trick he played, "oh yeah, just so you know that Wolf fella is for real, says tides are ideal to start seeing Blackbeard's loot wash-up on shore. He'd appreciate it if you find any to turn it over to him. Says there's a reward involved."

After being bled dry by the Judge none us could recall the specifics of why there was archeologist staying at Mrs. Cartwright, so we didn't take the matter very serious. Of course, situations have a way of changing one's mind.

*****

Next morning Thomas brought the coffee, it was my turn to bring the bait. We alternated so it wouldn't get monotonous. Strutting down the beach in our hip-waders slugging tackle boxes and buckets to sit on, we had our hearts intent on making a go of it. Headed for that slight curve of the beach where it narrows, knowing that just offshore was a sand bar, and if we cast our lines and jigged them over the bar they would find a deep spot as they made their way ashore. It was here, what we referred to as our fishing hole, that flounder would lay on the bottom ready to pounce on bait, and if we did our jobs the way you're suppose to, could land a kettle full in no time at all. We were almost there when we stopped dead in our tracks. Sometimes you are confronted by the unusual, situational matters which seems so out of place it'll strike you dumb. Well on that day we couldn't get any dumber. There before us was a ditch in the sand, and when I say a ditch I mean it was at least 10 feet deep and 20 across. This was not the work of some overzealous child with a toy shovel. This was the labor of a man, maybe two, over the course of the wee hours of the night intent on finding something most hadn't seen in a long time.

Thomas and I crept slowly, not knowing what we would discover. Peering over the edge we saw what you might expect at the bottom of a deep trench in the beach, a pool of water, but more importantly, nothing else. Now there's all kinds of entertainment, and I would be the first to acknowledge what floats my boat ain't necessarily what gets others all goose-pimply. But I think most would agree that digging a hole of these dimensions isn't done on a lark. Whoever was behind this work was looking for an article, perhaps of some value and the fact the hole was empty meant one of two things, they came-up short-handed. Or?

Almost everything unexpected or unusual is likely to capture the imagination of islanders, and it wasn't long before word got out that crazy folk had been diggin on the beach. Sheriff Stone was called-in to make sure there wasn't any funny business. Standing with one hand on his hip and other rubbing his chin it was pretty clear the incident had him baffled. Just to be on the safe side, he had the area fenced-off and warned people to stay away, but for curious types that was practically a formal invitation to poke around at will.

Some days later Cooper brothers found what looked like a barnacle crusted scepter sticking half-way out of the sand, just 100 yards or so from the ditch, which by now tides had filled-in. They weren't talking, but I had it on reliable information they turned the scepter over to that TJ Wolf from Richmond and were now walking around with an extra 5 bucks in each of their pockets.

Pretty soon the beach was pock-marked with diggings looking like foxholes that doughboys had hastily dug in the soil at Verdun during the Great War. Very surreptitious, done during the shadow of night when good people should be sleeping. When asked, Bankers wouldn't admit to it, but it was odd so many had bags under their eyes and all of them with a look of insomniacs.

More of them artifacts started showing-up in tidewaters and soon the fever had caught, transforming sensible people into irrational money grabbing treasure hunters. Rumor of Blackbeard's treasure had caught-on like wild-fire. Even Thomas and I found what looked like a flint-lock pistol, which seemed a little too convenient in retrospect, but with Wolf's money in my wallet I wasn't asking a lot of questions.

Island was in an uproar, Jack's Bait and Hardware had sold-out of shovels and spades, people didn't bother to wait till still of the night and were seen digging everywhere in broad daylight, some were even seen fighting over turf. I never experienced anything like it, our world was coming unhinged, and if something wasn't done soon there might not be enough island left to put back together. Sheriff Stone had reached the end of his rope, called a town meeting, and asked TJ Wolf to address the rumors of hidden treasure.

Just about everyone showed up. Place was a beehive of men and women, some pushing to get seats, others standing on barrels to see over the crowd, everyone shouting incoherently.

"Alright, alright, everyone quiet down! If you keep carrying on like you are no one is going to hear anything and I swear I'll call this meeting to a close." Stone was doing his best to contain the rabble which had worked itself into a lather. But he meant business, which no one would challenge, and so little by little Bankers settled down to a low roar.

"Now you all know I've asked Mr. TJ Wolf to speak to us tonight about speculations regarding Edward Teach's buried treasure, which he has graciously consented to. I don't what you nit-wits barraging the poor man with a lot of silly questions while he's trying to say his peace. There will be plenty of time at the end for that. Do I make myself clear?" Crowd churned with murmurs, but it was obvious he had their agreement. "Good, Mr. Wolf, if you please."

"Thank you, Sheriff for inviting me here tonight and I want to thank you good people of Bogue Banks for turning-out. I hope I can share with you what I know and what I don't know." Wolf made a good start, and I think most expected to get to the issue of treasure and where it was buried within a couple of minutes. Instead the man from Richmond embarked into one of the most elaborate descriptions of archeological mumbo-jumbo any audience has had to endure. It wasn't good enough to confine himself to scientific evidence regarding Blackbeard's treasure, or for that matter pirates treasure in general, which he never got to. Nope, the man had to drone-on ad nauseam about King Tut, other pharaohs, Hongwu Emperor of the Ming dynasty, Peter the Great, mad King George of England, and so on. After nearly 2 hours of lecture delivered in professorial monotone, most people had reached their limit. Comatose and on the verge of expiring from boredom some had drifted-off, others looked like they weren't too far behind. Had Sheriff Stone told everyone to go home they would have bolted like horses for the feeding trough.

But just before everyone had given-up, TJ Wolf cleverly snuck one past us, "and in conclusion, there is little to say regarding the whereabouts of Mr. Teach's treasure, except this, beware his ghost doesn't find you before you find it! Thank you for having me here tonight and good night." At which point the man slipped into the darkness leaving islanders slack-jawed wondering if their ears had deceived them, or had they really heard a veiled threat of Blackbeard's ghost from that archeologist from out-of-town.

As I was going on about intelligent people and rumors, you would most certainly expect them to dismiss the ludicrous notion that a ghost was loitering in the vicinity of their neighborhoods. But then you would be wrong. Not only did they not dismiss the ridiculous, they embraced the concept of a headless specter wandering about our island on nightly crusades to count the loot in his treasure chest buried some 200 plus years ago. Being a somewhat spiritual fellow, I'm not for one to poo-poo those who hold to good and evil spirits floating around those spaces between here and the hereafter, but I thought this one might be stretching the imagination a little too far. At best that is what I stood on until Thomas and I were returning from a lively exchange of ideas and cards at the Optimist club a week later, roundabout 11 pm.

Thomas was regaling me on the merits of a fake tell, you know giving the impression you got a winning hand when in-fact your cards add up to squat. "Robert, there is no harm puckering your lips, or twisting an earlobe, before you bluff your opponents into submission. I know you think the cards should speak for themselves, win, lose, or draw. But, you're missing the whole purpose of playing poker. For crying out loud sandbaggers have been pulling the wool over their opponent's eyes since the game was invented." Thomas had worked himself into a real tizzy trying to make his argument sound convincing, and I was listening intently thinking he might have a legitimate argument, kicking a can down the path so I could focus my mind on the more salient aspects of his dissertation.

I don't think he had taken one breath since we left Jack's Bait and Hardware, but as we approached Shore House all of sudden he sucked in air making a gasping sound, the kind a man makes before their final goodbye, which caught my attention. He was looking straight ahead with eyes as big as saucers, complexion of his skin looked sickly like a man on the verge of dying, "didddd you see that?"

"See what?"

"Over there, past the gate leading down to Miss Alice's, it's ahh, it's ahh, it's ahh headless, it's ahh headless thiiingg!"

"Thomas get a hold of yourself! You're letting your imagination run wild, there's nothing there. I'll show you." To prove my assertion I swung the gate open and walked around the big post with the sign telling everyone to get lost, "see I told you there was nothing."

Never, ever tell anyone they haven't seen a ghost, unless you're willing to dance with the Devil. Feeling a little cocky for being the brave one, I stood there practically taunting the phantom to go boo. Which he pretty much did. Hearing rustling, I turned to see a creature, maybe 6 feet tall, draped in weapons, wearing nothing but black, and missing a fairly important body part. I would normally share my regards to those I've come upon unexpectedly, but on this evening felt a little unsure as to the protocol. Instead Thomas and I bolted down the road, praying our new acquaintance had other plans and I am very glad to be able to tell you we both survived the ordeal, which of course you could surmise since you are reading my account of those events.

It would seem we weren't the only islanders to be visited by the ghost of Blackbeard that night. Some five other people also claimed they had been visited and there may have been as many who were unsure they should be admitting to hallucinatory manifestations.

Nothing like a good ole fashion spook to put a damper on everyone's fun, those who had been throwing dirt and sand left and right, sweating at a feverish pace to out dig their fellow treasure hunters were now nowhere to be seen. Streets were empty and only a handful of brave souls would consider venturing out after day turned to night.

Nevertheless, there were a few of us who considered TJ Wolf's warning prophetic and wondered what additional information he might have on the subject. It wasn't hard to find him as he had become particularly fond of the sticky buns at Shepard's Pointe Café and could be seen frequenting the establishment every morning around 9 am. Thomas and I decided to call on him.

Entering the café, which on an average day does a respectable business, was a little surprised to see the place overflowing with patrons. Miss Alice, Mrs. Cartwright, and Gabrielle occupied one of the window booths. Judge Peebles and Newman another. Cooper brothers sat at the counter. Doc Stevens and Mr. Cavendish were situated at one of the tables and a host of fishermen who were occupied by victuals filled in the gaps. TJ Wolf sat alone, clearly absorbed by flavors of a cinnamon roll and slurps of hot coffee. He had an air about him, not aloof, not inviting, almost like he was taunting us with a secret, "if you dare come, and talk with me."

Thomas and I decided not to rush him, but would do our best to make our visitation look natural. So, we held back biding our time. After our second cup of coffee we nodded at each other; time was ripe to make our move. But before we could find our feet, them Cooper brothers moved from the counter and slipped in beside Mr. Wolf. Leaning forward they spoke in hushed tones, occasionally glancing around to see if others were eavesdropping. They weren't long and having concluded their business shook hands with the archeologist and parted ways.

Had my chair pushed back and was half-way standing when Newman and the Judge moseyed over to Wolf and preceding transaction was repeated with similar outcome. Next were Doc Stevens and Mr. Cavendish followed by Miss Alice, Mrs. Cartwright, and Gabrielle. The place was emptying-out fast. Finally, it was our turn.

"Ahem, excuse me Mr. Wolf, Thomas here and I would appreciate a minute of your time, if that is agreeable with you?"

"Gentlemen, it is my pleasure. What may I do for you on this fine day?"

"Well, it is a little awkward, and I'd be lying if I didn't say I'm a might embarrassed, but the recent goings-on, especially with spirits appearing here and there, has our curiosity peaked; and well, it seems you could be an authority on matters which are of particular interest to folks like Thomas and me."

"Do tell, and what might interest you sir?"

Thomas couldn't hold it in any longer and blurted, "Blackbeard's treasure!"

"I see. Well gentlemen, I am sorry to disappoint you, but it is highly unlikely it will be found anytime soon. Many amateur and professionally trained archeologists have been searching for over a century and haven't turned hide nor hair. I myself have been on the trail for a good part of my career and, with exception of a few tantalizing bobbles floating up now and then, have come up empty handed."

It was those bobbles, Mr. TJ Wolf referred to, that led the people of Bogue Banks to believe the treasure was closer than he was willing to admit.

"That may be so sir, but we'd sure appreciate it if you could lend aid to us humble folk who are willing to take any necessary risks, and who are keen on putting our best foot forward."

"I am not certain gentlemen. In truth I believe I would be doing you a disservice."

The harder he pushed back, the harder we pushed. Not threatening, more like pleading and appealing to his good nature. Back and forth we went, almost like he was playing us. Smarter fellas would have smelled a skunk.

"Alright, I concede to you good men, but what I have to offer you must swear to secrecy. Do you agree?"

Thomas and I nodded our heads like we were at the 5 and dime sampling every sweet in the store, "cross our hearts and hope to die!"

He scooted low in his seat, chin almost resting on the table, hand covering the side of his face so no one could read his lips, whispering, "in my possession is an extremely rare and intricate map, crafted by the very hand of Edward Teach. It is in fact the map to his hidden treasure. Now, there is only one copy gentlemen, and it is so valuable many learned scholars have offered me literally hundreds of thousands of dollars, just to peek at it. I know if I put it in your possession it will be in good hands and I am only asking a paltry $100, cash." If there ever was a more conspiratorial moment, it has happened in my life time.

I swallowed hard, "a $100?"

"Yes, but keep in mind the treasure is likely worth a thousand times as much. But, if you gentlemen would prefer I can offer it to someone else?"

"No! No, absolutely not, Thomas and I will get you the $100. Please don't sell the map to anyone else!"

"Very well, I will see you tonight at Mrs. Cartwright's at precisely 7 pm, I will be sitting on the front porch, and don't forget to bring the money."

"Yes sir, we'll be there like a tick on a dog, precisely at 7 pm. Oh by the way Mr. Wolf, not that it is any of my business, but I couldn't help notice you were engaged in what appeared to be serious discussions with some of our fellow Bankers a few minutes ago."

"Why yes, they were ever so kind to drop by and tell me how much they enjoyed my lecture the other evening on archeological wonders of the world."

I didn't say it, but I thought they couldn't have been at the same lecture I attended.

*****

That evening at precisely 7 pm, Thomas and I paid Mr. Wolf a visit. And, as promised, he was sitting on Mrs. Cartwright's porch.

"Do you gentlemen have the money?"

"Sure do, feel free to count it if you like."

"That won't be necessary. Hand it over!"

He seemed anxious, almost too anxious, to conclude our business, and I was beginning to have second thoughts. But that all changed when he produced the map. Parchment looked fragile and as I held it thought it might disintegrate in my hands. Crude markings from ink, bled through veins of paper fabric, scratched by the author, perhaps shaky in the skill of drawing. Thomas and I somewhat skeptical as to the authenticity of the document in our possession begged for verification, "so this is real deal, the one and only bona fide map to Blackbeard's treasure, conceived by one and the same?"

"That it is, indeed gentlemen. Now I will bid you a good evening and happy hunting." Mr. Wolf rose from the porch and without looking back entered the house locking the door behind.

No time like the present, Thomas and I studied our newest possession by flashlight and planned our attack. Vague outline of the island resembled that of Bogue Banks, and details of recognizable landmarks were clear enough for one who has spent their entire life passing them by on a daily basis. From our accomplished study of cartographic handwriting we surmised should we follow ole man Salter's path directly from his weathered homestead, without wavering, 103 steps by a man with two sound legs and a minimum of one good eye to see by, should bring us to a dot on the map marked by a skull and crossbones.

Giddy with the realization we were only minutes away from being the wealthiest men in Carteret County, maybe Craven too, we pursued our treasure at a pace resembling a slow run. Shovels and picks were clanging, legs sometimes getting ahead of us, reminded me for all the world of how we must look at the annual barbecue rushing to get to the front of the buffet line.

...54, 55, 56...78, 79...101, 102, and 103. I've never stood on a platform for a subway, and hope I never will, but as we counted-off our paces and ended with the magic number, Thomas and I were greeted by a gaping hole in the ground and hovering on its edge were Mr. Cavendish, Miss Alice, Gabrielle, Cooper brothers, Judge Peebles, Mrs. Cartwright, Newman, and Doc Stevens waiting for the outgoing subway to take them far from where they were standing. All were holding an identical copy of the treasure map, all with a look Christmas had disappointed them once again. We'd been had, taken in by a con man.

Sheriff Stone arrived soon after to share the sorry news. "I had my suspicions when artifacts starting popping-up all over the beach. Sorry to say I didn't act on them soon enough. For a couple of bucks reward, he had the whole island pretty near turned upside down. Figured on having me a little talk with that archeologist this evening, but he is long gone, and I am sorry to say so is your money. Found a Blackbeard costume he used to terrify you folks, one of his maps, and knew where I could find all of you. Do you want me to press charges?"

Of course, the idea of pressing charges was ridiculous, as it would only make us look like the fools we were. Wolf knew that, in fact it was how he designed his confidence, appealing to our natural instincts of greed while making us look stupid in the process. Rumor had taken seed and with a little coaxing by TJ Wolf, bore its fruit. Ashamed and humiliated all of us declined Sheriff Stone's offer and vowed we'd never speak of the unfortunate transactions ever again.

Time has a way of healing, shedding new light on old events, even reframing them into slightly more palatable memories. It isn't that I've found a way to decorate our culpability regarding witless indiscretions. No, I believe that will always sting a little, but there is a lingering hope that Edward Teach left behind more than a reputation.

Now and then, when winter winds blow from the north, and spooks wander the tidewater of Bogue Banks, I get to thinking perhaps that treasure may still be found, and who knows maybe my pocket knives as well. Just knowing it's out there somewhere makes me feel a little better. For all of us at some time in our lives have had dreams of a pot of gold at the end of the rainbow; but not everyone has had the courage to pursue theirs.

If you happen to be passing by my porch and see a shovel leaning against my backdoor, I hope you won't think poorly of me. For it is only a reminder of what things could have been.

Broken Record

"bad, bag, baggage, bake, balance, ball, band, bank, banker, bankrupt, bar, barber, bark, barn, barrier, bartender, base, baseball, basic, basket, bath, bathroom, batter, battery, battle, beach, bear, beat, beautiful, because, bed, beef..." On and on, all day long David Strom would recite words from the dictionary. He was working on the B's when I first took notice of his odd behavior. His brother, Frank, was never too far from his side and would every so often give David a good whack upside the head, which would cause him to repeat the entire vocabulary under the letter he had been working on.

"Frank, why is it David constantly recites the dictionary, doesn't seem quite right?"

"Not absolutely sure Robert, mama says when he was born the doctor dropped him on his head and ever since he could talk that's what he's done. Smack him once in a while so the song skips. Kind of like a broken record. If I don't, he'll just keep rattling-on, letter after letter."

"What's the harm in that?"

Frank gave me a look like I might not have all my marbles, "if David keeps on spitting out words he'll get to the end of the dictionary in no time...you understand, the end of the record. No one knows for sure, but once the record is over, maybe David will be too. Problem is whacking only works for a while. Recording eventually catches-up and he moves on to the next letter."

I imagine every neighborhood has a David, the kind of boy who doesn't fit-in with what folk consider to be "normal" Some will steer clear of the Davids of the world, others may not avoid them but ignore them just the same, and a few don't know what the fuss is all about realizing they've got a few of their own graces which may appear unusual. An island is no different, with one exceedingly important exception, there is no hiding. David would attend school with his brother, he'd sit in the front pew at church, could be seen at the emporium, or down by the beach. Everywhere he went the record played-on. He might have had an unfortunate habit of spewing the lexicon from sunup to sundown, but he wasn't stupid.

Guess I was one of those who didn't understand David's behavior, but it didn't bother me like it did others. I figured life is full of characters, and if you're goin to shy away from those who don't look and act like you, well it's likely to be a lonely place. Besides, I found David to be quite useful, especially at school when I needed a little help on my vocabulary.

Aside from reciting the dictionary, David had a few other peculiar traits. For one, he despised blue haired ole busy bodies that loitered in groups of three or four exchanging gossip in hopes of latching onto titillating morsels. I also disliked these women who would become aroused by the goings-on of others, smacking of voyeuristic peeping toms. From my way of thinking they belong to those bottom feeding creatures and have very few redeeming values. Evidently, David and I shared a common aversion.

It wasn't as if he went out of his way to find them, for who would, but at times it was impossible to avoid them. Should they have the misfortune of crossing paths he would be certain to express his displeasure in his own uniquely vocal addiction, "bias, bicker, bid, big, bind, bird, bit, bitch, bitches, bitching, bitchy..." He'd keep at it until their ears burned and ran away, assuming they didn't faint first, and as he got older, and with each new letter, the diversity of his vulgar exposition grew. Surprising how many unpleasant words there are in the spoken language. He seemed to know them all.

His other trait, which would catch folks off guard, was he liked to fight. David wasn't a bully and he was careful to take it only so far, but being different it was not uncommon to find himself accosted from time to time by those who made fun of him, and thought he was an easy mark. They were wrong.

Costenbader boys had a reputation for pushing people's buttons, and after getting all wound-up enjoyed nothing better than to start a fracas. They fought dirty. Youngest one would initiate a fight, but if he found his opponent to be too challenging would call upon his older brothers to lend their support. If you fought one, you had to be prepared to fight all. With all three banging away there weren't many who could withstand the beating. They had taunted David on several occasions, but for one reason or another they never got a chance to go toe-to-toe.

Guess my number was up, heading home from school one day I was tripped by the eldest and held down while the other two wailed on me. Managed to land one or two good licks, but it didn't take long to realize I was fighting a losing battle. Would have screamed "uncle", what little good it would have done, when David came upon our party and decided to dance. David ripped the eldest Costenbader off me and proceeded to knock his lights-out. Then, while I laid on the ground bleeding, he planted one blow after another wiping the other two faces in the dirt. It wasn't like he was angry. On the contrary, he seemed to be enjoying himself. I suppose up till then he didn't have a really good excuse to mess them boys up. Wasn't particularly keen on how things started, but can't say I was disappointed in how they ended.

Years added-up and by mid 1920's David found himself at the L's, "liberty, libidinal, library, lichen, lick, lie...". Then in late 1930's the S's, which fortunately took him a long time to get through, but by 1952, now middle aged, he eventually landed on the Z's. He was getting close to the end of his record and everybody was curious as to what would happen next. David was going to either die, or he was going to live, regardless it would be newsworthy at any rate for these parts.

Frank figured it would be a spectacle one way or the other and decided to make it into an event. Arranged for a band to play at the Circle, sold tickets, and managed to get a few concessions. It turned-out to be a carnival with David Strom the main attraction. Everyone was in a festive mood. This famous psychologist, Dr. Hans Asperger, traveled all the way from Vienna to attend, said he would like to have an opportunity to study David. Mr. Dunlivin, our undertaker, was seen lurking around the edges, making sure he didn't miss out on an opportunity. While some played games of chance and others danced to the music, David stood center stage, pleased as punch, babbling words to his heart's content.

It was getting close, "zulu, zucchini, zweig, zygote..."

The crowd was hushed, Frank looked desperate, as David was ready to enunciate the last words sealing his own fate.

Mr. Cavendish, as you may recall our town drunk, had been partaking of some of the local spirits and was attempting to grasp the import of the moment. He whispered in his loudest voice slurring his speech, as drunks are apt to do, "why iss everyone soo quiet?"

Someone in the crowd caught him by the arm, "hush you ole rummy, David is about to say his last Z."

"Ohh! Why don't you flipp it?"

Frank, was clearly irritated by the outburst, but also curious, "what do you mean Mr. Cavendish?"

"Welll everyone knows a record hass two sidess. You know side A and a side B. If he'ss done playing side A, then just turn it over and play side B, it don't take no brain surgeon to figure that out."

As the saying goes, "out of the mouths of babes", or in our case a drunk, a seemingly simple, but eloquent, solution had been found to David's lifelong problem and from that day on he would continue to expound as he had done during the first half of his life. However, as we are aware side A of the record was in English and side B, was as best I could tell in French.

"ablegat, ablepsie, aboi, abolitif, abomey, abondance, abortif..."

Funny thing, during all those years folks had treated David like an odd-ball, but now that he was speaking French he became real popular, especially with the ladies. Yep, almost every Saturday night you could see David with a new girl down by the breakwaters cooing in his best French accent. Some years later that Asperger fella became famous for his studies on patients like David, they even named a condition after him.

Life is a wonderful thing. Full of drama…

>   *…and intrigue, wonder and beauty, it provides an endless array of entertainment. Nevertheless, some of it may seem cruel, especially in-light of those challenged by disorders not of their making, like David Strom. But I would argue we make of it what we are given and for those who do, they find blessings beyond belief.*
>
>   *Bizzy not one of us doesn't have a handicap of some sort. For some it is a physical manifestation, and for others something different. Don't let them hold you back. Instead make an asset out of what cards you have been dealt, and live life to its fullest. In a way our opportunities make us a little more human and there is nothing wrong with that. David is a perfect example.*
>
>   *One more thing, acceptance of other people's limitations can help you accept your own and I hope, in my most sincere and contrite way, that over the years you have come to accept some of mine.*
>
>   *Father*

*****

It is beyond irritating when someone finds a raw sensitive nerve, and then proceeds to stick the truth in it all the way up to the hilt. Could have done without the philosophical pandering which leaves me pondering which one of the many opportunities that characterize my existence, I have neglected to capitalize. Like so many other things in my life, I've managed to bury those handicaps which Robert Guthrie implies are humanizing, and even enemies have allowed me to ignore. However, sooner or later it all catches-up with you and, no matter how unpleasant, are forced to confront that human hiding behind the image in the mirror. Well, not today! I've got enough rattling around inside my head with this blasted winter storm and Peggy nosing around.

Engrossed in the letters to Bizzy, didn't take notice power was now restored, lights were glowing and furnace had kicked-in. Good thing too, my apartment was now cold enough for me to see my breath. Snow was falling outside, but fury of wind driven spin-drift had diminished. Fangs of this Nor'easter were retracting leaving in its wake the remains of its anger, white fluffy coatings, surreal and sublime, not unlike what you might see in a Currier and Ives post card. If it were not for my age, and modest degree of common sense, I might be tempted to go outside and play in it. Thank God for both.

Resolved to take a break from the letters, which have cast a spell upon me and forced me to think in ways I haven't in many years. Not that it is all bad, on the contrary there is an unusually sophisticated outlook permeated with southern island flavor. I would call it an acquired taste. Yet it takes more energy than the usual blather I'm accustomed to read.

Poured another shot of fortification, grabbed a manuscript from the top of the pile, and settled in for change of scenery. "Oh Donald, how can I express my love for you? As far as the universe, as deep as the ocean, my love is even greater! Marlene, my sweet Marlene, now that you have spoken such words, words I have longed to hear for what has seemed an eternity, how can I not but pledge myself to you, and admit I too have an intense and burning love! Two lovers separated by war torn Europe, one a spy for the British MI6, the other a spy for the German Abwehr, must endure the horrible truth they are in fact sworn enemies. A fact they must confront in the most unlikely of circumstances..." Crap! Not just crap, but crap plagiarized from an author I recognize. Have half a mind to call him up and suggest he sues them for all they're worth.

It was work like this that makes me think I should get a larger trash can. Pulled the pile closer to my chair and did my best to locate one manuscript that wasn't nauseating. Best I could do was digest a couple of pages, assuming the title didn't offend me first, mind wandering back to the letters, and surprisingly to Peggy. Not that I am a man of tremendous conscious, but the trick I played on her was low, even for my standards. Do you think she discovered my fib? Oh, what's the difference, she probably wouldn't think the worse of me, even if I set her on fire. Nevertheless, I shouldn't get in the habit of deceit lest I begin to start believing my own fabrications and end up like mother.

Adjudication of my veracity was interrupted by the doorbell, a polite little ring-a-ding. Not the rude unrelenting screech which often attends the impatience of the plumber or superintendent who lean on the button demanding my immediate attention. This was delivered, measured by a light tap, to insure it would not rattle my nerves. Peggy's ears must have been tingling for there she stood.

"Thought you might like a little pudding for dessert, it's not too sweet and I put a few berries in the mix to make it brighter."

Suddenly overcome with the urge to confess my fiction, perhaps hoping in the scheme of things I might be spared judgment from a higher being, I spilled my guts, "Peggy, I am sorry, but the story of having a wife who has spent time in prison...it was untrue. I have no wife, in fact I've never been married."

"Oh John, I know that. You must think me a simpleton if I were to believe such an outrageous tale." She gently pushed by me and put the pudding on the counter. "Men are apt to create fantasies thinking it somehow will dissuade the fairer sex from their appointed duty."

"And what duty is that?"

"Now don't be so innocent. You know full well it's a lady's responsibility to subdue the male, to declaw and render them harmless. I'm not saying you shouldn't put up a fight, it wouldn't be any fun if you didn't, but at some point you need to concede the battle. There is no shame in surrendering, especially when you realize how well you will be treated as a prisoner of war. As your warden I can be particularly generous."

All I could think of was how father was tortured by mother all those years, but Peggy seemed different and I was convinced not all women were predestined to mother's predilections, certainly Peggy didn't fit the mold. As I ate the pudding she explained to me how it was the women's responsibility to take care of a man. How men were clever in some ways, yet in other ways were dumber than dirt, and needed to rely on a woman's intuition to help them through their lives. If a woman failed in this duty the man would evolve following his own sorry devices, lost to our society as a pariah. Man's responsibility was to be the woman's partner and appreciate the finer things which accompanied the tender mercies of a lady's touch.

I listened to her intently, as if she were delivering the State of the Union Address, and as I did, realized the lady in apartment 8D had qualities of persuasion I had previously not recognized. All this time I had been avoiding a superlative orator.

She got up, patted me on the head, and confidently made her way to the door, "it's time for me to give you some room, but I want you to think about what I've said, and we'll be sure to continue this conversation at another time. Ta ta!"

For the life-of-me I never expected that chat. I had been lectured by a pro, and despite all my education and degrees, was left feeling more than a little stupid and resolved that next time I lie I would make no admission. She had snuck-up on me with the pretext of food, but clearly had other things on her mind, and if I am not careful would likely do it again.

Proteus

July 8, 1952

My Dear Bizzy

It all started somewhere in the recesses of Miss Alice's brain. A little tickle ignited a few sparks, sparks lit flammable reasoning, reasoning started to smoldering, which grew into a small fire, and before long there was a full blown gray matter conflagration. No question, a seed had been planted inside her cranium and there was no way in this world, or next, she was going to let it go...

...Fond of ordering the men of Salter Path around and expecting to get her way, I wasn't surprised in the least when I was summoned to Shore House on a matter of extreme urgency, which you will learn has everything to do with that idea rattling around inside her head. You might call it a sixth sense, because before I hastened down the path, passed the padlocked gate, and no trespassing signs I knew whatever the emergency, it was going to be a real doozy and somehow Miss Alice would involve me in a manner which I would find either discomforting, regretful, or both.

Accustomed to rough edges and sharp tongue entitled by wealth and position, I was greeted by Miss Alice in her familiar tone.

"Don't know who you think you are Johnny Joe, but when I make a point to call on someone you can be sure I am on time. That is a common courtesy you Bankers have yet to acquire, and understanding you have limited intellectual capacity I am forced to endure your delinquency without any hopes of recourse!"

"Nice to see you Miss Alice, wasn't aware I was expected at any specific time. However, I apologize for-"

"Your apologies are as worthless to me as you are! If I had a dollar for every apology you have brought to my door, I would be able to purchase New York City, Paris, and still have change left over for a cup of coffee."

"Yes ma'am."

"Don't have time to elaborate all your shortcomings right now, I am expecting a large package to be delivered to the Morehead post office today and I need you to go pick it up and don't get side-tracked along the way with pastries at the café or poker at the hardware store. You can piddle-away precious hours of the day when you're spending your own time. Do I make myself clear?"

"Yes Miss Alice. Ma'am, I am going to need to borrow your car."

"I expected as much, but don't you think for one minute I am going to pay for the gasoline. It is bad enough, having to depend on people like you, without being drained of my life savings in the process because you haven't provided the correct tools to complete the job!"

Was going to respond politely with a yes ma'am, or other affirmation, but I'd had enough kowtowing and didn't think she'd hear me anyway.

*****

Miss Alice was right about one thing. It was a large package. Actually, it was a large crate and weighed almost as much as I do. If it weren't for the postmaster, not sure I could have wrestled it into the car by myself. Tied the trunk lid down as far as it would go; and was careful driving back to the island to avoid pot holes and ruts, uncertain if it was fragile.

Return address on the box was La Spirotechnique, Toulon, France. Wrenched my back getting it out of the car, and as I stood messaging my sacroiliac pondered what them Frenchies had that was so important to Miss Alice. Wouldn't have to wait long.

"Don't just stand there like a dolt! Get a crowbar and get it open before I get any older!"

Getting a little steamed, but figured sooner I freed the contents the sooner I could get back to my own business and be rid of Miss Alice, at the very least for the time being.

Cautiously jimmied 2 by 4's and leveraged the plywood without splintering. My experience with big packages is most of the time the box can be more interesting than what's inside. And, I would have come to that conclusion, except I didn't know exactly what I was looking at. From first appearance it looked like a plumbing nightmare, but there were also some unusual paraphernalia thrown in, black fins, a mask and a belt with lead.

"Miss Alice, what is it that you have purchased?"

"Your imagination, or should I say lack thereof, never ceases to amaze me Johnny Joe. What do you think it is?"

Bizzy, wouldn't say I am an imaginative man when compared to those folks who have spent their early years engrossed in books becoming doctors and lawyers. But, I seem to have had just enough of that stuff to get me this far in life, and if I can amble from one day to the next, then I'm OK with that.

"Miss Alice, sorry to say I don't have a clue."

"Figured...what you are looking at is a modern Aqua Lung, first of its kind."

Turning back the pages in my mind, I recall reading about this device in the Sunday Post. Turns out two Frenchmen, an engineer Emile Gagnan, and Naval Lieutenant Jacques Cousteau, invented the self-contained underwater breathing apparatus, what they called the Aqua Lung, back during World War II and started shipping them to the US in 1950, launched this new fad called scuba. Amateurs without too much common sense, could strap tanks and a regulator on their backs and proceed to find a scenic underwater vista so they could drown themselves. Fact that some did not is practically a miracle.

"Now Miss Alice what do intend on doing with this here Aqua Lung?"

"Salvage Johnny Joe, salvage. Just off-shore within eyesight of where we're standing is the graveyard of the Atlantic, littered with shipwrecks going back to early 1700's. Some of them are worthless, some of them contain curiosities from another time, and some of them. Well, some of them contain enough pickings to buy us New York, Paris, and still have change left over for a cup of coffee."

Miss Alice had been born in mid 1800's and was now on the shady side of the mountain, the downhill run to eternity. I guessed she had to be 88 if my reckoning was accurate.

"Miss Alice, I may be out of turn to say this, but don't you think you're a might old for this scuba adventure. Just the tanks alone weigh nearly 80 pounds. If you put them on, you'll fold like a deck of cards."

"Don't be a damn fool! I have no intention of putting all this machinery on, or going underwater."

"You don't?"

"No. You are."

This is the point in our story where I find out I'm not driving, but alas am sitting in the back seat watching as oncoming traffic whizzes by. World as we know it is full of imponderables and for those curious types, experiencing the unknown is too much of a temptation to resist. However, I find getting from sunup to sundown sufficiently challenging and am more than happy to leave the discovery of the tops of mountains, Amazon rain forest, and most importantly the deep blue sea to others who don't mind dying just to say they've done it.

"Miss Alice you and I go back a long way. By now, you probably have a pretty good idea what talents I may have, and those I do not. Understanding I am somewhat adverse to sticking my neck out there for someone to chop it off, you can appreciate why I am a little reluctant to take you up on your offer. You done said it yourself, I ain't got no imagination or intelligence."

"First of all this isn't an offer, as you have said. I'm not looking for a volunteer, if I was I'd put an ad in the newspaper. Secondly, you don't need imagination or intelligence, which are only likely to get in your way. You just need to do what I tell you, and do it when I tell you. Third, if you are going to be a big cry-baby, whining like a coward, it's going to be more work for both of us, but it will not deter me on my quest; and, you will go under the waves to recover riches and baubles! We'll figure your cut after we've assessed the value of any salvage."

I was beaten and she knew it, "yes ma'am. How does this Aqua Lung thing work?"

"Don't bother me with details. If you want to know how it works, read the manual. But I recommend that you do so before tomorrow comes, because you're going to need it. Cap'n Chisholm has agreed to charter our trip. See you bright and early at the docks; and for goodness sake, try to be on-time!"

*****

Over the years I've learned reading in bed is a sure fire way of sending me off to la-la land. A few lines into whatever's caught my fancy, regardless of how interesting it may be, and I can be found with drool running down my chin and eyelids resting on my cheeks. If I have to start a paragraph over it's almost guaranteed I won't find its end. Why I thought reading a boring how-to on the operation of the Aqua Lung and scuba diving was going to be any different, I don't know.

Manual was in simple English, which was convenient for me, and learned if I wanted to breathe underwater I just had to inhale and air from the tanks would fill my lungs like it does on terra firma. Regulator was designed as open circuit, which meant my exhaled breath would be expelled into the water leaving a trail of bubbles. Got as far as the J-valve on the tank, but had to start the paragraph over twice, "when the tank pressure drops below 500 psi breathing will become difficult, pull the lever down to feed the reserve gas. Once the reserve is released it is time to ascend. Warning, it is critical when filling the tank to make sure the J-valve is in the...in the...in..."

Next morning came faster than expected. Sun pouring through my window caught me unawares with the manual on my chest and realization I was already late, and whatever I would need to know about scuba diving, and in particular the J-valve, I'd have to pick-up on the fly.

Down by the pier found Cap'n Chisholm's boat tied-up with Miss Alice in her cockpit fuming. Cap'n was at the wheel, engine was humming, and was surprised to see Thomas coiling lines.

"Thomas why are you here?"

"Moral support."

Should have made me feel good having Thomas onboard, but instead wondered why he thought I would need moral support from him. I had to let that sink-in.

"Johnny Joe, you're late again! If I could force you to give me back all the time you have wasted me over the years, I would live to be 200! Get those tanks filled and get on this boat!

Was already on the wrong side of Miss Alice; and, if I didn't shift it into high gear it was likely I'd stay there. Drug the double tanks over to the compressor set-up by the truck delivery and flipped the switch to the electric motor. It whirred and wheezed as pressure built in the tanks emitting pinking sounds as metal expanded under thousands of pounds per square inch. Took less than 5 minutes to fill. Hoisted them on my back to carry and found they were warm to the touch. Sprinted down the dock to drop the hot potato and as I stepped aboard, the boat eased away from her berth, free of lines and those constraints contrived by mother earth.

It is one thing, once a shipwreck has been found, to dive under water and commence a search for loot; and, it is another to find a shipwreck to dive-on in the first place. Watermen all know the best fishing grounds are often strewn with decaying hulks of once upon-a-time ships and boats, which create nooks and crannies for fish to call their home. Many commercial trawlers, in the process of pulling their nets, have recovered fragments of wreckage confirming their last resting place. Our strategy would be simple. Cruise to one of many popular fishing coordinates and drag a grappling hook to see what we could latch onto. Sticking something was a good sign, as the bottom over the continental shelf is relatively flat and sandy. There are in fact very few natural impediments to interfere with probing.

First two tries turned-up little, a couple tires, fishing net, a toilet, other sundry items which folks have lost or dumped since the beginning of time, but no indication we had found us a sunken ship. However, on our third try we hooked something that wouldn't budge. Under these circumstances your fancy takes over and suppositions regarding what may be at the other end of the line run the gamut from row boat to ocean liner. Notwithstanding, any enticement to find out exactly what was down there was dampened by reality I would be the one doing the looking. In spite of reservations I harbored, the scowl from Miss Alice dispelled any notion I might have of shirking my new responsibilities and decided now might be a good time to take a second look at the diving manual.

Lots of letters, sentences, and paragraphs on lots of pages, but nothing jumped out at me. Decided to scan illustrations, hoping the old adage a picture is worth a thousand words. One photo depicted a man donning scuba gear. Mask, snorkel, tanks, regulator, weight belt, and fins were all neatly arranged on a physique which could be described as almost superhuman, probably a Marine drill sergeant or Olympian and given the contrast between model and me, wondered if I was up to the task at hand. Another showed this same fella underwater, muscles bulging, casually swimming in a prone position using fins to propel him through the water. Seemed simple enough, at least I hoped so.

"Shake a leg Johnny Joe, times-a-wasting!"

Miss Alice was getting antsy, and if I told her I had only got through a few pages of the scuba manual, she probably would have shown me even less sympathy then she already was.

Thomas helped get the gear on. As the moment of truth approached it seemed heavier, my mouth turned to dust, knees started knocking, and I had a sudden urge to employ the privy.

Cap'n Chisholm seeing the state I had found myself, had a sincere expression of worry, "Robert, you sure you want to do this dive?"

"No sir, I do not! In fact, I would prefer to be on the beach fishing right about now."

Miss Alice pushed Cap'n aside, "if you don't mind Cap'n Chisholm I would appreciate it if you would leave this man alone. He is on an important assignment, the particulars of which do not concern you. You take care of your boat and I will take care of other matters." She grabbed me by the arm with a grip which surprised me for a woman her age and pushed me to the fantail where I was unceremoniously launched into the vast and dreadful sea. "Go find something!"

Immediately overcome with panic, thrashing like a banshee, water sloshing so close to my face, sucking some down my windpipe, was convinced I wouldn't need to submerge, but would expire right there at the surface. Then it dawned on me, dying now there would be nothing to show for my sacrifice; and not that I am altruist, but if I am going to perish then in any case it should be for something worthwhile. Blinked a couple of times, closed my eyes and slid beneath the surface.

Water seeped into my mask and up my nose choking me. Face plate fogged so I couldn't see. Lead on my weight belt, obviously excessive, pulled me down accelerating my descent with each foot, pressure on ear drums was unbearable and I hyperventilated like I was giving birth. But for the most part everything was going according to plan.

My short journey ended when I crashed landed on the sandy bottom. Lying on my back I could see the silhouette of our shrimp boat above me with Miss Alice, Cap'n Chisholm, and Thomas peering over the side.

118

Decided to stay put long enough to gather my composure and prepare myself for what lay ahead.

Turning, was startled to see what looked like a passenger freighter sitting upright. Rolled on my belly and attempted to swim, using fins attached to my feet as depicted in the illustration. But, weight from the lead pinned me to the bottom like a thumb on a nat. Was either going to walk around in slow motion, or I was going to lose the weight belt, opted for the later.

Having discarded my shackles found I was able, without too much effort, to swim in the direction of the object which now framed the world inside my mask. She was a monster, maybe 4 or 5 hundred feet long with cables haphazardly dangling about the decks and drooping over the sides to sand below. Learned quickly if I wasn't looking straight ahead I couldn't see anything, as my peripheral vision was blinded by the mask skirt, which is why I didn't see a school of toothy Tiger Sharks thick as a swarm of mosquitoes munching on pompano. Seen plenty of sharks fishing from shore and always minded where I stepped if wading into surf to cast. Instances of swimmers and anglers getting bitten aren't unheard of, although experts say it was because sharks mistook them for prey. To my way of thinking it doesn't much matter whether it was an accident or intentional. Folks got bit just the same.

Can't say I was real happy about the situation, and was ready to bolt when one of the bigger boys floored me. Made no attempt to veer out my way, just body slammed me like he was a football tackle, and swam off. Couple other Tigers bumped me as if we were on a crowded bus, made no apologies. Figured I was an uninvited guest dancing in the midst of a gang of exceedingly hungry, overzealous, and giant-sized guppies. Clearly they were not intimidated by my presence. No matter which way I maneuvered it seemed to be wrong. Needed to extricate myself from this predicament, but decided they might smell fear if I sprinted to the surface and resolve to eat on me a little. So, in spite of my instinct, waited to see what they would do next and am glad to tell you nothing. Occasionally they would speed-up to swallow an unsuspecting fish but for the most part swam in circles making me dizzier than when I was on the loop-to-loop. And so it would go, if I stayed out of their way and didn't stick my nose in their business, they wouldn't stick theirs in mine.

An amicable departure from predators of the deep brought me to the purpose at hand. Scanning the deck and hull for holes to penetrate, I found very few that would fit-the-bill. It wasn't obvious what had sunk her. Elected to start at the top and work my way down. Windows of the bridge had been missing for a long time which afforded me several options for entry. Ambient light illuminating exterior spaces, struggled to reach confines of the helm. Not dark, but made a mental note should I make a return trip, I'd need to bring some kind of flashlight if entering spaces of the ship which would be pitch black. Telegraph, speaking tube and other equipment familiar to ships of the time were festooned with sea life growing in odd shapes. Corals and fans swayed rhythmically in the surge of currents flowing in and out of hatches. Frame of the captain's chair was intact, cushions had deteriorated, metal railings looked frail from corrosion, yet overall I got the impression if she could be floated there was a chance she might sail.

*****

Wasn't sure how long I had been underwater, certainly long enough to drain the tanks, and determined it was better to be on the outside of the ship when they ran low. After exiting the bridge swam around the weather deck struggling to stay at one depth. For some reason was now buoyant. Was tempted to recover the weight belt, but was rudely interrupted when I inhaled and got nothing. It was like the regulator was stuck, sucked a couple more times with the same outcome. Then I remembered I needed to pull the J-valve down to open the reserve. Reaching back was horrified when I pulled on it and realized it was already in the down position. I had run completely out of air, there wasn't any reserve, and was looking at an ascent of roughly 75 feet. It wasn't fair, if I had known I was going to run out of air I would have taken a couple of deep breaths to make sure my lungs were full. But I guess that's the point of running out of air, if you knew it was going to happen, assuming you're a sensible person, you would get out of the water before you embarrassed yourself, or worse.

Most wouldn't call me a determined fellow. Have my strong points, but purposeful isn't one of them. Nevertheless, at that point in time I thought it was appropriate to step out of character. Single-minded I pointed my nose in the direction of Capn's boat and kicked like there was no tomorrow. Fortunately, I became progressively more buoyant as I ascended which aided in my salvation. By the time I made the surface I was moving at a pretty good clip, breaching the water like a whale, flying into the air 4 or 5 feet, and landing like a dead fish belly-up.

Gasping and sputtering I was immediately accosted by Miss Alice, "well don't just lay there all blue in the face. Say something! Did you find a ship? Well, did you? Johnny Joe, you are the most obstinate person I know! All this time I have been on this boat pining away, patiently waiting on news of a miraculous discovery and here you are resolutely withholding news as to the future of our enterprise. Have half-a-mind to strangle you when you get aboard!"

Cap'n Chisholm seeing I was indisposed pulled me to the stern with a boat hook and hoisted me into the cockpit where I lay taking stock on matters pertaining to my own personal physiology.

Thomas didn't bother to look up but was engrossed in the how to scuba manual. "Says here, if you hold your breath while making a rapid ascent your lungs are likely to burst, and divers have been killed instantly from brain embolisms. Seems you came-up awfully fast Robert. Did you hold your breath?"

Wanted to tell him the truth, but denial was the response less likely to run into long winded explanations and one thing I didn't have at that moment was a lot wind.

Thomas continued to recite from the manual. "When descending, you can relieve pressure in your middle ear, by swallowing and wiggling your jaw every few feet. That's an interesting fact. Robert did you have any difficulties with your ears?"

Wish I had known that one before I plunged to the ocean bottom.

"Oh, here's a good one, it is critical when filling the tanks to make sure the J-valve is in the up position; if left in the down position the diver will not have a gas reserve and will likely drown."

I was beginning to dislike Thomas's litany, not so much because it was information I should have known. No, it was because Thomas knew I hadn't read the manual, and he was rubbing my nose in it, making sure before I dove again it would be memorized cover to cover and that night instead of lying in bed attempting to peruse the mysteries of the deep, I sat in my living room with feet on the floor, and did just that. What I learned made my toes curl. Seemed I broke every critical rule of scuba diving on my first try. There were all kinds of dangers and if you didn't mind your p's and q's one could end-up in a world of hurt.

Next few dives were uneventful and devoted almost exclusively to testing underwater flashlights, for without there would be no hopes of entering the wreck far enough to find anything of interest. First one I tried was light-weight aluminum, epoxied to seal it from water. It worked fine for the first few feet, but after descending past 30 the canister crushed like a Dixie cup. Tried a couple others, but they also succumbed to the pressures at some point.

All this experimentation irritated Miss Alice, which by then had lost all patience. "Relying on you Johnny Joe to get this job done was a calamitous debacle, for which I regret. It would have been faster for me to drain the ocean and explore the wreck on my own."

"But Miss Alice, can't find your valuables if I can't see."

"Light a match for all I care, but get back in the water and get to work!"

Hounded to distraction I prevailed upon Sheriff Stone who offered me his police flashlight made of carbon steel, which when sealed worked perfectly from the surface all the way to bottom, below. Once again, we were back in business.

With flashlight in hand I sliced the dark as a warrior slices his foes with razor sharp rapier. Wherever I pointed my weapon shadowy recesses retreated, revealing anomalies of time and space. Along a corridor was a discarded doll, in a corner a lost shoe, and on the bridge evidence of the captain's log on the chart table, impressions of entries dissolved by measures with each passing year.

What stories would they tell if they could but speak. And then there was the ship's bell; a magnificently preserved brass dome, with clapper at the ready. I let the light play on its features, toying as if awaking it from the inanimate. This pleased me, and was completely lost to my game, blissfully ignorant I was fathoms below the surface. In bold raised letters etched upon the bell by skillful hands was the ship's name proudly proclaimed, "Proteus". No scholar, but it sounded of a potent Greek name and must mean something significant.

With new found knowledge we had power, power over past events and an opportunity for discovery. Then it dawned on me I was in a place where no man has stood since she met her untimely end and slid beneath the waves. It presaged of things found, should I continue my quest, which perhaps should be left well enough alone. Maybe a skeleton or two is lurking in the dark, anxious to drive me from their tomb.

Too onerous a thought, would suspend these invectives, for now I was compelled to return to the surface and report my finding.

*****

For once, in a very long time, Miss Alice seemed pleased. Wasn't sure if it was directed at me or the news, but I wasn't about to press the point and ruin the moment. Upon returning to shore we visited the portal of enlightenment, which I am sorry to say was unfamiliar. The Beaufort library. There Miss Alice pulled as many books from shelves as was relevant to our study of local shipwrecks. Divided between Thomas, Miss Alice, and me we scoured for any information related to the Proteus. Admittedly, I was less motivated by the task and permitted my mind to wander to neglected duties. Fishing, for example.

After what seemed like hours Thomas stood and shouted, "eureka". Which elicited a strong "ssshhh" and stern look from Miss Mumford, our local librarian. Amongst the pages of the Annals of Maritime Disasters of North Carolina, for years 1915-1920, he found a dispassionate almost bland entry related to the ship and events which sent her to the bottom. "On August 8, 1918, cruising from New Orleans in route to New York, blackened due to wartime regulation, Proteus was struck by an oil tanker which was unable to see her in the dead of night. Proteus's captain, Harry Boyd, immediately ordered abandon ship. Of the 95 passengers and crew on board, one perished. All personal valuables and ships safe were never recovered." This bit of news definitely piqued Miss Alice's interest and learning the ship had been built by the Cromwell Line, she immediately got off a letter requesting detailed diagrams of the ships interior.

As you may have gathered, patience is not one of Miss Alice's strong suites. Every day for near on 2 weeks I was dispatched to the post office to badger, beg or steal news from our poor postmaster regarding the expectant letter from Cromwell and every day I had the sorry detail of informing Miss Alice there was no response in the post. She was beside herself, almost prostrate and was careful to give a wide berth to Shore House knowing I made a perfect target for her frustration.

After giving-up any hope Cromwell Lines would respond to her request, quite unexpectedly a package arrived addressed to Miss Alice containing the floor plans of each deck as laid down by the builders some 50 years earlier. It took her less than a minute to find what she was looking for.

"Johnny Joe, there is but one place to look if we hope to find our treasure. The pursers office. For there, we will also find the ship's safe, and most likely passenger's money and valuables, which many would entrust to the purser for safe keeping during their voyage."

In a dramatic and grand motion she extended her arm and slowly allowed her index finger to trace the diagram landing on a small somewhat insignificant looking room, and in tiny barely legible letters was written, "purser billet"; two decks down and immediately astern of the bridge, a distance less than my first digit of my pinky.

"There", she exclaimed triumphantly! "That is what we have been looking for!"

From what I could discern, the area of interest could be accessed through a companionway from the bridge, a relatively easy job assuming nothing blocked my passage. However, retrieving the safe, of unknown dimensions and weight was to be a quite different matter.

Once again, I descended into the depths to merge with those elements which constitute an absolute barrier for man's existence. Yet there I was, sustained by pistons and valves of questionable reliability, certain should I dwell on such matters they would prove their fallibility. I needed to switch channels to a somewhat lighter topic, before I became overwhelmed with doubt. So, I thought to myself about all the good eating fish. "Blues were fun to catch, but too oily for my taste. Wahoo is good, but you have to be careful not to cook it too long so as it becomes dry. Same with swordfish. I like drum a lot, but if truth be known trigger fish is for my money the best eating fish there is." And don't you know, my recitation on good eating fish calmed right down.

From the bridge I found my stairwell which during its day conveniently directed traffic of stewards and crew through labyrinths at the business end of the ship, shielding sensitive eyes of passengers from the mundane. Effortlessly I glided down without having to place foot upon a single step, first one deck then another. Merging with ghosts known to haunt every shipwreck, I traversed a short distance from companionway pedestal turning to see billowing clouds of silt stir in my wake, telltale signs of specters born upon the seas and with it the realization my enthusiasm must give way to more cautious movements if I hoped to find my exit.

In my mind's eye I visualized the passage of the purser during the course of his day dispensing the duty of his position. In essence he was the business manager, attending to payment of bills, salaries, and acting as liaison between passengers and ship's owner. His role was not insignificant, and as such, would report directly to the ship's captain.

My plan was to count doorways on the starboard side of the ship as I progressed to locate my objective. Light from the flashlight gleamed brightly reflecting minute particles suspended in a distracting and confusing array; redoubled my focus looking beyond the dangerous glare. One...two...three, this must be it. A rounded door was left ajar, probably by the anxious purser as he hastily fled the doomed ship leaving behind a legacy for which I was now bound and determined to recover.

Spartan in design and decoration it suited its purpose and represented to those who would entrust their valuables an air of respectability. Beyond the single table affixed to the bulkhead, protected in a corner by supporting walls, stood a small safe, perhaps 2 feet on all sides. Carefully, gently, I pressed and found it shifted ever so slightly, thankful that fanatical owners had not welded it into place.

I had found that which should place me in esteem, unshakable even by Miss Alice's venomous tempers. I would be lauded and hoisted upon shoulders of Bankers, paraded as a hero to those generations who before were forced to collect the detritus of shipwrecks washed upon their shores to survive. I, Robert Guthrie, would no longer be an ordinary man!

Shaken from my reverie by resistance on my regulator, I knew it was time to pull the J-valve and make my departure and as I did, placed a light line from the purser's office, along the side of the hall, and up the stairs to the bridge. This would be my trail of crumbs which would afford the security, regardless of visibility, that would facilitate my escape during future forays.

My report to Miss Alice was well received and found her in very favorable humors, she could not disguise a smile and look of contented victory.

"Robert, you have done well my boy."

This was the first time she had used my proper name. Not that she hadn't known it all along, but calling me by any number of irrelevant appellations seemed to amuse her. Now, I had earned her respect and the right to be Robert.

"Yes indeed, you have done extraordinarily well. And, I forgive you for being indolent and stupid. I now realize you can't help yourself, but with a little constructive guidance from me you have accomplished what I consider to be a good day's work."

OK, could have done without the back-handed complement, which under closer scrutiny didn't sound like a complement at all. Nevertheless, she wasn't screaming at me and I figured that was an improvement, and the best one should hope for.

Over the next few dives I engineered a system of pulleys and ropes that would progressively drag the safe from its present location to the threshold of the door; down the hall; and in stages, up the companionway to the helm. There I would attach a sling to bring it to the surface and waiting arms of Miss Alice. Working slowly, stopping when silt blinded my progress and threatened to undo my efforts, I managed to raise the safe to the level of the bridge. It worked flawlessly. Almost home, the easiest part of the journey lay ahead, but final trek to the surface would have to wait for another day.

*****

Dawn broke. It looked from all appearances to be a text book picture perfect day. Sun was bright, not a cloud, light winds, and Carolina blue skies set the tone for our sprint to the finish line. At the dock a crowd had formed of people cheering us on, which initially I considered very thoughtful and was buoyed by all the good wishes. Nevertheless, our adventure was meant to be a secret, can't have moochers stealing our claim. Someone had to blab, and of course, once word got around the island there was no stopping the cascade of events precipitated by loose lips.

Considered our situation and concluded no harm was done, as there was no way anyone could beat us to the punch at this point. After all, how many people had an Aqua Lung? However, hidden behind false confidences I would learn it wasn't necessary to be equipped with scuba equipment to steal what was rightfully ours.

By mid-morning was back in the water again, and lighting upon the bridge was relieved to see our safe precisely where I had left it. Scooted it out to the adjacent wing and in no time secured it with a sling. Tied with so many loops there would be no way it could get away from us. Two tugs of the rope and off she went making its way to the surface for the first time in many decades. Gratified, I made no attempt to ascend, but basked in the glory and image of treasure found. Only after it broke the surface did I make my ascent and in my last few feet wondered if I would ever dive again. Could there ever be a more compelling reason?

Encouraged by Miss Alice's entreaties, Capn' Chisholm opened the throttle and pointed the bow in direction of Beaufort Inlet making good time in light chop which had developed. Passing Fort Macon on our port, we entered the harbor. Cap'n idled her down for a triumphant return of warriors fresh from battle. Miss Alice, Thomas, and I stood proudly in the cockpit hoping everyone on shore was getting a good look at our safe, absorbing envious stares from our admiring Bankers. Helm was spun hard-over and engine backed at a roar bringing our stern into its berth as pretty as you please, drawing our venture near its end and what an end it would be.

People pressing in from all directions, some taking photos, others shouting questions, it wasn't surprising we neglected to see North Carolina State Troopers amongst the melee. But their presence would become known to us soon enough. As we brought our safe ashore four large uniformed officers with those funny looking hats stepped forward, "you're all under arrest."

Miss Alice isn't the type to be easily intimidated or bullied, "you knuckleheads have got the wrong people! Go make yourself useful and catch some real criminals!"

"Sorry ma'am, I have a warrant for your arrest, and of those who aided and abetted for stealing the property of North Carolina as per laws of the Department of Natural and Cultural Resources governing salvage. We have been made aware of your unlawful procurement of a safe, which formerly was aboard the ship, Proteus."

"Listen here you oversized, under-brained gorilla. If you think you can waltz down here, flash your badge, say a few fancy words, and expect to take what, through our hard efforts, belongs to us, you have another thing coming! Now back-off before I really get mad!"

To say I was wincing and hoping Miss Alice would control herself would be an understatement. Handcuffs appeared when she started swinging her purse, and before you could say zip-a-dee-doo-dah Miss Alice, Cap'n Chisholm, Thomas, and I were in the back of cruisers on our way to the county jail. Our safe was confiscated and taken to a locksmith to extract its contents.

Let me tell you, an overnight in lock-up is a sobering experience. Accoutrements were either intentionally undesirable, or neglected from inadequate funding. Didn't matter, they were heinous! Mattress thin as paper, smelling faintly of urine, and should I have considered sleeping there was an incandescent light bulb hanging directly over my bunk which remained on all hours of the day. Sink for washing and drinking, discolored from rusty plumbing, was attached in a bizarre and extremely unhygienic manner to the toilet, discouraging any notion of bathing or pooping. Air stale from sweat of prisoners lingered like an uninvited guest and moaning from individuals who from all appearances were uncooperative with the gendarmes amplified my discomfort. To add icing on the cake I was rooming with a guy named Bubba. He was a menacing looking individual, larger in proportion then most men, and festooned with unpleasant tattoos covering his torso, arms, and neck; graphic expressions of discontent, poignantly expressed in terse sentence fragments, "hate", "I hate you", "I hate everyone". It was purported that Bubba had murdered his wife, yet in a very short period of time became awfully fond of me. Made up my mind, if I wasn't released within 24 hours, I was going to ask for the death penalty.

Seems Judge Peebles had some influence and we were arraigned and tried the next day. However, his hands were tied and, unfortunately, would be sitting for our trial. State would be represented by their chief prosecutor, Alastair Finkelstein, and the defense would be represented by our very own Newman Willis.

I could immediately tell Mr. Finkelstein was a fastidious individual, the kind who preens in front of the mirror before leaving his house in the morning and throughout the day frets should his hair get mussed or a little mustard stains his tie. He had pencil thin neck which could barely support his head, very thin lips, and beady eyes suiting his profession. Newman, on the other hand, could care less what he looked like. As long as he bathed and wore clothes to cover his nakedness everything else didn't much matter. Judge Peebles, neither a fastidious snob nor a slob, and was on this day madder than a wet hen, "let's get these ridiculous proceedings started! Mr. Finkelstein you will present the case of North Carolina versus the defendants."

"Thank you your honor, however, I request a postponement of these proceedings until such time we can either locate owners of the recovered property, obtain signed quit claims to such property, or prove in fact the property under consideration has truly been abandoned according to the laws of this land."

"Request denied! Mr. Finkelstein it would take weeks, maybe months, to arrive at verifiable determinations you have so cleverly petitioned. It has been many decades since the Proteus and its passengers wrecked and it is likely that owners of the recovered property are either impossible to find, or dead. I don't want this trial to be prolonged by your nonsense and therefore, rule all property in question has been abandoned. Another thing Mr. Finkelstein, I don't much like you. Not that I don't care for supercilious prosecutors, which I don't. It's because you are using the laws of North Carolina to build a mountain out of a mole hill. Now get on with it or I'll hold you in contempt!"

"Yes, your honor." He cleared his throat, "the laws governing the disposition of salvaged property in North Carolina are unambiguous. All recovered artifacts, valuables, and currency belongs to the state as defined by Article 3 of the Department of Natural and Cultural Resources. It is at the discretion of the Department to determine any rewards to be paid to salvors based upon cultural heritage and value assessments. Article 3 is also clear in the requirements of salvage. Those parties contemplating reclamation must be able to provide proof of their qualifications in proper management of excavation. They must also be licensed. Defendants in question have not been properly trained and accredited as to their abilities to preserve the integrity of historical finds, nor have they acquired the requisite license. By law they may suffer up to 2 years imprisonment and fines not to exceed 1 million US dollars."

This last bit of information echoed in my head replaying over and over, sounding for all the world like we were hardened criminals.

"So, Mr. Finkelstein, you have eloquently stated the case for the Department of Natural and Cultural Resources. Now what is it you want me to do with the defendants?

"Your honor, it is the state's position that we make an example of these individuals to discourage other would be thieves contemplating stealing property from North Carolina. We, therefore, are asking that they receive the maximum prison sentence and pay a fine of $10,000 each."

Thomas, Cap'n Chisholm, and I lowered our heads as the reality sank-in, our lives were about to change forever. Miss Alice, reacted differently, "you gas bag! When I get done with you your gonna wish you had become a doctor, not a lawyer, cause you're going to need one!"

"Order, order, any more outbursts from you Miss Alice and I'll send you to prison for 10 years! Newman, if you please, try not to make this circus look any more absurd than it already does!"

"Yes, your honor." Not being a lawyer, Newman felt no compulsion to follow those principals and standards of conduct the men of our judicial system are bound by. Nor did he feel compelled to respond to the specifics of his client's indictment. Instead of addressing Judge Peebles or the audience, Newman looked straight at the prosecutor, "Mr. Finkelstein, that is a very handsome suit you're wearing today. Did you purchase that at Sears and Roebucks by any chance?"

Somewhat irritated at the suggestion the prosecutor smugly responded, "thank you, but no. I acquired it at Ivey's in Charlotte."

"Oooh! Ivey's, do tell. That must have cost you a pretty penny?"

"Well it wasn't cheap if that is what you mean."

"That is precisely what I mean. A suit like that, probably hand tailored, made from fine gabardine wool or pure silk, with a little extra fabric at the seam just in case you put on a few pounds and need to let it out, if you know what I mean, probably cost somewhere around $200. And them fine I-talian shoes you're wearing, I would guess cost almost as much. How much do you spend on clothes each year, Mr. Finkelstein? A thousand, two, I'll bet three? Do you know how much people in these parts spend on clothes? Most, if they're lucky, can afford a suit for $25, and it will need to take them to the grave. Most good folk, the salt of the earth, are forced to live off the produce of our ocean, as their ancestors before them did, and over the course of one year of intense labor don't make $1000 in income. My, my, what these folks could do with the money you spend to make yourself look pretty."

At this point there were two things happening in the court. First, the good folk, as Newman put it, were grumbling and if their expressions were any indication they were ready to lynch that prosecutor fellow. Second, Mr.

Finkelstein, squirming like a greased pig, scooted his I-talian shoes under his chair so no one would see, and slouched trying to hide from threatening looks that were clearly and intentionally directed at him. If I were to guess, he was going to have a heck of a time getting out of town in one piece.

Newman had a gleam in his eye as he mosied over to the prosecutor's table and leaned in close to whisper, "I have an offer to make you Mr. Finkelstein. It's plain and simple. After these proceedings are over, I will personally drive you to the station and see to it that you get safely on your train back to whatever hole you emerged from. All you need to do is make a little compromise. Do I have your agreement?"

Finkelstein shook his head vigorously affirming he was willing to trade.

Newman stood, and in his most professional flair zipped his fly, which he evidently neglected before leaving from home. He was now prepared to address the Judge, the prosecutor, defendants, and audience. He was what I would call in a bellicose mood, "Mr. Finkelstein, what is the value of the recovered property found in the safe?"

"Not absolutely sure, we've made only a preliminary evaluation at this time."

"That is perfectly fine Mr. Finkelstein. No one is going to hold you accountable for a misplaced penny or two."

"If you say so. We have found gold coin, some valuable jewelry, diamond necklaces, rings and such, which is conservatively estimated at $200,000."

"Very well, and what percentage does the Department of Natural and Cultural Resources typically offer as reward to salvors for recovered state property?"

"It depends, but somewhere between 10 and 20 percent."

"Excellent, then I propose your honor, the prison sentences be commuted to time already served and that the state offers a reward of 20 percent to the defendants which would amount to $10,000 each and I would recommend the defendants use their reward to pay those fines suggested by our prosecutor."

Judge Peebles chuckled and was well pleased by Newman's proposal, "Mr. Finkelstein, I find what the defendant's lawyer has suggested to be very fair. Do I have your agreement to these terms?"

Mr. Finkelstein didn't need to think twice, "your honor I agree", practically shouting to make sure everyone in the court room could hear his conciliatory and generous offer.

Judge Peebles, relieved the nonsense had concluded satisfactorily, stood. "Given both prosecution and defense have amicably arrived at a resolution, the court rests its case. Defendants are free to go!"

Some say the cheers and shouts of "here here" could be heard all the way out to the island. I don't know about that, but I can tell you everyone was relieved. Thomas, Cap'n Chisholm, Judge Peebles, Newman, the whole darn courthouse, everyone except Miss Alice. For once in all the years I have known her she looked small and whipped, vulnerable isn't strong enough a word. I felt truly sorry for her disappointment, so close to recovering a small fortune, only to watch it slip between her fingers. It's not that the rest of us wouldn't have enjoyed a slice of that pie, but we were happy enough to be free and done with the legal mumbo jumbo which almost sent us away to live with men the likes of Bubba.

I put my hand on Miss Alice's shoulder and handed her the doll I had found on the ship, the only artifact of our adventure not stolen from us. She had a tear in her eye and held that doll to her chest like it was a living breathing baby, "thank you Robert. From the bottom of my heart...thank you."...

...From that day on, Miss Alice would never again say a cross word to me, and I saw her as more than just a prickly ole spinster intent on making my life miserable.

Love,

Father

It Was Just Her Time

Peggy had proven that strength of will comes in all sizes and shapes, and belief in those matters of the heart, as evidenced by her confidence, can melt even the most tenacious of icebergs, or at the very least make a puddle or two. Should I hope to protect my freedoms I would have to devise a more plausible lie, one designed to disgust even the most amorous of females and send them running for their lives.

I sat in my favorite chair pondering several distasteful scenarios, some more questionable than others. What could I come up with that wouldn't sound absurdly contrived, but would be so repulsive Peggy would disavow any desire to pursue her aforementioned scheme? Disappointingly, I had reached the age where the list of plausible iniquities had shrunk and was left with a short inventory of disaffections requiring little or no effort to execute. The passive role for my life, whether good or bad, had now become the norm.

Perhaps a disease. Yes, but what kind of disease? It has to be incurable, one where scientists have plumbed the depths of research to no avail. It has to be nasty, where body parts fall-off and all the super-glue in the world won't help. But most importantly, the disease must be highly contagious, so viral that being on the same planet puts one at risk. HIV, not likely. Flesh-eating disease, too rare. Ebola, wrong continent. Tuberculosis, wrong century. Herpes. Yeah! I think I can sell that one.

All I would need to do is to fake a script and leave it in a conspicuous location for Peggy to find. Went on-line found the recommended medication, cyclovir, and daily dosage. Printed an officious looking prescription from the desk of a fictitious doctor, D. Abrams M.D.; scribbled his signature; indicated for treatment of infectious Herpes and of course my name. ..Voilà! It would have to be Peggy's discovery. Calling attention to it might seem suspicious, so

I made a number of copies and spread them about my apartment so there would be little chance she could miss them.

Feverish, I had worked overtime developing my fiendish plan, but despite the despicable nature of my scheme, was comforted in the knowledge it would produce the desired results. Now, impatiently, I would have to wait upon an opportunity for another casual encounter, one where curious eyes would unearth the dreadful news.

In the meantime, I pulled the last box of letters next to my chair and was resolved to discover the mystery of who Robert Guthrie was, and why mother had his letters.

March 16, 1953

My Dear Bizzy

Those who we are drawn to in life aren't always the most logical or lovable. But chemistry and chance conspire to create bonds which transcend rational thinking. It certainly was true for the relationship that evolved over the course of years between Miss Alice and me...

...sadly, that was all about to change.

March usually brings tidings of warmer weather and hopes for an early summer to Bogue Banks, but on this day there was a little chill as wind blew from the north reminding all that until the official date for start of spring, ole man winter was still in charge.

Met with Mrs. Cartwright to go over the list of renovations and repairs needed to be completed before the onslaught of renters took over our lives and it made nearly impossible to do anything but cater to their appetites. Was hoping to whittle-down my things-to-do no later than beginning of May and although preoccupied with my punch list, wasn't surprised when I got a call from Gabrielle informing me Fred, Miss Alice's runabout, was feeling poorly, and I should endeavor to come quickly. Found my way to the back of Shore House, down to water's edge and small dock where Fred had made his home for the last 40 some years. Miss Alice looked a tad shaky, and being concerned for her wellbeing, I determined to act as if nothing was amiss. A ploy I have used unsuccessfully from time-to-time. Ignoring the obvious will get you nowhere, but it does allow you to ease into painful truths without embarrassing yourself or others; and for some, the fantasy is appreciated.

"Mornin Miss Alice, you're looking spry and fresh as a button today!"

"Thank you, but I don't feel so spry." She pulled her shawl tighter around her neck, "to be honest I'm feeling a little thin, and worrying about Fred has got me shook-up. I'm nothing but a bundle of nerves and can't shake this beastly feeling something awful is going to befall him. Oh, please Robert, do what you can to get him back on his feet!"

"Now Miss Alice, don't you start fretting over Fred. It won't do you, or him, any good."

I was worried this day would come. I had kept Fred afloat for the last decade with patches, chicken wire, and bubble gum stemming arteries and leaking hull. His backbone was broken in no less than two places I knew of, and chances were his ribs and spars were so rotten that, should I get the motor started, it wouldn't be safe to take him more than a few feet away from shore. To try to squeeze any more from his tortured frame would have been cruel, and to promise Miss Alice there was any hope would have been even more cruel. I was attending to Fred, not in the capacity of his physician, but as his coroner.

"Miss Alice, why don't you let me go over to Morehead City and shop around for a new boat? They've got these modern aluminum hull travelers which are nearly indestructible. Put a Johnson motor on one and you'll be able to sail the seven seas."

"Robert...?"

"It ain't happening Miss Alice. I am truly sorry, but it is time for us to lay Fred to rest."

Like I said Bizzy, those who we are drawn to doesn't always make sense. The cord formed by uncommon matches knit together misfits and the sensible alike, and with time, devotion develops into a mystical union. It is a teeter totter for sure, one where the whole is greater than the sum of the parts. However, destroy one side of that union and you risk destroying the entire shebang.

Miss Alice and Fred had been companions from her early days on Bogue Banks. And as funny as it may sound, Fred had been the partner in life she was never able to find in a man. What sustains us while we're breathing isn't the same for all of us, but most would agree a broken heart can be lethal. I guess the pain of losing Fred was too much for Miss Alice, and so she decided to call it quits. Yesterday, March 15, 1953, Miss Alice died at her beloved Shore House.

90 years old is not untimely by any figuring, but particularly inconvenient for those few who counted her as a friend. I've known a lot of people whose behavior was nicer than Miss Alice, but none truer to themselves, and for that, none more honest.

Funeral was to the point. She lived. She died. Wake was what you might expect, men stood around in awkward poses, fidgeting, with hands in suit pockets, gagging from neck ties wrapped in lethal tourniquets, uncertain what to say, but obliged to make their presence. Women chattering about this and that, making themselves feel useful by forcing food onto the unsuspecting over fed, and apologizing for the one person who couldn't do it for themselves. Only ones who didn't seem either bewildered or uncomfortable were the children who played in ruckus disregard for the deceased and Pastor Tully of Salter Path Methodist Church, who managed to balance a platter piled high with every item from the buffet in one hand and a sweet tea in the other, while regaling anyone who would listen about his pathetic golf game, this, of course, was not how he characterized it.

Overall, I'd have to say the event was well attended, some came because there was free food, others because it was the polite thing to do, and perhaps some had come to make their peace with a New Yorker who had stormed our island at beginning of this century and left in her wake a confusing array of emotions. Many familiar faces, Bankers aren't hard to identify, but there were five which I'd never seen before and I assumed they had to be family from up North. Turns out I was right. Eleanor Butler Roosevelt, Miss Alice's niece, and her four adult children managed to find their way from their retreats and compounds to our very door step to pay their last respects.

*****

Roosevelt's would stay on the island for almost a week attending to personal effects and legal documents for disposal of Miss Alice's property. Eleanor, a stately woman composed of manners and grace, kept mostly to herself. However, her eldest son, Theodore Roosevelt III, grandson of our 26th President, was an affable fellow and was inclined to mix it up with locals. He and I took a liking to each other, almost immediately.

I spent as much time as I could with Theodore, he liked to be called TR, sharing with him the history of his great aunt, as could be recalled since her arrival on the island in 1915. Told him about her early years, spared him some of the sordid details of fights she had with citizens of Salter Path, and embellished the more adventurous enterprises she got up to, those she might herself have told during her epitaph, had she been able to attend. He was most appreciative, as her life on Bogue Banks had remained a mystery to him and his family.

In return, TR divulged that Miss Alice died a pauper having squandered her wealth over the years on ill-advised business ventures designed by nefarious scoundrels promising quick riches to the naive. Bankrupt on numerous occasions, she regrettably left a trail of unpaid creditors stretching from Beaufort to New York City. Her only assets, at her death, were Shore House and adjoining property, which she bequeathed in her will to TR and his brothers and sister.

Truly, this was sad and hard news to bear. His words shattered my image of Miss Alice. She was always the grand dame to me, nurtured at the teat of the golden cow, born with a silver spoon in her mouth, sustained by blue blood coursing through her veins. Her demeanor was a testimony to her upbringing and a reminder that some are more fortunate than others. There are those who despise this ilk, but there will always be rich people in our world, regardless of how jealous we may be, and it was fitting Miss Alice belonged to this tribe. How far she must have come to fall from her days as a young lady, the queen of society from Paris to New York, flowing in the opulence of riches, to what must have been her shameful poverty.

Looking back now, a few things began to make sense. I was never sure why Miss Alice had fallen for that archeologist's scam of Teach's buried treasure. Slogging with spade and map, pacing off steps to locate and recover stolen property. It borders on desperation to engage in such foolhardy and rash endeavors. It is one thing for folks like me to put their faith in fallacious hopes, it is another for the wealthy to stoop to such nonsense. Then there was the Proteus and the purser's safe. Certainly a woman of means would not have to resort to extraordinary efforts to make a few dollars? Instead she could have contacted her investment counselor and made more money in less time and with less risk. On the other hand, if she was penniless then the pieces of the puzzle come together to form a picture of a prideful independent woman holding a secret too distasteful for her to admit. Pity, I wouldn't have thought less of her.

My memory of Miss Alice can't help but be flavored by this unfortunate news. However, it does not change the person she was, and either you liked her or you didn't. I, for one, did.

*****

TR, now a property owner on Bogue Banks, would be frequenting our shore and he promised to be a good steward of Shore House and what his great aunt had worked so hard to build. Of course, that remained to be seen. Was never certain when he would appear, preferring to keep his travel plans under his hat. One day there he would be greeting me in a familiar and courteous manner as if we had been friends our whole lives then, just as quickly, he'd be gone.

While he was on the island he was sure to take time to fish with Thomas and me, and I have to admit was surprised how good an angler he was. Not that he shouldn't have been, but with rich people you never know what they can and can't do.

Charitable, he was always happy to share stories of his famous family. His father was a brigadier general and war hero, and by the way TR spoke of him, was also his idle.

Once I got over the awkwardness of fishing next to American royalty, it was perfectly natural to be a little curious about his grandfather, "TR, what was it like being the grandson to the President of the United States?"

"Oh I don't know, I guess no different than any other grandfather. He was always telling stories and was glad to see us when we were little, dotting on us to the annoyance of our parents. Offered advice when he thought it might be useful, you know like any other patriarch would. Only thing was, he was leader of the free world, but as a little boy I didn't take any notice of that stuff. I cared more about candy and chocolates he snuck to me when mother wasn't looking."

When he wasn't fishing, TR was engaged with lawyers and bankers in serious discussions, the subject of which was held in close counsel. Comings and goings of officials from the state and local community lead to speculation, some believed he was scheming to subdivide Shore House and its property, deeding it to developers who planned to destroy our island and way of life in exchange for money, or worse, to sell out to a seedy hotel chain. Others were certain he was going to throw the people of Salter Path off their land and to make Bogue Banks his own exclusive estate. Something his aunt had contemplated, and there were those who claimed the apple hadn't fallen far from the tree. Fear has a way of growing in the hearts of men kept in the dark, breeding all sorts of wild ideas. For me, I wasn't sure what was going to happen, but I didn't think TR was the kind of person to destroy the memory of Miss Alice and the homes of innocent natives.

In subsequent years TR frequented Bogues Shores less and less, fueling even more onerous suppositions. Nervous prostration had gripped our tiny island, and from all appearances there was no relief in sight. Then one morning over coffee and donuts at Sheppard's Point Café, Thomas paused in his ritual of silently devouring the newspaper, "listen to this! Says here":

"Theodore Roosevelt III, guardian of property inherited from his late great aunt, Miss Alice Hoffman, has negotiated an outcome for the disposition of her estate which can only be hailed as brilliant. In exchange for unspecified tax benefits, he and his siblings have decided to gift a significant portion of property to the State of North Carolina. Described as a man ahead of his time and lauded for his devotion to the outdoors, in a truly magnanimous gesture, he has set aside 298 acres of their property for naturalist purposes."

On occasion I hear something that rubs me the wrong way and without giving it too much thought, arrive at the wrong conclusion It's not too often, but when it happens I feel like an idiot.

"Thomas, I am as liberal as the next guy, but the thought of folks peeling off their clothes, running around our island in their birthday suits, and peering out from behind brush like a bunch of demented pixies has got my blood boiling. I don't care if TR is ahead of his time, the very moral fabric of Bogue Banks is at stake, and if we let them get away with this, then what else can we expect? I don't know about you, but I'm going to sign a petition to stop this nonsense. Mark my words, I'll get the Judge and Newman to sponsor a bill to block the use of Miss Alice's property for nudism if it's the last thing I do!"

"Robert hold your horses, you're off half crazy running down the wrong path. You're thinking of a naturist, they're the ones that prance around naked as a flag pole. What we got going on here is a naturalist, which is a totally different kettle of fish. Them Roosevelt's intend on dedicating land which is to remain in its natural state, undeveloped, and as pristine as the first day our Lord created it. This is a good thing Robert, and you would have benefited with a few more years in school!"

Of course, being caught by my ignorance I did the only thing one can do when cornered, "you said naturist."

"No, I did not! You know darn well I said naturalist! You're saying I did to cover up your own stupidity!"

"No, I'm not!"

"Yes, you are!"

"No, I'm not!"

Belligerent defiance and stubbornness took on a life of its own and during the next week or so, long after we had forgotten it origins, Thomas and I continued to trade jabs. Only the best of friends feel comfortable getting-up a head of steam without the worry of damaging a relationship. Ours was unflappable; and, for some strange reason, I enjoyed the game.

*****

Land within the confines of the reserve, now hosts a variety of foliage which includes oak trees, loblolly pine, cedar, salt grasses; and, because of plentiful marsh lands, also an abundance of wildlife. Egrets, ospreys, pelicans, gators, turtles, snakes, and believe it or not even a manatee or two, can be found in the watery reaches which constitute this monumental state park. 298 acres is a big stretch, I had no idea there was that much land on the whole island, but ciphering was never one of my strong points.

Ironic, the very thing Bankers had been afraid of was exactly what TR had prevented. These lands would never be touched by developers. Named after his grandfather, he stipulated the park be kept in its natural state as a preserve for education and recreation. Nevertheless, it would be sheer fantasy to think their generous act would somehow forestall the tidal wave of development that would eventually arrive on the shores of Bogue Banks for the undesignated land. It did not; but, what it did do was establish, no matter how many structures are built, a place to see our island as it once looked when the original Bankers settled here in the mid 1800's. And Thomas was right, that is a good thing.

Some intelligent people believe that once we become spirits after passing into the next world, we still are able to view all the comings and goings of this one. I don't know about that, but if it is true, then I can't help but think Miss Alice is looking down and is well pleased.

She Was From Out Of Town

Time has a way of chasing you down the paths of your life and unwittingly, years add-up. When young we don't take notice of the subtle changes to our bodies. A few grey hairs poke-up on your head and chin, a little more fat here and there, skin not quite as elastic, but all-in-all hardly noticeable. Middle age brings a few surprises, crow's feet and wrinkles, receding hair-line, enough pudge you're forced to suck in the gut when a pretty girl walks by, cheaters replace perfect vision, yet it hasn't gotten out of hand, and we all retain a false hope one step backwards would set us straight again. Gracious souls are likely to say you look distinguished, friends will tell you different.

Then one day you wake-up, there is no mistaking, age has caught-up, and you ponder what happened to that young man full of vitality who, without warning, has disappeared to be replaced by a stooped-over and broken version of the original. Can't help but wonder who the hell is staring back at me from my mirror. Certainly not me! Wrinkles look more like furrows in a corn field. Age spots instead of freckles. Belly protruding like a women in her 2nd trimester. Knees click loud enough to scare sleeping dogs. Unusual aches and pains gets you to thinking what's next, and lordy, even man boobs. It isn't as if I have sat around my whole life doing nothing, but failures in those biological systems which drive our metabolism and facilitate our joints bending back and forth have contrived to work against me. I know there remains a man within, he's just harder to find.

Elderly are easily dismissed, perhaps because our years of contribution to society are behind us. To the rest of the world we have become transparent, it is obvious when unseeing eyes dismiss you as an object of derision. If they only knew me when I wasn't any different than they are, maybe even better? All they perceive, or want to, is the old man I've become, and without too much imagination can't conceive there was anything but. On occasions I have been tempted to pull-out a photo to prove them otherwise, but who am I kidding? They don't care, and faded black and white photographs are hardly convincing. Ugly truth brings the realization our time has come. And it has gone. I have fought back as long as I should, and now letting go, have arrived at that place where wistful dreams have been replaced by resignation.

*****

Mrs. Cartwright has always been selective as to the tenants she keeps and even more careful who she invites back for future seasons. As most property owners she has been burned by careless interlopers who have neglected and abused her cottages and, as a consequence, prefers to keep a list of reliable renters who have demonstrated their respect for what doesn't belong to them. Which is why I was a little curious when I saw on the manifest for *Lost Horizon*, a quaint little cottage nestled in the dunes just this side of Atlantic Beach, an unfamiliar name, a Mrs. Dorothy Stanford. She had leased the cottage for the season. Scribbled in the margin, in Mrs. Cartwright's handwriting, was a notation, "from out of town", indicating that she knew little or none about the particulars of this individual.

"Robert, be a dear, and go on over to *Lost Horizon* at noon to check in our newest guest, Mrs. Stanford. She is traveling alone and is new to our community. First day is always the most difficult finding your bearings and I don't want her to think us Bankers are inhospitable. So, do what you can to help her settle in, you know, groceries, beach furniture, and let her know we are here for her if she has any specific needs. I always like to leave new renters with a good first impression."

"Yes, ma'am, more than happy to oblige"

This was standard routine for me. I would make sure they knew where fresh linens were stored, how to turn on ceiling fans, which restaurants were good and which to avoid, remind them not to get too much sun in the first few days, so-on-and-so-forth. It also gave me an opportunity to size them up, determine if I was going to have to become their wet nurse and hold their hands during their entire stay, or have a little peace and quiet.

Not sure what I expected with Mrs. Stanford. If she was traveling alone she could either be a matronly widower, or one of those modern women who vacation without husbands when their whereabouts are uncertain. We've even had a few that gave up on married life and run off to the beach to make a new start. Regardless of the circumstances I was always taught not to judge, as it is more difficult to back pedal out of irrational prejudices then to pedal forward into rational conclusions. Whatever this lady turned out to be I was intent on greeting her with respect.

Made sure I was early as many vacationers like to get a jump start on their sojourn and arrive well before check-in. If it were me I'd do the same, and so, if I can help it, I try not to disappoint paying customers. Found a little shade on the wrap-around porch, melted into one of the rockers, propped my feet up on the railing, and let my eyes rest a while.

I must have drifted off because I didn't hear the car approach, and was only enticed to rejoin the living by a large four-legged retriever licking my face. Figuring I might be a new best friend, he seemed supremely happy to see me. Smiling from ear-to-ear, wagging tail, trying his best to jump into my lap, carrying-on like dogs are apt to do, which is why I didn't take notice immediately of the woman standing behind him.

"Hello, my name is Dorothy Stanford. His name is Buddy, and from the looks of it, I might have some competition."

Now I am here to tell you when I saw that lady standing before me I was in a state of confusion. I was bewildered, perplexed, stupefied, and muddled. I am not normally disoriented by the opposite sex, in fact, can say for the most part I am immune to those wily voodoo spells women cast upon unsuspecting males. She was different, not what you would call beautiful, for I have indeed seen examples of more beautiful women and there was nothing in her looks or behavior you would call lurid. I would guess she was in her mid to late 40's, with delicate features, kind eyes and a smile that was slightly sad, certainly not contrived. Truly, I would have described her as average looking, except she wasn't. For in some measure I saw her in a most agreeable light. I have been told that in rare instances a man can be smitten by the presence of a woman, well it would appear this woman had done just that. Without waving a wand or snapping fingers I was attracted to this person, who only a few weeks ago agreed to lease *Lost Horizon* from Mrs. Cartwright. Is this how it works? Someone gets an urge, motivated by events or seasons in their lives, makes a decision triggering a series of consequences, resulting in two people passing like ships in the night. Sometimes they pause, sometimes not.

"I beg your pardon ma'am! I must have dozed-off. Mrs. Stanford, my name is Robert Guthrie and I apologize for what must appear to you as my slothful deportment. I can assure you it is not normally my nature to greet guests as I have done. Please don't think the less of me for this momentary indiscretion." I babbled on and on like a wind-up doll spitting out regrets and pleas for forgiveness as if I was a condemned man before an executioner.

"Calm down, Mr. Guthrie. Goodness, I just arrived, and your only crime is napping! I have not taken any offense, so I would beg you would not ask for absolution, as none is required. Please, you must call me Dorothy and I would prefer to call you Robert, if it suits you?"

140

Yep, I was afflicted, caught in my own trap, ready to relinquish better judgment. However, this would be only a temporary affliction, wheels of my brain were already turning faster than my emotions, arriving at its destination in the nick of time. Revelation was hurtful, one minute I was lost in a make believe where imagination is free to run wild, next brought back into reality recognizing the man I had become would not be the kind of man a woman could find attractive, certainly not Mrs. Stanford. Momentarily stunned, I reverted to the young man who was long gone, now left in his place was a self-conscious and timid replacement. This would not do, needed to dispel any ideas of the familiar and get back in-line where I belonged.

Slightly flushed, unlikely Mrs. Stanford would make the connection, "thank you Dorothy, Robert suits me fine."

Did my best to get Dorothy situated while I tried to pull myself together, unloaded her car, opened blinds, ran some water for the dog, jot down a list of produce and staples she requested from the emporium and as I handed her the keys to the cottage our hands touched, lingering for but a moment. Nothing she would notice, but I certainly did.

After I dropped off her groceries, in spite of more sober inclinations, I promised, "will look in on you tomorrow, see if you need anything." This, of course, was a ploy that went well beyond polite concern, and I regretted it immediately knowing it could lead to only one thing. Disappointment.

Next day I came by the cottage to find it empty, she probably went for a walk along the beach. Good thing, I could claim I kept my promise without awkward posturing that accompanies individuals who are beset with my condition. I would let it alone, and found over the course of a few weeks Dorothy occupied my thoughts less and less. Pangs which pull on the cords of our hearts become dull, and with time mental torture associated with withdrawal symptoms dissipate.

*****

My employer seemed outwardly to be comfortable with her new tenant. Inwardly, however, she wanted to know who this person was and why she was alone. Insidious prying and open-ended questions queried by Mrs. Cartwright over casual encounters eventually achieved their design. Piecing together fragments of a private life, she learned that Mrs. Stanford, of Raleigh, was indeed a widow of some means. Her husband, a bank executive, was sadly killed during World War II at the Battle of the Bulge, leaving her to raise a son and daughter. Now grown and off on their own, she had more free time and money than she knew what to do with, which prompted her decision to repose by the sea. I listened intently to Mrs. Cartwright as she divulged the secrets on my favorite subject, and found I could listen dispassionately without the slightest hint of my secret attraction. Confidentially I congratulated myself for self-restrained deception.

By summer solstice I was up to my eyebrows in alligators, trying to keep up with work orders on properties stretching from Fort Macon to ole Salter's homestead. If I could just drain the swamp I might be rid of the pesky annoyances, but as soon as I thought I was making headway, a fresh crop of renters would arrive with complaints that would test the patience of Job. Sprinting from one task to another left me with little idle time and as such, I kept that space between my two ears clear of distractions.

Don't remember what day of the week it was, they had a way of running together, pick-up truck already packed with tools, thermos was full, and was likely not to cross paths with Mrs. Cartwright until sundown. Slid behind the wheel and started the engine, but before I could escape the boss lady caught-up with me.

"Robert, sorry to have to add to your list, but I just got a call from Mrs. Stanford at *Lost Horizon*. Her door to the beach is jammed shut and won't budge. With all this heat and humidity chances are it is swollen in its frame. Be a good lad and run on by there sometime today."

I hadn't thought about Dorothy in over a week, but the idea of having to be in her general proximity appealed to me. Nevertheless, wouldn't want to give Mrs. Cartwright the wrong impression, so I did my best to sound aggravated, "I'll do what I can, but I am only one man and there is a limit to how far I can be stretched." Had the ring of man who knows his services were in demand, and was at the brink of saying no.

"I understand you have been working your tail off, come winter we can all rest, but until then I need you. Without Mr. Cartwright you are the only person I can rely on."

Working all kinds of hours, it wasn't unusual for the two of us to get a little testy, and today Mrs. Cartwright had pulled out the big guns. It was almost guaranteed that once or twice each season she would resort to guilt in order to keep me in check. Careful not to overuse this tact, unknowingly she had just used-up one of her chips, as it was my pleasure to be attending to Mrs. Stanford. In fact, I intended on making *Lost Horizon* my first stop.

Found Dorothy on the back porch stretched across a hammock, sublimely content, absorbing one of the many wonders of God's hands. Ocean swells languidly tracing the shoreline in white foam, birds relentlessly chirping songs hoping to attract a mate, gentle breeze chasing perspiration from nape of her neck, unwilling to relinquish warming rays of the sun, and who could blame her. Is there any better place on earth to let go of the past and embrace the present?

Buddy was first to greet me, waking from a dead sleep bathed by iridescent waves of heat. Lifting his body from the spot where he slept, wagging from head to tail, this boy affirmed the belief I have always harbored of the connection that exists between man and dog.

"Mornin Dorothy, hope I'm not disturbing your pleasure."

"Oh, hello Robert, didn't expect you so soon. I only just called Mrs. Cartwright."

"No problem, I was heading this way and it was easier to make you my first stop", which was a lie. "How you been gettin-on?"

"Wonderfully, never imagined there was a place where I wanted time to stand still as much as here. Each day is better than the last and I hope they never end. My only distractions are pods of dolphins parading by my front door and pelicans swooping soundlessly. Has it always been like this?"

Certain questions demand an answer, impolite to ignore, others are ruined by man's feeble attempt to reply. I just smiled.

Splendor of our moment was rudely broken when an impudent young man pulled his shiny brand-new red convertible Cadillac into the sandy pull-out of the cottage next to *Lost Horizon*. Blasting from his radio was that equally impudent singer from Tupelo Mississippi, belting-out one of his rockabilly tunes girls fawned over, name of Elvis Presley. Driver stepped out of his car, acting like he owned the place, slicked back hair too long for my liking, tight chinos, and loud shirt monogrammed with e-lectric geetars emblazoned on the lapels, completing an ensemble which I can only describe as trashy. Would like to say I never saw his type before, but that would be a lie. Almost every season one of his kind show-up, cruising the beach in search of one thing, wealthy, unattached, and naïve women, older the better. Gold diggers, cads, gigolos, call em what you want, they all have one purpose, to prey on the lonely in order to line their pockets. This fella was probably in his mid-30's and by his expression was already honing in on Dorothy.

"Hello there good looking, my name is Dick." He was right about that. "I'm going to be your neighbor for a couple of weeks, and who knows, maybe more. And what should I call you, lovely lady?"

Not cold, but definitely guarded, "my name is Mrs. Stanford. My friends I choose, and they may call me Dorothy." Her perception and caution were impressive. Dorothy had sent a warning shot across his bow and if he was smart he'd take note.

"Well, let's see if I can't convince you I'm the kind of guy you should want as a friend." With a flare that would put Errol Flynn to shame, Dick lifted his valise from the back seat of the Caddy. As he receded into the cottage, he winked, smiled over his shoulder, and made sure the resident of *Lost Horizon* saw the gleam of his pearly whites.

Got down to business, while Dorothy rocked in the hammock, I proceeded to attack the stuck door. She wasn't fooling, I pulled and pushed, banged with a rubber mallet, swore a little, but it wouldn't move. Finally resorted to pulling pins from the hinges and with all my weight forced the door from its frame. It landed on the porch with a crash, for which I apologized profusely. It wasn't just swollen, the darn thing was warped. Probably made from cheap wood, it curved at an angle from which there would be no recovery.

"Dorothy, sorry to say I am not going to be able to fix your door today. It is so out of whack I have no choice but replace it. But don't worry, I'll plane the edges down so you can close and LOCK IT overnight, be back tomorrow with a new one." I hope she was considering my not too subtle hint.

Set up my horses, got the door clamped, and proceeded to plane the edges with long slow even strokes, peeling back ribbons of wood. There is something very satisfying about tools of carpentry in the right hands, and if a man has the skills there is no lacking for work.

Dick, not satisfied to leave well enough alone, reappeared in a pair of swim trunks, no shirt, ostensibly to wax his car. But he didn't fool me. In less than 15 minutes beads of sweat were collecting down the middle of his back, running from his neck over a hairless chest, muscles rippling with the sheen of male virility, while he whistled some tune resonating as a siren for lovers. In the heat I was considering unbuttoning the top few of my shirt, but he had a way of making me feel self-conscious. There was no way I was going to give Dorothy an opportunity to compare the two of us, and not wanting to embarrass myself, remained wrapped tighter than a turban on a sheik. Couldn't tell if the half-naked jerk was having any effect on her, but she was after all a woman, and there was no denying Dick was a man.

Replaced the warped door, made sure it would latch and its lock found the brass plate, lingering as long as I dare without appearing obvious. Figured if I hung around he might get restless and wander off in search of different prospects. Reluctantly, I had other jobs to attend to and was forced to make my goodbyes to Dorothy, promising a new door tomorrow, leaving her at the mercies of that creep. For the rest of the day and long into the night I couldn't get my mind off the fox in the chicken coop. Was hoping Dorothy was able to defend herself and prayed Buddy would sink his teeth into Dick's fleshy buttocks. My invocation gave me some comfort.

Jack's Bait and Hardware opened at 7 am, I was there at 6:45. I'm sure I seemed rude as I brushed past Jack headed for the isle where he stored doors, hoping he had one in stock. I was intent on getting a replacement, and necessary hardware, so that when Dorothy woke I would be poised to shelter the ramparts of her heart. No such luck. There were screen doors aplenty, a couple of windows, even a porthole for a boat, but the place where doors were stockpiled was empty. Must have stared at it a good 5 minutes thinking one might appear, if I would only eyeball it long enough.

"Jack, what kind of hardware store are you running here? There isn't one door in stock. If you can't keep up your inventory I am going to be forced to take my business to the mainland!"

"Hold on there Robert, sold my last one yesterday. Can't keep every item on the shelves on a lark, not knowing when you're goin to show up and buy it from me. Nobody does business like that. Don't worry, got some comin in this afternoon. You come back then and I'll be happy to sell you one."

Going over to the mainland to buy goods really wasn't an option for Bankers, and Jack knew it. If we gave all our trade to them people on the other side of the sound it wouldn't take long before our island would sink into the Atlantic. I was just going to have to bide my time and wait.

After I had finally procured the door and made my way to *Lost Horizon*, it was already too late. Down by the water's edge sat Dorothy on a beach chair, Dick laid on a blanket close enough to listen to Dorothy's thoughts. Hooted and waved a greeting acting like nothing was amiss. Being a servant so-to-speak to those who rent, I was obliged to make nice to Dick, which I did begrudgingly for Dorothy's sake. Nothing for me to do but finish the job I had come for, yet I mulled-over how this would play-out, and despite my own disappointment, hoped the lady from out of town would be spared the pain and embarrassment of extorted love.

*****

A few days had passed, Mrs. Cartwright had seen the couple ensconced in what she called "rapturous conversation", not realizing the sting her words would cause and I had resolved to do what men must do when they are vanquished in battle. Pout. It was the first Monday of the month, my day for delivering fresh linens and instead of making *Lost Horizon* my first stop I planned on making it my last, knowing there would be less time to dwell on things I would prefer not to see.

Sun was already dipping into the ocean when I pulled up alongside Dorothy's cottage. Tooted the horn, to give them fair warning in case they were in what you might call in-flagrante-delicto. Kept my bundle of towels, sheets and pillow cases held high peeking around the pile just in case they didn't hear my toot. Mercifully I was spared the contortions of mismatched lovers and found Dorothy sitting alone staring out to sea.

"Hello Mrs. Stanford, sorry to bother you, but I needed to drop off the linens before it got too late."

"Mrs. Stanford, that sounds formal Robert, have I made you mad?"

"No ma'am, I would just prefer given recent developments not to presume an informal posture. One which might be difficult to explain to certain individuals who might take it the wrong way."

"I am sure I don't know what you mean?" She did in fact know what I meant, but had the good sense to let it drop.

Gave Buddy a pat and stepped off the porch headed for my truck.

"Robert, do you know there is a dance this Saturday at the Circle?"

In season there was always a dance on Saturday nights at the Circle, "no, I was unaware."

"Well there is. Why don't you come? It would be nice to see you when you're not working, and it should be fun!"

"I'll think about Mrs. Stanford."

"Oh please, call me Dorothy. It sounds so much better coming from you."

I was confused again. Had she dumped stupid? Was she shining-up to me, maneuvering so I would ask her out on a date? Wasn't sure, but hope springs eternal even from those whose hearts have been trod upon. "Ok, Dorothy, I'll come."

"Wonderful, I can't wait to see you there, let's say around 8 pm!"

That seemed clear enough, I wasn't being asked to pick her up.

*****

Rest of the week toddled along, kept myself busy, but as Saturday approached I couldn't help getting excited at the prospects of spending time with Dorothy on the dance floor. Shaved twice just in case there were some cheek-to-cheek numbers, made sure my shirt and suit were pressed, and wore my lucky tie, the one with prints of fish hooks and catfish. Parked close enough to the Circle so I wouldn't get too sweaty as I made my way up to the pavilion and as I got closer heard the band play my favorite song, "I Love You For Sentimental Reasons."

"I love you for sentimental reasons
I hope you do believe me
I've given you my heart"
Don't that beat all, it must be a good omen.

Men and women, holding hands, filtered in from darker edges of the Circle following rhythm of the brass section. White lights ringed the dance floor, cabaret tables with white table clothes and candles defined its borders and gave couples a place to rest their feet and sip cocktails. There were a few good dancers, but for the most part women kept one eye on their partner and other on their partner's hooves hoping to dodge misplaced steps.

It had been some time since I had attended a dance. Last time I was cornered and cajoled by one of our older female Bankers promising the company of attractive young ladies, and consented to give it a shot, but found neither the courage nor the girls to sustain my interest. Most evenings ended the same way, walking home alone wondering why I bothered in the first place. But tonight was going to be different.

Stood on my tip toes, head stretched at the end of my neck, scanning the crowd in search of Dorothy. Caught the eye of Capn' Chisholm and his wife, exchanged a quick wave. Newman and Judge Peebles were absorbed in a conversation completely oblivious to the festivities and Mr. Cavendish was where you might expect, planted on a bar stool wearing a halo of alcoholic fumes. Was beginning to think I had been stiffed, when out of nowhere there Dorothy stood, directly in front of me. She wore a sleeveless red and white polka dot dress down to her knees, black high heels, a little rouge on her lips and cheeks, and of course her smile. She was stunning. Funny, I had been looking forward to seeing her, but now she stood before me I was as nervous as a snowman in summer.

Tongue tied, brain racing to think of what to say, "wow, Dorothy you sure look fine! I mean you look very nice. I am real glad you showed up, not that you weren't going to, but some women say one thing and do another. Sorry, that didn't come out right." Harder I tried to say something intelligent the worse it got and the probability of getting the train back on its tracks was rapidly fading.

I had to come up with a distraction and it had to be fast, then it came to me, "Dorothy, let me get you something to drink."

"Alright Robert, but where is your..."

"Hold that thought Dorothy, I'll be right back!"

Retreating from the fray isn't very manly, yet it gave me a temporary reprieve so I could grow a spine and think of something to say that wasn't offensive or inane. However, when I got to the bar I realized I hadn't even asked what she wanted to drink. Decided to play it safe in case she was a teetotaler, purchased two cokes. As I found my way back to where we parted I practiced the prattle of small talk, "nice weather, are you enjoying your stay, Buddy is a handsome dog", one liners that might allow me to ease into a real conversation.

Dodging swaying couples, weaving through the crowd, I retraced my steps ending where I left. Took me a moment to realize something was different, and something was wrong. Like the time I accidently walked into the lady's room at the theater. Didn't sink in right away, some of the facilities looked familiar, some things were missing, confirmation I was in the wrong place came when a girl emerged from a stall and screamed her head-off. And tonight, I found myself in the wrong place again, for there, with his sleazy arm wrapped around Dorothy's shoulder, was Dick.

"Robert, you remember Dick don't you. He's decided to stay an extra week, isn't that great!"

"You bet, real glad to see you again...Dick." Although laced with sarcasm, there was actually a thread of truth in what I said, for there was no chance Dick would have extended his stay had he already accomplished his goal of trading favors for Dorothy's money.

"Robert where is your date?"

Having accidently stepped into the ladies room was embarrassing; on the other hand, realizing I had accidently thought Dorothy was interested in me was shattering. "Oh, she took ill at the last minute, decided to come out alone, catch-up with a few friends. Well, here are your cokes. Hope you both enjoy the dance."

Made my way home, hung-up my suit, put the shirt back in the closet, still clean, flopped on to the porch glider, and proceeded to beat myself up for being so dumb and thinking Dorothy was actually interested in me. I rocked back and forth till dawn broke over the horizon. It was easier than trying to sleep.

*****

Boys were in rare form, heads bowed, unwilling to make eye contact, at least with me. Only words I could coax were lame bets they made while staring at equally lame poker hands. Optimists were holding court, but something wasn't right. Never experienced the silent treatment before and wasn't sure what was going on. Was I being censured? Men don't behave this way with other men, maybe I was losing my mind?

"Alright, what's eating you guys? You ain't acting normal!"

"We aint acting normal, Robert, it is you that ain't acting normal!" Newman shared his sentiments as if he was spitting something foul tasting from his mouth.

"I don't understand?"

"Well let me explain it to you. Ever since that woman from out of town showed up you've been on her heels like a puppy dog. Professing you don't care for her, all the while mooning over her like a nincompoop. And, if that wasn't bad enough, you've been treating your friends like dirt." A little grumbling from other members, as they nodded their heads in agreement.

I hated to admit it, but he was right, I had been ignoring my friends, even been short with a few, "sorry, I didn't realize it was obvious. I'm also sorry if I have acted like a jackass."

Judge Peebles in his own way extended an olive branch, "Robert, don't take it too hard, we've all been tempted at one time or another by the female gender. My advice to you is to be real careful. Women share all the idiosyncrasies of a diesel engine. Hard to get started, but once you do they run hot, require a rich mixture of fuel, and if you're not attentive they'll quit on you. You're better off staying away from things that are high maintenance."

"Thank you Judge, I appreciate the advice."

I didn't want to sound impolite, nevertheless, I was not unfamiliar with the tendency of men to lump all women into one disagreeable lot. Their inclinations are usually not based on personal experience, but born from a fraternity of like-minded brethren who find comfort in the solidarity of shared thoughts and adhere to the idea that women pose a threat to their God given freedoms. And, as with most generalizations, they are typically wrong, but it is easier than defending the notion women have different personalities, and as such, there may be some who are actually nice. By degrees that was what I was thinking as I was agreeing with my fellow members of the Optimists Club.

Thomas was silent throughout the affair, but as the game broke-up shared his own opinion. "Robert, them boys mean well, but they don't always know what's best. I don't know this Mrs. Stanford, but I do know you and I trust your judgment. If you like her, then that is good enough for me."

"Thanks Thomas, but it really is only academic. I've gone around the bend a little too far and certainly no competition for that Dick fella."

"Now you listen to me Robert, there ain't no one who doesn't feel like you. We are all moving in the same direction and none of us like the changes are bodies are going through. You can choose to be ashamed of yourself, or you can choose to accept the person you have become, it's up to you. I guarantee you that your Dorothy has her own doubts, gets a little disgusted with her figure, remembers when she could turn men's heads, and wonders how anyone could find her attractive the way she now looks; which is why Dick has been able to weasel his way into her good graces. And as for him, he can't last much longer. Trust me, he doesn't have the savvy or patience to endure. I don't know how, but I do know it is only a matter of days before he self-destructs. You've got to hold-on there and show Dorothy you are the better man."

*****

Turns out, Thomas was right. Only a few days later under a full moon, Dick decided to make his move. Invited Dorothy for a ride in his fancy Caddy, rode down to the beach and parked only a few feet from water's edge. Turned the radio to a station playing romantic tunes and figured the time was ripe for a little smooching.

In the morning evidence of the previous night's escapades were plain to see. Caddy hadn't moved an inch, buried up to its hub caps in sand, waves threatening to submerge the lavish car as tide changed directions. Dick being questioned by Sheriff Stone, was sitting on the hood wearing a shiner earned when his plan didn't meet with Dorothy's approval. Not that I care, but he learned a valuable lesson. He should not underestimate women, for they can throw a right hook good as any man, especially when advances are uninvited.

A small crowd had collected, keenly interested in what was going to happen next. Sheriff was in the process of reorganizing Dick's thoughts, "you must be some kind of natural born idiot to drive a street vehicle, one as nice as yours, out onto soft sand and park in the surf zone. I'm not in a frame of mind to lecture you, cause something tells me I'd be wasting my breath. However, I am here to ticket you and collect the fine before I allow one of our Bankers to pull you out with their tractor. Parking overnight on the beach, that's $50. Driving on the beach without a permit, is $25, and polluting a nesting sanctuary for turtles with oils and grease from your undercarriage is $75. Be real careful of what you say next, because I have half-a-mind to throw you in jail for trying to assault Mrs. Stanford."

"Sheriff, I don't have the money."

"Well, you better get it and get it fast, for it won't be long before your Caddy becomes a submarine!"

"But it might take hours to get money wired to me!"

"Son, why is it you think the crisis you've created should send me into a panic? Personally, I hope you can't raise the money and from the look of the crowd it would appear as if I am in good company."

Dick took off running in a dead heat headed for downtown Atlantic Beach and nearest bank. It would take him over 3 hours to acquire the necessary funds to pay off his fines, and in the meantime the water rose inch-by-inch. You couldn't pay most folks to sit in a movie theater for 3 hours, even if the show was action packed, but the spectacle of a sinking Caddy had our Bankers glued to where they stood. Mesmerized, they remained sentinels testifying to the power of nature as it won out over man, and justice was served to one in particular. By the time Dick made it back and tractors extricated his car, the sea had swamped the inside ruining the beautiful red and white tuck-n-rolled leather bench seats, electricals had to be fried, and chances are his motor would have to be rebuilt. All-in-all I'd have to say Dick's vacation turned-out to be pretty expensive.

No one likes to be made a fool, and I am sure that was exactly how Dorothy was feeling. Not the cleverest man, but I had enough common sense to leave her alone until she could sort the whole mess-out. As for me, I didn't feel vindicated, although maybe I should have. Instead, I made it a point to recognize the brilliance of my youth, accept the fact that it was now gone, and appreciate the season in which I now lived, which is really the only thing any of us can do.

I Promise

Season was drawing to an end. Saw Dorothy infrequently, out and about on errands, smiled and waved hoping she might be inclined to strike up a conversation. Polite, but she kept her distance, and I respected that. Occasionally drove by *Lost Horizon* just to see telltale signs, beach chairs stacked against the shed, towels and swim suits hanging from the porch railing, lights in the window. Then one day, nothing. Along with the rest of our summer crowd she had packed-up and left. Returning to their homes where some would work, attend school, get on with mundane comings and goings of life, leaving behind happy memories of lazy days spent on Bogue Shores and empty cottages which echoed of fun now past.

As crazy as it gets, and trust me it gets pretty wild, I can't help feel a little remorseful when the last vacationer departs. First few weeks aren't too bad, cleaning and winterizing Mrs. Cartwright's properties keeps me busy, but at some point I make an end to the work and find myself filling time. This year wouldn't be any different, except I would have to cope with some awkward images etched in my brain, constructed by a brief encounter with the lady from out of town. Maybe she'd come back next season, maybe not.

It doesn't take much to take us off our feet, fragile creatures at best. A couple of hard knocks and we aren't the same people we'd been. Contortions we're forced to go through to bring back some semblance of normalcy is painful, especially once we realize those routines we counted on for years no longer provide satisfying distractions. Sure, I had the Optimists with make believe regality, funny hats, secret handshakes, penny ante poker, and an occasional rally to raise money for local charities. Sometimes I'd go by Shore House to help Gabrielle with yard work, which would only evoke a flood of memories of Miss Alice, both good and bad. Food had lost some of its taste, sunrises and sunsets seemed bland, those things which had grounded me and

151

brought pleasure to my life were thinner and, as a consequence, only managed to irritate me.

But of course, I could always count on Thomas for an early morning or late afternoon sojourn, wrangling, through luck or skill, fish from the sea. A stalwart defender of those who live on the shores of Bogue Banks, and especially anglers, he could always be counted-on to raise my spirits. Regrettably, time waits for no one, and I was about to find Thomas and I had cashed one too many checks.

*****

"Come on Robert, you've been dragging your fanny from one end of this island to the other. It's about time to snap out of it. I know you had set your mind to saddle-up with Mrs. Stanford, but it simply weren't meant to be, at any rate not this season. Pining all day and night won't change matters; and frankly, at your age it's unseemly to be carrying on like a forlorn teenager. Grab your rod and tackle box we're going fishing."

Thomas meant well, and Lord knows I deserved a good talking to, but it wasn't a simple matter of waving a magic wand and presto-chango everything was back to normal. Once you make-up your mind to get on with living it still takes some time to catch-up. Nevertheless, I was determined to try. So I put on a good face, fetched my gear, and did my best to go through the motions.

As Thomas and I made our way down the beach some our fishing buddies told us, "you guys should have been here yesterday, we slew them", which is a line of crap. It's always the same, "you should have been here, when." In the 50 plus years I've been fishing on the island I have never been where I was supposed to be, when I was supposed to be. But you can be certain there is someone who claims they were.

In spite of my present mood, gentle lapping of waves bringing surges of warm water curling round my toes felt good; and despite my stubbornness, a smile emerged unexpectedly. Sound of squawking gulls fighting over a fish reminded me how most animals have to toil just to stay alive and how lucky modern man was to be free of those burdens. We even have idle time to enjoy nature.

It was the time of year for Spanish Mackerel to be running, what little good that would do me. It was just one of those days, where I couldn't keep bait on the hook to save my life. Devilish pin fish, size of the palm of your hand, would sneak-in and steal what doesn't belong to them. Put a fresh piece of shrimp on the line, throw it out, few subversive nibbles, and reel in a naked hook. Every cast turned out the same. I would've had more luck swimming out to deeper waters with a knife between my teeth. Thomas, for some strange reason, had always been immune to the pillaging of pin fish.

On this day, however, he was struggling with the elusive vermin. Moreover, he appeared distracted and listless as if something wasn't normal, didn't show his usual vigor, and didn't seem to care.

"Thomas, what's ailing you?"

"Ummm, ummm, think I'm getting a sore throat. Had a tickle when I woke, but ignored it hoping I was wrong."

I've tried that strategy as well, but rarely found it effective. Put the back of my hand on his forehead, "you're burning-up. You best pack-it-in and get to bed. If you need Doc Stevens I can get him over to your place in a heartbeat."

"I think you're right, starting to feel a little achy. I'll let you know if I want the Doc."

*****

All kinds of things were catching when I grew-up, mumps and measles were pretty bad, but let me tell you there were others much worse, like infantile paralysis. The name has a way of striking terror into the hearts of parents. Insidious, tiny virus associated with the polio disease had been the scourge of millions of families during the 19th and 20th centuries, and even before. Leaving many children, and adults as well, with withered limbs, some confined to wheel chairs, and others unable to breathe without aid of mechanical devices. By early 1950's little had been done to effectively combat ravages of the disease, and collective fear had built to a feverish pitch sending the nation into a panic. One couldn't help think if Franklin D. Roosevelt, president of our United States, could succumb, then what chance did us common folk have? Many did what they could to avoid public exposure, abstaining from swimming pools, water fountains, and even rest rooms. Always in the back of your mind was a lurking premonition that fork or spoon you had in your mouth from the diner didn't look as clean as it should have. But no matter how hard folks tried, news of some new victim was never too far round the corner.

It wasn't until Jonas Salk developed the first effective vaccine did America get a grip. Individuals, families, entire communities stood in long lines at clinics, schools, and churches to receive their immunization. Sure hope you got yours Bizzy.

My own recollection was vivid. Managed to escape infection up to that time, but queued with other Bankers had me wondering if my number was up. Approaching the finish line I was besieged with apprehension, and negative images invaded the sanctity of my thoughts. An almost ridiculous and ironic question pressed upon my mind...what if standing here, near the end of the race, I was to be inoculated? Anxiously waiting my turn, I held my breath hoping to avoid infection, gulping shallow breaths so I wouldn't faint. As the line slowly snaked, time drew to a crawl, anxiety took over, and I was convinced it was already too late.

One moment had me already in the grave, next I was right as rain. Bite of the needle pricking my skin brought immediate relief in the belief, however misguided, I was now free from the threat of this perilous disease. Many felt the same way I did. Not many would decline the vaccine, but there were a few, and, sadly, Thomas was one.

*****

Helped Thomas organize his fishing gear, and got him as far as his door step, made a futile attempt at humor, "I'd feel sorry for you if you weren't so ugly." Thinkin better of my rude comment, "you'll feel better tomorrow."

Didn't give much thought to his complaint during super, and by the time I headed to bed had completely put it out of my mind. However, sometime around 3 am, I was to be reminded.

Island life is fairly quiet off-season, especially after the sun sets. Bankers are inclined to find comfort of their homes more appealing then carousing and running amok at all hours of the night, which is why I nearly messed my pants when I heard pounding on my door, beam of a flashlight franticly searching interior spaces of walls and floors for something or someone, and bellowing of Sheriff Stone.

"Robert, Robert Guthrie, are you in there? Robert, if you ain't dead open this door right fast!"

Out of my mind and confused, I tripped over the lamp cord trying to pull on my pants. Almost had them zipped, when I got to the door, "Sheriff Stone, what in the world are you screaming about at this time of night! You practically scared me half-to-death!"

"Robert, come quick, Thomas is real sick! Doc is with him right now. He sent me to fetch you!"

Barely got one foot in the vehicle when Sheriff Stone's squad car sped off, first over paved roads and then along the bumpy sandy two-lane path down towards sound-side, springs squeaking complaints as we lifted off the ground and bottomed-out. Took a couple of turns on two wheels and screeched to a halt digging deep ruts in the pull-out next to Thomas's cottage. Found Doc standing over Thomas in the bathroom. Thomas was submerged in a tub full of water with chunks of ice floating about him like he was some fancy cocktail, and for all the world as incoherent as a box of rocks.

"Robert, glad you're here. Thomas is doing poorly and I'm afraid we need to get him to a hospital. You're closest thing he's got to kin on the island so I'm going to need you to go with us."

"How sick is he?"

"He's got a temperature pushing 105. I don't want to be an alarmist, but there's a chance he won't make it if we don't get him cooled down; and, quick. Get a blanket and soak it, we'll wrap him in it with as much ice as we can find."

Sheriff and I ran around like chickens with our heads cut-off trying to make ourselves useful; and despite our panic and flailing-about, finally managed to get Thomas cocooned in ice and situated in back of the squad car.

Don't remember much of the ride, siren whaling, headlights warned of oncoming traffic as we passed cars like they were standing still, Doc taking Thomas's vitals every few minutes. Took us over an hour to get to the emergency room in New Bern where he was ushered into intensive care. From window in the door I could see doctors and nurses pouring over him. Had to answer some annoying questions an administrator insisted were essential, as if they would determine Thomas's prognosis. Provided the name of his only surviving sister, didn't know her street address, thought she still lived in Winston-Salem. And once having done that, there was nothing left to do but settle-in and wait. Bright lights of the waiting room weren't meant to be comforting, and they weren't. Stark and cold there was no sympathy as their glare was an unpleasant reminder that for those who entered this façade, some would leave and some would not. Shuffling from uncomfortable chairs to water fountain, Sheriff Stone and I took turns pacing back and forth, occasionally exchanging a furtive glance or shrug, anxiously holding on for any news.

Doc Stevens eventually came out looking bedraggled, "doctors have done everything they can. It's now going to be a waiting game. Next 72 hours will be crucial."

"What's he got Doc, the flu?"

"No, Robert it isn't the flu. Can't be sure until spinal and throat cultures come back, but he has all the symptoms of polio. You boys might as well go home. I'll let you know if there is any change."

Daylight was breaking over the beach when we coasted to a stop in front of my cottage. I got out and looked back at the Sheriff, there were no words. How could there be any? We were facing off with an adversary for which there was no hope for victory and who held the life of our dearest friend in the balance. Any attempt to provide a rationale for what was happening would be lame. Some medical conditions are the cause of neglect or carelessness, but the randomness of disease defies logic. Even if I wanted to say something I had a lump in my throat that would have choked the life out of me. Instead Sheriff Stone simply reached out and squeezed my hand.

Rest of the day I puttered about. Did a little cleaning, mended a screen, straightened out the shed, was never more than a few feet from the phone. On pins and needles, I waited for someone to call from the hospital, finally rung-up the Sheriff to see if he had heard anything. Nothing. Made a sandwich, ate only half, and drifted off in my easy chair listening to the radio.

Woke to a storm lighting up the sky, darkness splintered, followed by distant rumbles. Nothing unusual about that, except it felt peculiarly ominous, portending of something sinister waiting in the dark for its prey. I resolved to call the hospital.

"Yes, my name is Robert Guthrie. Could you please tell me how Thomas Jackson is doing?"

"Are you family?"

"No, but we are good friends."

"I'm sorry unless you are family or listed as a guardian I'm not permitted to share patient's information. It is confidential."

Not one to normally question authority or policies, but under the circumstances I made my protest, "you must be kidding! He has been very sick and I am worried out of my mind! I need to know how my friend is doing!"

"No I am not kidding, and I don't like your tone"…click.

Callousness of petty rule makers is enough to drive a man to violence, and what's worse are those who voluntarily salute such insanity. If I could have reached through the telephone wires I would have shook some sense into the operator at the other end. Instead I was left with a dial tone, fuming, wondering how my friend was doing, and why it took so little to set me off.

Minutes on the clock, hours in the day, days in the year, passing of the calendar proceeds always at the same rate for those who wait on nothing. However, give a man a reason to calculate, think, worry, hope, and for some strange reason the earth's rotation screeches to a halt making days and night interminable.

*****

Phone rang, my waiting had ended, "Robert, this is Doc Stevens. Sorry I haven't got back to you sooner, but I really didn't have anything meaningful to report until now."

"How is he doing Doc?"

"Robert, there is no way to make this easy, so I'm going to just come right-out with it. He is not doing well at all. Thomas's muscles have no strength and are not responding reflexively to stimuli like they should. What's worse he's struggling to swallow. Cultures have confirmed he definitely has polio. If this trend continues he will likely be paralyzed. We're moving him to Greenville. They have better facilities to treat neurological disorders and a staff familiar with progression of polio symptoms."

Few words have caused more pain in my life, in their utterance time sped up and I saw images of Thomas and me pass before my eyes.

And so it would go, as his polio progressed, and Thomas's condition deteriorated, they moved him further and further away from Bogue Banks.

From New Bern to Greenville, where his legs stopped working, then to Raleigh, and when he finally could no longer breathe on his own, they sent him to Hickory, center of the world so-to-speak for patients who were confined to ventilators. In 1944 the citizens of Hickory built a hospital in 54 hours to save their children from an outbreak of polio. Of the 13 wards, 1 was dedicated to patients whose lives were sustained by iron lungs. It was here Thomas had now made his home. It would be here he would live out his remaining life. For Thomas it was a one-way ticket.

*****

Disease and death arouse some powerful and unusual emotions, fear, anger, even embarrassment. I had walked to the ticket counter and turned around so many times I'd lost count. Even if I managed to find the courage to buy a bus ticket to Hickory, what would I say once I got there? Last time we talked it was to on his front porch arguing over when the tides were running and what time I should come by to go fishing. Seems like a million years ago now.

The ride took over 8 hours, at each of the many stops during our journey I got out to buy a new magazine for Thomas. Field and Stream, Outdoor Life, Sport Fishing, American Angler, all those I knew he liked to read and a few he didn't. In any case I wouldn't come empty handed. Walked the 6 blocks from the station to the clinic, arms loaded, must have looked like a salesman peddling periodicals.

Nurse at the reception desk wasn't unkind, but she didn't smile. I remember it was very quiet, if people were talking they had to be whispering. Mood seemed very somber and I knew this wasn't the place for joking.

Introduced myself apologetically, "excuse me, sorry to bother you, but I'm here to visit Thomas Jackson."

"Yes of course, please follow me."

Hallways smelt faintly of antiseptic, not a single decoration to interrupt the cold sterile environment testifying to pain and suffering of those unlucky enough to have found their ways within. I knew I had to keep this appointment, but I swear it was the last place on earth I wanted to be.

As she opened the door to the ward I was overcome with a sight that was profoundly depressing, one I will never forget. Row after row, men, women, and children occupied metal cans. Sound of clicking motors working wheezing mechanical bellows resonated off barren walls. Within each coffin was housed a poor soul, barely alive, sustained by sucking air in-and-out of broken lungs. Pull the plug and they wouldn't last more than a minute.

As they lay there, the sum total of their lives was now defined by what they could hear and see from their confinement. Nothing, there was absolutely nothing for them to do, but exist. Their vacant stares shrieked agony. I was reminded of a sci-fi book I had read as a boy, where a mad scientist had extracted the brain of his unsuspecting brother and kept it alive. The brain sustained the personality of its owner, had all the faculties of thought and reasoning, and yet had no tangible connection to the world. It had no means of escape, and rambling wayward thoughts finally drove it to insanity. It was terrifying. And here in this ward the terror of that book had been brought to life, and was real.

"….I said your friend Thomas is third from the end, on the right. Did you hear me?"

"I'm sorry, I was distracted. Yes, third from end, on the right"

"Visiting hours are over in 30 minutes. Please abide by our curfew in respect for our other patients."

"Of course, 30 minutes", I thought to myself I'd be lucky to last 30 seconds.

Leaden legs pulled the rest of my reluctant body past the unfortunate. I did my best to avert my eyes from their situation and hoped when I found Thomas I would have the fortitude to say something to him, instead of bolting and running for the door.

"Hey ole man, looks like you found yourself in a bit of a pickle! They feeding you well? Here, brought a few magazines, read some of them already, not much new, but there is one article on jigging for flounder with plugs you might like."

"Robert, what are you doing here?"

"What da ya mean, I came to visit. Don't tell me you got so many visitors I'm not welcome, came all the way from Bogue Banks by Greyhound, just so I could see your sorry puss. Listen I'll argue with you later, got to go pee, hold tight and I'll be right back."

I didn't have to go pee, I had to puke. Made it to the john, burst open the door, knelt over the toilet and blew my lunch. Curled next to cold porcelain, I cried my eyes out and vomited some more. Appearance of Thomas entombed, except for his head, in that ghastly shroud of pumps and valves was more than I had anticipated even as a man of color, I could tell he was pallid, his skin looked thinner, and eyes were vacuous. It sickened me and now that I had broken down, how would I recover to face my friend?

Men are tested when forced to confront their fears, and I was either going pass or fail. Running out of time, it wouldn't be long before someone would come looking to kick me out of the hospital. Perhaps I could make that my excuse. What? Is this how I wanted to remember my time with Thomas? Washed my face in the sink, managed to soak my collar and tie, shirt tail out, red-eyed I drug myself back to my friend.

"Robert, you look a mess."

"Well that's something coming from you."

"Now you listen to me, there's nothing you can do for me. I've had my run, and all we got here is some bad luck. Can't have you hovering over me pretending things are ok, do you understand? All you can do for me now is to fill my mind with the use-to-be's. Well there gone, and it's too damn painful to dwell on. I need to deal with the now and that's hard enough without being drug into the past. You're my best friend, but I need you to promise me something."

"What?"

"You need to promise never to come visit me again. Don't write me, don't try to leave a message. You have to promise!"

"Thomas, I can't do that!"

"Promise!"

Mamma always told me never to make a promise I couldn't keep, it's easy to make them, it's harder to keep them. But, sometimes you tell the people you love what they want to hear, not that you necessarily believe it yourself.

Sound of my own voice, as I said those words, was not totally convincing and under my breath I prayed to God, who discerns truth from lies, that I might be forgiven.

"I promise...I promise."

The Storm

Winter seemed especially long and cold. Too many days wind blew from the north pushing warmer air offshore. Vague aches and pains, and other complaints seeped through cracks in windows and doors, along with a family of mice looking to find relief from frigid crown of winter. I could tolerate the mice, but wasn't too fond of the other stuff. Maybe it was my age or bleak notions rattling around my brain, whatever, a melancholy became my constant companion shadowing my every step. Hounding me like a door-to-door salesman. Not that I am a snob, but I prefer to pick the company I keep and well, he wasn't welcome.

Doc Stevens told me Thomas was holding his own, but I wondered for how long. A man's spirit is sustained through hope. Without it, spirit will die and body follows not too long after. Thomas was strong-willed, I prayed he was strong enough.

Somewhere around end of March I noticed wind shifting from the south-west and signs winter had finally broken. Soon thereafter the jacket was replaced by short-sleeves, long pants with shorts, and my uninvited guest was kicked to the curb. Been through a rough spell and determined that I was done with it. From now on, I was going to count my blessings and look for a more positive outlook, regardless of circumstances. I might not be able to pick my fortunes. But it's my choice what I do with what I've been given.

Weather is far less predictable sticking out into the Atlantic, but as is often the case here on the island, colder than normal winters are followed by hotter than normal summers, and with it some nasty storms.

*****

Got my head around the upcoming season and even made a few suggestions to Mrs. Cartwright how we can improve our bottom-line. She was a dear soul and generous to a fault, sometimes to her own detriment. I had an idea or two which was likely to rub her the wrong way, but knew they were fair and would cut costs.

"Now hear me out Mrs. Cartwright. All I'm suggesting is we take a step backwards and look at this from a fresh angle."

"Robert, I'm no cheapskate and the last thing I want to do is to send the wrong message to renters who have been loyal!"

"I understand, but what I'm suggesting shouldn't pinch their wallets and is unlikely to offend anyone."

"Alright I'm listening."

"Ok, good. First, folks staying at your properties treat linens as if they belonged to them. They use them to clean their cars, take them down to the beach and sometimes leave them for tides to snatch out to sea, and it's not uncommon for sheets and towels to grow a set of legs and disappear with renters at the end of their stay. Now, if you were to ask for a refundable deposit on linens folks would realize they need to take better care of them, especially if they want their deposit back, and trust me they will. I am not absolutely sure how much money you'll save by not having to replace linens each season, but I would bet it's substantial. Second, you get people making reservations and cancelling at the last minute, which means a lost opportunity for you. If lucky, you can find someone to fill the gap, but more often than not the property remains empty. If you were to ask for 10% of the rental fee upfront, of course credited to the lease, and make it clear if they cancel within 2 weeks of their scheduled arrival it becomes non-refundable, I guarantee you that last minute cancellations will become a thing of the past. I got a few other thoughts, but I'll save them for another day. You go on and chew on what I put on your plate, in the end, it's your decision."

"I don't know, sounds reasonable, really no additional cost to renters if you think about it. Hmmm, let me ruminate on it a little."

"You do that Mrs. Cartwright, in the meantime let me take a look at your reservation book so I can start prioritizing my work." This was a half-truth. I did need to get my projects prioritized, but the real reason was to see if Mrs. Stanford of Raleigh had made a reservation for the summer. To my disappointment, she had not. But season was early and there was still time for her to make up her mind.

However, there was one registered guest whose name I did recognize. Buford J. Pettibone, richest man in North Carolina, and perhaps the entire south. Now it's not that Bogue Banks hasn't hosted the wealthy, for they like the beach same as anyone else, and our shores are certainly some of the finest, but a man of Mr. Pettibone's pedigree gracing our little island, and more importantly, staying in one of Mrs. Cartwright's properties, well that's something to raise an eyebrow or two.

"Mrs. Cartwright, you are aware that Buford J. Pettibone is to be one of your guests?

"Why of course Robert, I penned the date myself, why wouldn't I be aware?

"And you realize he is one of the most affluent men of our southern states?

"Now that really doesn't concern me. I will treat him with the same courtesy as any other guest and expect you do the same."

"Yes ma'am, I certainly will!"

Somewhere in one of my letters Bizzy, I am certain I have shared that I am not the most educated man that has walked this earth, some would say the wheels are turning, but ain't much happening. Nevertheless, I wasn't born yesterday and the more I thought on it the more skeptical I became as to the purpose of his visit. Could be he was coming to partake of our splendors, could be he was sojourning with an ulterior motive. Little did I know that before long there would be a collision, one of stupendous makings between one of the wealthiest men to set foot on our shores and a storm of frightening proportions. We'd see who would win.

*****

It didn't take long to find out what Mr. Pettibone's intentions were. Word got around, as it is apt to do, Pettibone was planning to visit our island in a speculating mood, scrutinizing a stretch of beach just west of the Circle to build a high-rise hotel, an Olympic-sized pool and hundreds of beach cabanas. A hotel associated with his name was destined to bring lots of folks from all parts of the country...lots and lots of folks.

As you might expect the response of the islanders was mixed. Actually, calling it mixed would be a tad too generous, as they evolved two camps diametrically opposed to the other. There were those who were delighted in the idea and saw an opportunity to bring more money to our island and then there were those who were adamant that no hotel be erected on their island. They could build a hotel, but only as long as it was on the mainland far from the natural beauty and quiet of their homes. It weren't rocket science figuring out who would join which faction. Shop keepers, restaurant purveyors, dance hall owners, and everyone else who figured their revenue would skyrocket were definitely in favor of a new high-rise hotel. They were led by our very own Newman Willis who was more than happy to facilitate any and all permits. Then there were the rest of the native islanders who could only imagine how an influx of rude over-demanding itinerants would thrust their world into chaos, just short of the Tribulation. This group was led by Sheriff Stone who would own the fallout from traffic jams, flared tempers, and petty crime that would most certainly follow on the heels of such an undertaking. I of course was against the insanity, but would have to bite my tongue as long as Pettibone was the guest of Mrs. Cartwright. Poor woman, she was undecided how she felt about the notion of a new hotel, until I informed her it would most likely cut her business in half.

Day of his arrival was attended by a spectacular display of supporters, and detractors. As Buford J. Pettibone's limousine crossed the causeway onto the island there, front and center, was Newman sitting on top of a float decorated with banners heralding a warm welcome to its newest son. A marching band banged-out "For He's a Jolly Good Fellow", not exactly sure, but I think that's what they played; and, as they ambled down Fort Macon Road crowds edged in from both sides of the street, some cheering good wishes while others yelled for Pettibone to get lost. Keep in mind the only time islanders are motivated to have a parade is when one of our great wars end, or when one starts.

Mrs. Cartwright and I waited on the front porch of *Carolina Day-Dreams*, largest and most accommodating of her properties. As the entourage inched their way down the island we could hear the sound of horns blaring and confusion of cheers and jeers.

A conga line of vehicles wound their way down the sandy drive, some peeling-off to park on shoulders, others persisting to the bitter-end. Finally, Buford J. Pettibone's limousine glided to a stop. From the rear seat I could see the prominent investor sitting as natural as can be, waiting for someone to open his door for him like he was royalty; which of course, his chauffer executed without delay. As he emerged the cut of his fine wool suit, monogrammed shirt, silk tie with pearl stick pin oozed money and warned that although we may look, we should not touch.

Newman out of breath and beside himself stuck his right hand almost in Mr. Pettibone's face hoping to shake the hand of our prominent guest, "Hello Mr. Pettibone, my name is Newman Willis. I am mayor of Atlantic Beach and would like to be the first to welcome you to our humble…"

He never got the chance to finish his sentence. Buford J. Pettibone brushed his hand away and curtly responded, "you may speak to my lawyers when they arrive," and then proceeded to walk right past Newman, past Mrs. Cartwright, and past me directly through the front door and shut it behind without as much as a how-do-you-do.

Newman clearly disappointed was always quick on his feet and knew just what to say, "thank you all for coming out. It's obvious Mr. Pettibone is worn out from his trip and we should let him have his rest. I will be conversing with his people over the next few weeks regarding potential developments (*wink-wink*) and will endeavor to keep all of you informed."

I was dubious anyone from Pettibone's staff would be talking with Newman regarding any plans for development and even more dubious if they did Newman would keep anybody informed.

Didn't take long for this enterprise to heat up, surveying crews poured in from every direction on the compass traipsing through folk's yards, trampling flower beds, spying through them optical thing-a-bobs at lackeys holding yard sticks in the air downwind. Commotion they created screaming numbers back and forth, pounding stakes in the ground with different colored ribbons. It was enough to drive our islanders insane. Business types wearing 3-piece suits would wander in and out of the background talking serious as if they were extras in the cast of a movie. Drama they fashioned from total disregard for what once was, had many of us wondering if this wasn't the beginning of the end for our way of life. Imagination spun exaggerated outcomes where every native's home was bulldozed only to be replaced by row after row of cinderblock monsters reaching skyward obscuring sun and moon, fencing-off the beach from all who were not registered paying guests of one of Pettibone's hotel chains.

I was always busy at the beginning of the season sorting out petty little problems at one or more of Mrs. Cartwright's properties. Some miscues like forgetting to turn on water heaters, frozen door locks, and such, always had to be rectified as quickly as possible, which kept me on my toes during the first few weeks. But never in all my days had I met anyone who could find fault in the totality of service we provided. His Highness didn't like the creaking floor boards in the living room so I had to lay carpet. He found the only sticking blind in a back bedroom and threatened to call his attorney. Linens were not soft enough. The screen door opened the wrong way. The list was endless, and I found myself being pulled away from real work to attend to his capricious impulses. And, I wasn't the only target for his discontent. Sheriff Stone had started collecting complaints from all corners of our island. Even Newman was none-to-pleased how events were progressing.

I admit to having little patience for those arrogant son-of-a-guns who use their money as a weapon against the less fortunate and I was losing patience. Like so many of the other wealthy, Pettibone had never learned any limits the rest of the world were forced to comply with, and would satisfy every moral or immoral fancy that pleased his appetite. I would cater only so far to this one-man wrecking crew and decided there was going to be a reckoning of ways if things continued as they had, regardless if he was a guest of Mrs. Cartwright, or not. The show-down didn't take long in coming.

Mrs. Cartwright had decided she should make a visit to *Carolina Day-dreams* and call upon her guest to make sure everything was to his liking, and she asked me to accompany her. We found the rich bon vivant sitting on the porch in one of the rocking chairs.

"Good afternoon Mr. Pettibone, I hope I am not intruding, but was anxious to stop by and see how you been getting on. I hope all is well, but would be all too happy to attend to any of your needs which we have neglected, which is why I have asked Mr. Guthrie to join me."

Not even looking up from his Wall Street Journal he took a deep breath as if winding up, "my dear lady, you are in fact intruding! As to how I am getting on, as you say, well that is none of your business. And as for my needs, they are many given the distinctively deficient condition of this property, which you should be ashamed of. I will in fact rectify the paltry accommodations available on this island shortly, once my 5-star hotel has been erected. Until then I would appreciate it if you would leave me in peace. If I require anything of you, you can be certain I will have you summoned. Have I made myself clear?"

That did it! I took one step, grabbed the newspaper out his hand and pulled the bully up by his collar so he was standing on his tip-toes. "Pettibone, I am not sure where you were raised, or by whom. But in these parts, when a woman is standing we expect you to stand as well, as a sign of respect. You might think you are pretty special given all your money, but let me tell you there isn't enough money in the world to forgive the way you just spoke to Mrs. Cartwright and if you do it ever again I will drag your sorry behind down to the swamps and let the gators nibble on you a little. Have I made myself clear?"

It takes a lot for me to get so excited, and I'm normally not the threatening sort, but every man has got his limit and he found mine. White as a ghost slipping back into his rocker, papers strewn across the porch, he had the look of a man that just dodged a bus. It is unlikely anyone had spoken to Buford J. Pettibone in that tone in quite some time. I marched Mrs. Cartwright by her elbow back to my truck, and before we departed, I glared back at our guest to make sure he understood I meant business.

Funny thing, after our little tête-à-tête we didn't hear a word, not a peep, from the man in *Carolina Day-dreams*, which suited me just fine and although it appeared the boss had been put on ice, his project continued unabated. A construction shack was erected on site and rudimentary outlines of a foundation began to take shape. Architects carrying blueprints under their arms hustled from the property to the court house and back, by the hour, like ants scurrying to and from an ant hill. And with it, the tension which had beset our community ratcheted to the breaking point. As tiny cogs in the massive machinery directed by those who took no notice of our existence, all we could do was watch.

Summer hadn't even got a head of steam and I was already exhausted from the ordinary, and the extraordinary. Couldn't tell you what day of the week it was, just kept my head down and worked on one list while Mrs. Cartwright created another. Was checking on outdoor spigots to make sure renters didn't leave them running after rinsing sand off their feet, when out of nowhere I felt someone touch my sleeve.

"Hello Robert, I was hoping I'd run into you."

Oh my goodness, it was Dorothy Stanford! Somehow, she snuck under the radar and found her way back to Bogue Banks. "Dorothy, you surprised me! I'm so very pleased you came back. Where are you staying?"

"I'm staying at *Heavens Ocean*, just down the road. Guess I waited too long to reserve *Lost Horizon*, but I am enjoying this cottage just as much."

"Is Buddy with you?"

"Sure is. I left him napping. Something he's very good at."

"Wow, it's nice to see you." Uh-oh, looks like I found myself trying to think of something intelligent to say to her again and all I can come-up with is drivel. Smart move would be to wait till she says something and let her lead the conversation. Our pause was painful.

"Robert, I want to tell you I am sorry."

I certainly didn't expect her to lead off with that. "What do you have to be sorry about?"

"Well I guess the way I handled that situation with Dick last summer and for not saying goodbye, which after I got home I regretted. You were polite and gentlemanly and I should have thanked you for it. And, I am very sorry to hear about your friend Thomas. What a dreadful thing to happen. I hope you can accept my apologies, please say you do."

More than anything I wanted to scream hallelujah! I've waited months for her contrition, for her acknowledgement she had slighted me, and God only knows for an apology. But I had another thought, which can only come if you're willing to calm yourself and listen to what you're thinking. How many times have I, either intentionally or unintentionally, hurt someone, someone who waited on my apology, and it never came, maybe too many times. In that moment it was reaffirmed for me that none of us are perfect, least of all me. It took courage for Dorothy to confront what had happened and courage to say she was sorry; and, if I responded to her in any way that was demeaning, then what kind of hypocrite was I?

"Dorothy, seems you have been carrying a burden heavier than the crime you believe you've committed. I accept your apology, but I am sorry the pain all this fussing has caused you, and I am sorry for my friend Thomas. Certain crosses aren't worth bearing, lets lay it on down and not speak of it anymore."

Gratitude finds its way to your doorstep at odd times, her nod affirmed for me things had been set straight and all was well. I would like to tell you after that day Dorothy Stanford and I were inseparable; but, truth was my days didn't get any lighter and what free time I could steal was spent on mundane tasks of keeping my life intact, washing clothes, cleaning my own house, you know chores. When I was able to see her, I am happy to say, we were right cordial as we had found familiar ground, and there is nothing more pleasing when you're in the company of a woman who you respect, and respects you in return.

*****

It was turning out to be an extremely hot summer, which given the colder than normal winter wasn't too surprising. But there was somewhere that was even hotter than Bogue Shores; the Sahara Desert, all the way over there in Africa. Now you might think that's not all that abnormal, I mean everyone knows the Sahara gets pretty hot. Nevertheless, what you may not know is when the Sahara gets as hot as it did this summer, it's not uncommon to kick-up some strong winds. These winds move in a westerly direction and when they meet warm waters of the Atlantic bad things start churning. There they pick-up moisture, energy, and spin and if they organize like a labor union then we got the makings of a hurricane. Well, guess what? That's precisely what was going on, and all the while, us islanders had no clue.

Wasn't as if National Hurricane Center was playing their cards close to their chest. They knew things were brewing, but without verifiable proof a storm was headed to the eastern seaboard they were reluctant to alarm folks unnecessarily. All they would say was conditions were ideal for serious weather. On Bogue Banks conditions are always ideal for serious weather. Even on sunny calm days things can turn ugly without warning, which is why no one paid too much attention to the babble coming out of the Hurricane Center. But truth be known, no one on the island wanted to get guests nervous with threats of evacuation without a reason.

Storm winds swirled from Cape Verde Islands due west and by the time it passed Bermuda the tropical depression had morphed into a full-blown hurricane and was gaining strength. Not to worry, our best meteorologists, at least by their own definition, were predicting it would veer north and miss the coast completely, which is what we all believed when we went to bed on Saturday. However, by Sunday morning hurricane Amelia, now a category 3, had not budged and was headed directly to our shores.

With sufficient warning, houses can be boarded, water and gas turned off, and the process of moving people inland can proceed in an orderly and safe fashion. It was too late for that now. Any attempt to evacuate people would likely cause massive confusion and traffic jams placing those who we hoped to save in greater danger. No, the only course left to us was to follow the wisdom of the original settlers of Salter Path in times like this, hunker down, and pray.

I did my best to get around to all the properties to ensure guests had lanterns, bathtubs were filled for drinking, and encouraged them to stay in-doors no matter what. My last call was on Dorothy, I knew she was would be scared, heck I was scared, and offered to ride it out with her and Buddy, which she gratefully accepted.

By mid-afternoon the barometer had dropped from 29.6 inches to 27.0 and continued to fall. Winds on the beach were gusting at 80 mph and waves were pounding the shore-line, some 15 feet high. If the hurricane hit the island at high tide storm surge could erase any evidence it ever had been inhabited.

Dorothy had positioned herself on the couch with her legs tucked under, grasping her knees trying to find, or create, some comfort in what had become a terrifying situation. Sounds emanating from outside were deafening. Debris and lawn furniture were pelting the house in a constant staccato. It couldn't get any louder if a locomotive had busted through the front door. Her cottage shook to its very foundation with each blast of wind, creaking and bending, I wondered if it would hold. Poor Buddy was inconsolable. Panting, eyes bulging big as saucers, fear coursed through his vein like molten lava. He ran from the back of the house to the front and back again looking for some place to hide from what he didn't understand. I tried to intercept him and hold him, but he would have none of that.

Myself? By my presence I had been elevated to a position of protector, which was absolute nonsense. I had no more power to resist the onslaught and restore peace and sanity than anyone else. But, if I caved-in to my own fears the fabric of our sanity, in what had become a close-knit enclave, most certainly would have come un-glued; and so, it was up to me to keep it together. Hour after hour I played games in my head, multiplication tables, reciting the pledge of allegiance, trying to recall what I did on each of my birthdays, alphabet forward and backwards, anything to distract my thoughts, promising if I could hold-on for just 5 more minutes it would be 5 less minutes of torture.

It was pitch dark and the dreadful shrill of the winds had reached a feverous pitch, all other sounds were consumed in the void it created. Strain of persistent insults had seriously weakened nails, screws, and those materials in which they were intended to hold together. I knew our situation couldn't last much longer, something had to give. What gave was the front door. Bolted, and locked it began to bulge inwards stretching like rubber. Instinctively I jumped on top of Dorothy as it exploded sending thousands of splinters flying in every direction. Buddy, terrified and confused, lost his mind and ran straight for, and through, the breach. Dorothy tried to chase him.

"No! You'll get yourself killed if you go outside!"

"I've got to find him!"

"Not on-my-life! Buddy is gone! Going out there won't bring him back! I'm sorry!"

I sat on her using all of my weight to pin her to the couch. Dorothy fought me, screamed, kicked, did everything in her power to break my hold, but I wouldn't let go. Although she came close several times of breaking free, I knew if somehow she managed, her chances of surviving in that storm were nil. Eventually the fight left her, limp and exhausted she surrendered to my restraint. We would lay there the remainder of the night as the storm slowly spun itself out. Spent, it eventually died.

First light brought evidence of the destruction rendered by Amelia. Roofs missing, windows smashed, even a few houses collapsed. The beach was eerily distorted, dunes pushed some 20 to 30 feet inland. Shingles, boards, and insulation were scattered everywhere. People curious as to the outcome walked like zombies in a trance trying to come to grips with their new reality. Dorothy and I spent the day and better part of the next looking for Buddy, calling out his name till we were hoarse, searching ocean and sound sides with no luck. I didn't want to tell Dorothy, but I didn't think we would find him. For all I knew Buddy was blown all the way to the Smokey Mountains.

Only good news was that the hurricane was fast moving. Had it not been, who knows how much worse it would have been. One other bit of good news, there was no trace, not a shred of evidence, of the outline of Buford J. Pettibone's hotel. Excavation markers, construction shack, rudimentary foundation were completely erased, as if it had never existed. In its place was sand.

No one knows how Pettibone had weathered the storm, but it evidently made an impression on him, for without delay he packed his bags and exited the island with his entourage pretty much the way he entered, never to be seen or heard from again.

It was a relief to most everyone on the island and Newman, being the consummate politician, decided to seize the opportunity as only he could, "I want everyone to know that after receiving many complaints regarding the construction of a high-rise hotel in our town; and, after consultation with Sheriff Stone, I recommended to the town's commissioners that we should not approve the siting permit, and politely asked Mr. Buford J. Pettibone to consider an alternative location. As you all know by now, the situation has been resolved."

What Newman neglected to tell everyone was, even though he thought of having that conversation with Pettibone, it never occurred. It was the power of God's hands, elements out of man's control, that made a more powerful persuasion than any small-town politician could exert.

Some folks swear that during the most stressful moments of this entire transaction, women of the island formed a prayer circle for the purpose of beseeching our Lord to wash away the sinful contrivance of that singularly greedy rich man. Now, that may be a stretch of the truth, but there was a storm, and Buford J. Pettibone and his edifice are definitely gone.

Aftermath

In the aftermath of such a devastating event it is hard to know where to begin. There is so much to do at a time when your energy level is at its ebb and one can't help but feel overwhelmed. But you do what you can, knowing down the road, a month, a year, maybe even longer it's possible to put your life back together. To reassemble a past in a fashion that satisfies the present.

Picking up the first bit of trash is the hardest, then there is a second and a third and with each small step forward it gets a little easier. Community begins to come together helping each other, encouraging each other, and before long you find your stride tackling each one of the many catastrophes you'll be forced to face before there is light at the end of the tunnel.

I was fortunate to come through with only minor damage to my cottage. Mrs. Cartwright was less fortunate. For her it was a numbers game. If you own enough properties probability was high one or more was going to be seriously damaged. Many of our guests, having endured an unimaginable ordeal, quit their vacations by the sea, and as many cancelled not wanting to wade into the residual havoc left behind. Hard to say there was a silver lining, but with fewer renters to cater to I was free to do my best to put humpty dumpty back together again and when I wasn't hammering and sawing I spent what time I could with Dorothy.

*****

I could see it in her eyes. Same thing I've seen in the eyes of others who have faced near-death at the mercy of forces of nature. It's a look that says, "oh, I get it, Angel of Death is always around the corner and if he wanted me, there is nothing I can do to stop him." It's the same look you see in the faces of soldiers who have survived terrible battle. With time it fades, but never goes away completely.

Dorothy had to contend with a close call with the great divide, but also with the loss of her beloved Buddy. Most dog lovers would rather not put it into words, but silently they mourn their companion, maybe even more so than those of a spouse, or parent; which, with the added sense of guilt, compounds the pain of loss.

Did my best to avoid topics which one might consider controversial or depressing, but at some point in every relationship curiosity gets the better of you and you wonder who has trod upon the ground you now occupy. Hoping enough good will and trust has been built up to forgive any missteps you forge into the murky unknown.

So I asked the question that had been on my mind, "Dorothy, what was your husband like, I mean if you don't mind me asking?"

"Steven, I guess he was a good man. Certainly had lots of energy, worked long hours, sometimes 6 days a week. He poured his heart and soul into his profession and from what I've heard, did the same when he went to war. We never lacked for any physical need or want, however, it would have been nice to have spent a little more time together. Nevertheless, we had two wonderful children and I guess the best way to sum him up was he was a good provider."

Don't consider myself an expert in the affairs between men and women, however, when a woman describes her spouse as a good provider and deflects to the qualities of their offspring, it's usually because they can't think of anything nicer to say about their husband. Had enough common sense to know the difference between love and caring, caring and respect, and respect and indifference. Wasn't absolutely sure, but I think she opened the door for me. Maybe just a crack.

Responded with the one thing that seemed to fit the moment, "hard to lose someone you love."

"Robert, why didn't you marry? As gentle and giving as you are I can't imagine you couldn't find a woman to love you, even way out here on this island."

"I was married."

"You were! I'm sorry I didn't mean it to sound like that." Clearly, I surprised her with my admission.

"Yes, many years ago."

"Are you comfortable talking about it?"

"I'm comfortable enough, but truly there's not much to tell. I had just turned 19, newly returned from World War I."

"I had joined allied forces late in the war, thinking it was my patriotic duty. It was in the spring of 1918. Germany had our backs against the wall. Artillery barrages were incessant. Mustard gas filled the trenches with poisonous clouds blinding soldiers who opted to discard their hideous gas masks. Those who weren't blinded lay in feet of mud and their own excrement, shell-shocked, delusional, many already having succumbed to nervous breakdowns. No sense going into too much detail, you can trust me it was unpleasant. Dumb luck or providence got me through those blistering days of combat, sometimes hand-to-hand.

By beginning of August the tide had turned and we gave it back in spades. Our counter attack during the Battle of Amiens pushed the Germans in the opposite direction beyond their western front. They teetered on complete hopelessness. After Megiddo, in September, the enemy had decided enough was enough and sued for peace. I would be coming home."

"Funny, most folks think World War I started when Arch-Duke Ferdinand of Austria was assassinated by Princip, the Bosnian rebel fighter defending his Slavic independence. His assassination triggered a face-off between triple alliances, Britain, France and Russia versus Germany, Austria, and Italy. However, truth be known World War I's origin was a result of intense royal jealousy. From the day Kaiser William II took power in Germany he made it crystal clear he was envious of Britain's naval prowess, ruled by his grandmother Queen Victoria, and eventually her son King Edward VII, William's uncle. There wasn't a family get together where Willy didn't find some way of endearing himself into the good graces of grandmamma, or Uncle Bertie for the purpose of stealing glimpses at the magnificence of Britain's navy. His jealousy spilled over from family feuding into prejudicial national superiority, eventually driving him to an unqualified arms race with the Brits to build the biggest battle ships, what they called dreadnoughts, ships of enormous dimensions. Britain had 12-inch guns on their ships, so Willy built ships with 13 -nch guns. Britain responded with 14-inch guns and Germany rushed to build 15 inch, and so on and so on. Doesn't sound a whole lot different then what we're doing these days with them Ruskies. Escalation in armament occurred uninterrupted over a 20-year period. Tension between Germany and Britain intensified with each new ship. War was inevitable, it was only a matter of time and it didn't really matter what triggered the first shot. Anyway, I got myself caught-up in the whole mess thinking I was part of some greater noble cause, when the insanity of war could have been avoided if grandmamma had taken Willy over her knee when he first started acting-up."

"When I returned home I learned my older brother Mathew had been killed not more than a few miles east of where we were fighting during the German spring offensives, and my parents had died weeks after I left for Europe from the Spanish influenza. For the first time in my life I was alone. Personal tragedies aside, I was lost in an unfamiliar world and gravitated to any safe harbor in the storm."

"Loneliness drives people to make some pretty rash decisions. Turns out my rash decision was to marry the first girl that took notice of me. Beatty was her name, from Charlotte on holiday with a few of her girl friends. I met her at a dance on the Circle. She was pretty in an ordinary kind of way, quiet, and she didn't pretend she didn't like me. Compatibility, shared values, those things couples test at some point in their relationship never came-up in our conversations."

"We were fond of each other, but it would be a lie to say we were in love. Each of us knew what we wanted and didn't waste any time exploiting the other in the guise of marital sanctimony. I married to find a replacement for the family I lost, she married to fulfill a childhood dream drilled into every little girl of the time. Get married, move into a house with white picket fence and clapboards, raise 2 ½ children, maybe keep a cat or dog, and go to church every Sunday. All the articles necessary to parade in front of her friends and family to validate everything was as it should be. Heck, I was just a boy, didn't know really who she was or for that matter who I was. Turns out who we were wouldn't work. Harder I tried to recover my family in our marriage, the harder she worked on trying to create the perfect image. Our desires were shallow and selfish. Neither of us tried to find any middle ground or each other, and as a consequence, neither of us got what we wanted. Instead of growing together we grew apart. Both of us frustrated, our marriage was doomed before it started."

"Did you have any children?"

"Yes, one daughter, Elizabeth. I liked to call her Bizzy. She was a cute little girl."

"Can't remember the specifics, odd given the impact of such a decision; anyway, one day we fell out of marriage. Bitter, she moved back to Charlotte to get away from me, but more importantly to get our daughter beyond my influence. I could have fought her in court, but thought it probably would have made matters worse. Over the years I've collected quite a few regrets, losing Bizzy was my greatest."

"Have you stayed in touch with your daughter?"

"Not at first. Too ashamed at the stigma of divorce, and not wanting to have to explain to Bizzy what I couldn't explain to myself. Then somewhere in the late 1940s I decided I had waited long enough and started writing to her regularly about this and that, thinking it might pique her curiosity. Heard she lives somewhere in Baltimore. She married a man, name of Tibbits. Turns out there are lots of Tibbits in Baltimore and I didn't know which one was her. So I've been sending letters to her mother, I expect she has forwarded them to Bizzy."

"Has she responded to your letters?"

"...still waiting."

*****

Good news Bizzy, Buddy is alive! Been nearly 3 weeks since he ran away, and without question I thought we had lost him for good. Have no idea where he got to, but by the looks of him he must have taken up residence in the swamp. Skinny and filthy, he is a shadow of his former self. But I am sure we can rectify both in short order. Dorothy is beside herself with joy and I won't deny I am pretty happy about this turn of events as well.

Suppose it's been a while in coming, but I think this is going to be my last letter, at least for a while. You know I hoped we could have been closer and my letters were an attempt, albeit perhaps feeble, to light a spark. Waiting for your responses has given me a lot of time to think about the could-of's and should-of's and all the things I wished we might have been as a family. I guess it wasn't meant to be.

I often think of your childhood, lost to me, and ponder if I had been involved would I have been a good father. Would you have looked up to me, or not? Those days are gone, I'm sorry for that and for any pain I've caused you. But most of all, I'm sorry for those left behind. It sounds lame now, but no man knows how the future will turn-out, or understand for certain how the consequence of their actions will move the dial this way or that; and, I wish I could go back in time, would have done things differently. As the saying goes, 'hindsight is 20-20.' I'm sure you deserve a better explanation, unfortunately there is none. It is not a good excuse, in fact there are no excuses. People are human and will do the oddest things. Sometimes destroying what is closest to them.

Well Bizzy that's pretty much it, but if I can offer any last advice, it is this. Don't turn your back on those who love you. Life is short, make the most of what you've been given before it's too late.

For now, your loving

Father

Not sure why I was surprised to discover the letters were from my grandfather. Why else would they have been locked away in mother's attic so many years? And as silly as it sounds, I was surprised I had a grandfather, something hard to avoid even for the most cloistered and aggrieved. He had been the person mother had prevented from entering our lives, a shadowy figure she avoided speaking of at all costs. Now that I think about it, was probably the central person about which most of her mysteries surrounded.

John M. Tabor

She undoubtedly had cowed father into submission, for when I made inquiries as to the particulars of a maternal lineage he would always defer, "you should ask your mother questions of that nature", creating a cyclical dilemma with no solution. Repulsed from a straight answer I eventually gave-up asking, but have never ceased to wonder as to the gaps in our family tree, reluctantly withheld. Where there is smoke there is usually fire and I have always subscribed there was more behind my ignorance than met the eye.

Now, after more than half a century, some of the pieces are falling in place. Occasionally you hear of cold cases, where clues to unsolved murders are run to ground and perpetrators apprehended after years living incognito amongst a community of unknowing. My mystery was less complicated. Mother was poisoned by parental estrangement, nothing novel. What is not clear was whether mother was fed distortions from my grandmother, birthing a lifetime of hatred or in the absence of a father figure created her own nuanced lies? She was certainly capable of the latter. Maybe it was a little of both.

It's also not clear why someone would keep the letters of a man which they held in contempt? Wouldn't it have been easier to discard the lot of them? Then again, it's possible she retained his letters as a tangible connection to the man she never knew. Although unread, they may have provided some comfort knowing they were there if she had a mind. Perhaps if she had read them she might have come to the conclusion her father wasn't the ogre she had portrayed him. Of course, dispelling perverted representations would steal the one thing she cherished most about her father, having someone to blame for all her disappointments and failures, a frailty for which I am sure she would offer no apology. Even in death the incongruities of my experience with mother astounds me and I will have to live with these few unanswered questions, as it is unlikely she'll reach back from the grave to provide clarity.

It's not surprising that over the years we acquire the prejudice, hatred, and anger our parents reinforce through subtle and not so subtle messages ground into our brains on a daily basis. Attitudes become generational, inherited no less than our DNA. It is the baggage of our lives stored in the overhead compartments of our bus, in the belly of our planes, in the closets and attics of our homes. Shouldn't there be a time we can let go of our complaints and animosity against those imperfect people who veered off the path? After all, it is not our role to judge; and, if we are not to judge then what right to we have to punish?

It would be all too easy to embrace my own beguiling and hateful stories of mother and pass down, to those who might listen, the same set of mutated genes which when inseminated allows us to defer responsibility for our own lives. No! What is done is done! Too many wasted days, hours, and minutes regurgitating the past. I must move on and leave the past where it belongs. I now have an opportunity to write that long overdue book, to herald a unique voice, and to heal.

And so, John Tibbits wrote that book which had been hidden within, the one good book which every man is allotted. Inspired by his grandfather he would entitle it, *Letters to Bizzy*. What of Peggy? Well, John had for too long dodged what in his heart he desired, and if his mother wouldn't follow the advice of her father, he would. Forgiveness of oneself is perhaps the hardest thing to do. Until we do, it may seem impossible to forgive others. Peggy taught me a little about forgiveness and letting go. And so, the fake prescriptions miraculously disappeared and Peggy became more than just the woman down the hall.

www.ingramcontent.com/pod-product-compliance
Lightning Source LLC
Chambersburg PA
CBHW051822170626
46807CB00003B/986